Prai

Mossy Creek

MW00657623

"Written in the tradition of Fannie Flag and Garrison Keillor."
—*Nola Theiss, KLIATT*

"Delightful."
— *Marie Barnes, former First Lady of Georgia*

"Mitford meets Mayberry in the first book of this innovative
and warmhearted new series from BelleBooks."
— *Cleveland Daily Banner, Cleveland, Tennessee*

"You won't want to leave MOSSY CREEK! These pages offer
readers a taste of country charm with characters that feel like
family."
— *Joyce Handzo, Library Reviews*

"If you have never entered the city limits of MOSSY CREEK,
then you should go there immediately. The books of this series
are among the most readable and enjoyable you will find anywhere."
— *Jackie K. Cooper, WMAC-AM, Macon, GA*

"Mossy Creek combines the atmosphere of an Anne River Sid-
dons' novel with the magic of a Barbara Samuel's character
study. The latest trip is worth the journey."
— *Harriet Klausner, Amazon.com reviewer*

"The characters and kinships of MOSSY CREEK are quirky,
hilarious and all too human. This story reads like a delicious,
meringue-covered slice of home. I couldn't get enough."
— *Pamela Morsi, USA Today bestselling author*

"MOSSY CREEK is a book you will not lend for fear you won't
get it back."
— *Chloe LeMay, The Herald, Rock Hill, SC*

"For those who like books with a strong sense of community
and place, engaging characters and stories that will take you
from tears to laughter and back again. It's very 'Southern,' and
very small town."
— *Renee Patterson, Alachua (FL) County Libraries*

Enjoy the Complete

Mossy Creek Hometown Series

Mossy Creek

Reunion in Mossy Creek

Summer in Mossy Creek

Blessings of Mossy Creek

A Day in Mossy Creek

At Home in Mossy Creek

Critters of Mossy Creek

Homecoming in Mossy Creek

Christmas in Mossy Creek

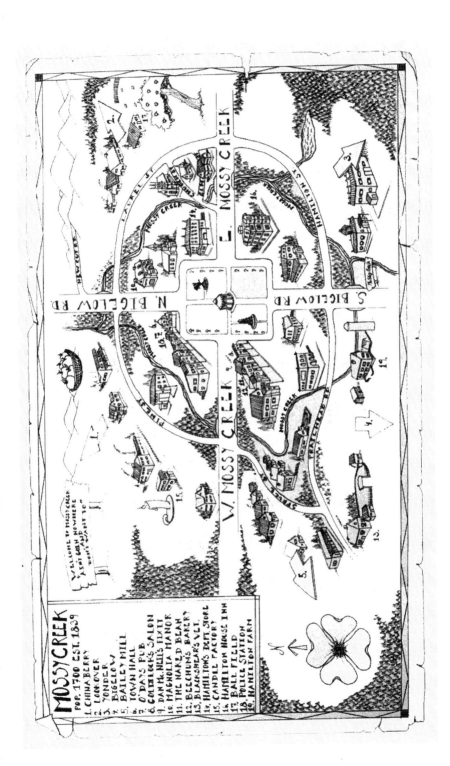

MOSSYCREEK
POP. 1700 EST. 1839

1. CHINABERRY
2. LOOK-OVER
3. YONDER
4. BIGELOW
5. BAILEY MILL
6. TOWN HALL
7. O'DAYS PUB
8. GOLDILICKS SALON
9. DAN McNEIL'S FEXIT
10. MAGNOLIA MANOR
11. THE NAKED BEAN
12. BEECHUM'S BAKERY
13. BLACKSMEAR'S VET
14. HAMILTON'S DEPT. STORE
15. CANDLE FACTORY
16. HAMILTON HOUSE INN
17. BALL FIELD
18. POLICE STATION
19. HAMILTON FARM

WELCOME TO MOSSYCREEK
AIN'T GOIN NOWHERE
DON'T WANT TO

MOSSY CREEK

E. MOSSY CREEK

W. MOSSY CREEK

N. BIGELOW RD

S. BIGELOW RD

LAUREL ST

HAMILTON ST

DEDICATIONS

A Special Dedication

To the memory of our beloved sister in writing
and BelleBooks partner,

Sandra Chastain

Sandra was a driving force behind the founding of BelleBooks
and the creation of the Mossy Creek Hometown Series.
A writer of over 50 novels, she inspired and mentored numerous
writers, many included in the Mossy Creek series.
A generous and loving spirit, Sandra was a true Southern lady.
There's no higher praise than that.

Author Dedications

To the newest joy in my life,
my grandson Connor Jackson Donahue.
—*Martha Crockett*

This story is dedicated, with love, to my dad, who had a big heart
and an even bigger laugh. And played an awesome Santa at the
local nursing home. We miss you.
And to my family, John, Brenna & Wil. I wouldn't be the person
I am today without your love and support.
—*Darcy Crowder*

To my wonderful grandma, Gladys O'Neill Hendrick Hardy.
I'll see you by and by.
—*Susan Goggins*

To my sisters Kathy and Eileen.
—*Maureen Hardegree*

I dedicate Joyeux Noelle to my great-grandchildren.
Ethan and Rylie bring a youthful energy and a freshness to my
life. Love to each of you . . . Nana.
—*Nancy Knight*

To Maja, who has looked after our critique group
nearly every Friday morning for ten years.
—*Carolyn McSparren*

Christmas in Mossy Creek

A collective novel featuring the voices of

Carolyn McSparren
Martha Crockett
Susan Goggins
Darcy Crowder
Maureen Hardegree,
Nancy Knight

Memphis, Tennessee

BelleBooks, Inc.

ISBN 978-1-61194-834-9

Christmas in Mossy Creek

Published by:
BelleBooks, Inc. • P.O. Box 300921 • Memphis, TN 38130
We at BelleBooks enjoy hearing from readers. You can contact us at the address above or at BelleBooks@BelleBooks.com

Visit our website— www.BelleBooks.com

First Edition November 2017

10 9 8 7 6 5 4 3 2 1

Images: Interior: © erikdegraaf, © Wilm Ihlenfeld | Fotolia.com
Images: Cover: © Wenani, © Milkovasa | Dreamstime.com
Book & cover design: Martha Crockett
Mossy Creek map: Dino Fritz

Lady Victoria Salter Stanhope
The Clifts
Seaward Road
St. Ives, Cornwall, TR3 7PJ
United Kingdom

Merry Christmas, Vick!

The Thanksgiving turkeys have been
consumed, the pecan pies are gone,
and the extra cans of cranberry sauce
have been put in the pantry for a few
weeks. Now Mossy Creek is turning its
attention to Christmas.

I know y'all don't have Thanksgiving
over there across the pond, but you
do have Christmas. Here in the South
we celebrate all kinds of ways. Of
course, we decorate our houses and
buy presents. We have church choral
celebrations and pageants and holiday
bazaars.

Mossy Creek's Christmas parade is
coming up soon. We'll have floats
from various community organizations,
the high school marching band, Santa
Claus, and even a depiction of Baby

1

Jesus fleeing from Herod's soldiers, complete with a local donkey.

We also decorate the town. Although they're up in the air at the moment, 'cause our committee can't decide on a theme. So Creekites are waiting with bated breath. Snowflakes or angels? *'Tis the Season* or *'Tis the Reason*? Reindeer or manger scenes? Who knows? I'll keep you informed!

Katie

Let's be naughty and save Santa the trip.

—Gary Allan

The Ninety-Sixth Annual Mossy Creek Christmas Parade

EARLY NOVEMBER — THE PLANNING COMMITTEE

"You're the only person in Mossy Creek with a miniature Sicilian donkey," Louise Sawyer said to me. "The Virgin Mary needs to ride Don Qui in the Christmas parade."

I choked on my coffee and coughed until my eyes streamed. It had to have been a full minute before I could speak coherently. "I will *not* be responsible for the Virgin Mary's losing the Baby Jesus in a premature birth before she gets to Bethlehem. You know what that donkey's like. In the ongoing battle between Satan and the angels, Don Qui bats for Satan."

"All taken care of, Merry. First of all, Kristin James is playing Mary in the parade. If she can't actually *ride* Don Qui, if he gets fractious, she's tall enough to jump off his back without getting hurt."

"With sofa pillows under her robe so she'll look pregnant on her way to that second-rate inn?" I asked. Louise, my best friend and sometime partner in my horse breeding and training operation outside of Mossy Creek, had volunteered herself and me to chair the Mossy Creek Christmas Parade committee.

Big mistake. I didn't like committees, and committees didn't like me. Nothing good ever came from being on a committee. For me, at least.

3

Louise was a retired school teacher and volunteer extraordinaire. She had time for boards and expertise at bossing everybody in Mossy Creek around. She'd taught most of them. I, on the other hand, was younger and anything but retired. I had a farm to run and carriage horses to train. Besides, I was an *incomer* to Mossy Creek, where your family had to have been resident for at least three generations before you were considered a native.

"Kristin can only be Mary if the parade supposedly takes place *after* the birth when the Holy Family is running off to Egypt to get away from Herod's soldiers," Louise said. "Her mother and father said that under no circumstances will they allow her to ride through Mossy Creek looking as though she has a bun in her particular oven."

"So Mary and Joseph are going to flee Herod, then swing back to the crèche so they can lay Baby Jesus *back* in the manger? Doesn't exactly follow the Biblical account, does it?"

Louise shrugged. "Kristin is seventeen. They don't want her showing up on Facebook looking nine months pregnant."

"Now *that* I understand."

"Kristin is borrowing one of her little sister's Cabbage Patch dolls to carry. Wrapped in swaddling clothes, it'll do just fine until they get to the crèche on Town Square to lay it in the manger."

"Where's she going to put him on the trip? In a saddlebag? Don Qui should love that."

"You can be extremely exasperating when you put your mind to it," Louise said. "Kristin will hold the baby in one arm and Don Qui's reins in the other."

I rolled my eyes. "Like that's going to work."

"Meredith Abbott, this is a Christmas parade in Mossy Creek, Georgia. It is *not* Macy's Thanksgiving Day parade. We do not have blimps that look like superheroes flying over the Square tethered to two dozen handlers. We do not have giant floats that we have been working on since New Year's Day last year. It is a small, local, everybody-wave-at-Santa-Claus-and-grab-candy-out-of-the air parade. Mary, who will *not* still be pregnant, will hold the Baby Jesus wrapped in swaddling clothes."

"That she has snatched out of the manger ten steps ahead

of Herod's soldiers with their scimitars. Are we going to have scimitars, by the way?"

"What is the *matter* with you?"

I was sulking, but couldn't help it. "I hate Christmas. And this one is already shaping up to be a disaster."

"Why on earth would you hate Christmas?" Louise asked. "Everybody loves Christmas."

"Not everyone." I sighed. Might as well tell her. She'd get it out of me eventually. "When I was growing up, my Daddy was always off somewhere getting ready for a horse show the day after Christmas. If he remembered and had time, he'd call on the phone, but since it was a landline at that point, it was expensive, so we couldn't talk long. It was always just me and Mom. We never had a turkey. The smallest was too big for the two of us, so we had one of those turkey roast things that come wadded up in a net and do not look, smell, or taste like real turkey. And the horses that Daddy hadn't taken to the show still had to be fed, watered and exercised by Mom and me. Invariably, whoever Daddy was working for that year had kids and grandkids who wanted to come play with the horses on Christmas afternoon. Guess who had to babysit the little brats?"

"I had no idea." I could see Louise's mind working. "You never said anything."

I shrugged, glad of her empathy but feeling self-conscious all the same. "It not the kind of thing that comes up in everyday conversation."

"We had a lovely little Christmas last year, didn't we?" she asked hopefully.

I hugged my dear friend's shoulder. "Thanks to you and Charlie. I would never have gone to the Nine Lessons and Nine Carols service at the Presbyterian Church or learned to cook candied yams . . ."

"Or hitched up Heinzie and gone for a lovely long carriage drive in the afternoon. Besides, the Mossy Creek Christmas parade is the Saturday after Thanksgiving weekend, not Christmas Day. It will be fun. You'll see."

"I will do this insane thing," I said, "if you promise to get Kristin to come out and learn to ride Don Qui."

"I doubt the head of the Spanish Riding School in Vienna could learn to ride that jackass."

"Probably not. But she's got to come out and try at least a couple of times a week after school."

"But she has cheerleading practice and football games and gymnastics and school. She's a senior. She has SATs."

"Take it or leave it. Ask her. Who's playing Joseph, by the way?"

"We lucked out on that. She's dating Meat at the moment. If anyone can handle that donkey, Meat can."

"Meat who was all-state tackle last year?"

"Right. Being heavily recruited by the University of Georgia, the University of Tennessee and LSU as we speak."

"Meat can toss them both over his shoulder and finish the parade on foot if he has to," I said.

Meat's actual name was Cal Reece. Until his hormones kicked in, he'd been a relatively normal boy, if a trifle outsized. When he topped six feet and two hundred pounds at age nine, his coach said he reminded him of Refrigerator Perry, the legendary pro-football player.

When Cal outgrew even the largest kitchen appliance, however, his teammates looked for a bigger nickname. The only thing they could come up with was *Meat Locker*, immediately shortened to "Meat."

"It's the perfect romance of the Titans," Louise said. "Since they were homecoming king and queen this year, they've been hot and heavy, so he's going to play Saint Joseph and wrangle Don Qui—at least keep him tethered to a lead line and walk beside him. He has good reason to keep his girlfriend intact. This will work, Merry. I promise."

• • •

Kristin James stood six feet tall and maybe weighed a hundred and fifteen pounds, almost all of which was muscle. Even Meat envied her six-pack abs. She'd always wanted to be an Olympic gymnast, until she came up against the hard wall of fact that they were usually under five feet tall and had no discernible boobs.

She then focused on leading the Mossy Creek cheerleading

squad. She was the anchor in any pyramid. The girls trusted she would never drop them.

Kristin decided against using some sort of temporary dye to turn her ash-blonde hair dark to play Mary. She'd once tried it on Halloween and wound up looking like a Tasmanian tiger with stripes ranging from black on the ends to blonde at the roots. She enlisted fellow cheerleader Shamira, even though her father disapproved, to show her how to fashion a hijab to cover her hair.

The Virgin Mary traditionally wore a blue robe, which suited Kristin's coloring perfectly. The blue hijab would enhance her blue eyes. The cheerleaders all agreed she'd look fabulous. Not necessarily virginal, however, or like a very young girl who has just given birth to a baby boy in a stable a long way from home with no midwife around.

I knew all of this within an hour of making Kristin's acquaintance. Like most teenage girls, she was a talker—with herself her favorite subject.

To get ready for Kristin's first attempt to ride Don Qui, I'd worked every day to attempt to turn him from a very small donkey pulling a very small carriage—his usual duty when he couldn't misbehave himself out of it—into a riding animal for a lanky girl carrying a doll.

I was almost as tall as Kristin and weighed considerably more, so I figured if I could get Don Qui to carry *me*, getting him to carry Kristin should be a piece of cake.

At least Kristin knew how to ride a horse. Her equine sport of choice was western pole-bending. While I considered that an even crazier horse sport than jumping five-foot fences, obviously Kristin had no fear.

Yet.

She hadn't met Don Qui.

But then Don Qui hadn't met Kristin.

Don Qui only lived on my farm because he and my big Friesian gelding, Heinzie, were much closer than David and Jonathan, despite the difference in their sizes. Heinzie didn't mind spending a few hours away from his buddy. Don Qui, however, usually spent his times of separation braying his head off. I'd finally given up and kept the pair together as much as possible. Today, Heinzie grazed happily on the other side of the arena fence where Don Qui could see him.

By the time Kristin showed up for her first encounter with the donkey—looking like some kind of Norse goddess in jeans and boots—I'd had limited success with him. *Very* limited.

Over several years and with great difficulty, I'd trained Don Qui to accept a harness, accept a bitted bridle with attached reins and pull a miniature horse cart. Usually. He had never before, to the best of my knowledge, worn a saddle nor carried a live human being on his back.

Over the last week, I'd gotten him to accept the saddle, though I had to chase him down to get it on him. But he nipped at me every time I tried to mount.

"This is crazy," I told Kristin. "He'll try very hard to kill you, and he may succeed."

"This sweet little old baby won't hurt me, will you, sugar?" Kristin scratched the donkey's face gently until his eyelids began to droop. She moved to his poll, then his neck and all over his little brown body down to his hooves.

I'd always said those dainty little hooves were secretly cloven, although they seemed perfectly normal.

Don Qui sighed in ecstasy.

"He's biding his time until he's lulled you into trusting him," I whispered.

"Why, he's the one being lulled, aren't you, baby boy?"

Don Qui leaned against her and sighed.

I watched the pair together, amazed. Kristin must be a donkey whisperer, or she'd secretly slipped him some drugs. Likely drugs.

I let Kristin groom him, pick his feet, all the while crooning to him. The horses in the paddock, including Heinzie, were now hanging over the fence watching and envying their small brother's massage.

"You have to wear a hard hat," I told her.

"But Mary wouldn't have worn a hard hat. I'll look stupid. No way."

"No hard hat, no Don Qui. As a matter of fact, nobody rides or drives any equine on this place without wearing a hard hat.

Bones mostly knit, but busted skulls can leak all over my nice clean arena."

"But Samira is going to teach me how to tie a hijab. I can't wear a hard hat over that."

From her place at the arena fence, Louise said, "Can't you wrap that hijab *over* your hard hat? Mary would have been wearing something like that over her hair, wouldn't she?"

"You know how big those hard hats are?" Kristin said. "I'll look like one of those aliens from *War of the Worlds* in drag."

"Borrow it and try it," I insisted.

Kristin sighed deeply. Don Qui echoed her. "All right, but I'm going to look ridiculous."

"Good. Here's one of my hard hats," I said. "Put it on and we'll try out Don Qui. I didn't know whether you wanted to try riding him bareback or in a regular saddle. I also have a side-saddle. Two thousand years ago, Mary would probably have been riding astride, although I suspect having just had a baby, she'd prefer to sit sidesaddle. Must have been hellish riding a creature with a backbone like a donkey, so they must have laid rugs across his back cinched somehow so they wouldn't slide off him."

"All the way to Egypt," Kristin said in awe. "It doesn't say the angels gave them any help on the trip, does it? And poor Joseph had to walk all the way." She scratched behind Don Qui's long ears.

If he could have purred, no doubt he would have.

"I did bring one of my bareback pads," Kristin said. "It's padded and has a bucking strap to hold onto. We can take off the stirrups. I'd rather be able to bail."

"Let's try it."

The bareback pad and the cinch obviously felt close enough to his regular harness that Don Qui didn't protest too much when they tacked him up. He only cow-kicked at me once and Kristin not at all.

He did protest the bridle, however. His big old donkey teeth snapped at my fingers and nearly nipped my hand, but I pulled away in time.

"Now, you stop that," Kristin said in a voice she'd honed on rowdy cheerleaders.

After the soft crooning in his ear, Don Qui's eyes snapped open at her tone. She went right back to the crooning, however. Possibly in surprise, he opened his mouth and let the bit slip inside.

"There. That's a good little angel," she said.

I could only shake my head as I snapped an eighteen-foot longe line to the bridle in hopes that eighteen feet between me in the center of the circle and him on the perimeter would be enough to keep me safe. So long as he chose not to charge.

Kristin walked into the arena beside the donkey, scratching and crooning.

She leaned against his side, leaned back and slid onto the bareback pad sidesaddle.

Stunned, Don Qui stood perfectly still. He took two steps.

I crossed my fingers.

One more step and all hell broke loose. He bucked high and hard. Kristin landed on hands and knees six feet away while Don Qui tried to kick the moon, brayed like a wildebeest being chased by a lion and took off to the end of the longe line.

I hung on by digging my heels into the arena sand when he dragged me.

After a fit of giggles, Kristin hopped up off her hands and knees. Then with a look of steel in her eyes, she took the longe line from me and hand-over-handed Don Qui—much against his will—into the center of the arena and up tight against her.

"Let's try that again. Unhook the line, please," she said calmly. "We're about to have us a goat rodeo."

This time she threw her leg across the saddle. No more of this sidesaddle stuff, apparently.

She was one heck of a rider, I had to admit, even if she was twice Don Qui's size. She stuck to him like a limpet while he performed amazing feats of bucking and kicking. She grinned the whole time, even when he started braying at the top of his lungs.

I figured they could hear him in downtown Mossy Creek.

He wore out before Kristin did, although I could see the sweaty patches under her arms and down her back. In twenty minutes, he was walking on a loose rein in figure-eights around the arena while Kristin crooned to him.

She finally walked him over to where I stood awestruck and slid off.

"Who's a good boy, then?" she crooned.

She was barely out of breath. I'd have been on my way to the emergency room if I were still alive.

"No problem," Kristin said. "Let's get him rinsed off and feed him some carrots. I brought some in case you were out."

She walked off with Don Qui trudging tiredly along beside her without a lead line or even a bridle strap holding him.

Later, after dinner, I said to Louise, "I don't know what she is, but according to Don Qui, she's not human."

"He's not broke yet, you know," Louise said. "This is just the opening salvo in Kristin's campaign. He'll probably behave worse when she comes back again."

"I am well aware of that. He still harbors a demon inside, but if Kristin manages to cast it out for the duration of the parade, I'll be satisfied."

• • •

"But we have to take Heinzie along or Don Qui won't move a step," Louise said at the next board meeting for the Christmas parade committee.

Hosting it at her cottage, she'd restricted the drinking of Mossy Creek mimosas until after the meeting was officially closed, otherwise nothing would get done. Nobody would be able to pass a Breathalyzer test on the way home, if Amos should be lurking somewhere close.

Comprised of Ida and all the Garden Club members Louise could wrangle, the committee members grumbled, but agreed it was prudent.

So far, I'd sat back, letting the committee be the committee.

"And what role do we have in mind for that ginormous black Friesian gelding?" Ida asked me directly. "I thought he and that donkey came as a matched pair."

"We could dress Amos up as a Roman soldier and have him chase the Holy Family down Main Street," Louise answered for me. "Waving a scimitar."

Everyone snickered.

Ida shook her head. "That won't work. Amos can't keep his

attention on the parade and be in it too. That's an all-hands-on-deck day for the police department."

"Well, who else is there?" Louise said. "I don't see Herod slaughtering his own innocents."

"How about the Magi?" Helen Overbury suggested. "That black gelding and a couple of quarter horses or Arabians with riders dressed up in robes could follow along after the Holy Family?"

"That's not a bad idea," Louise said. "We have plenty of horses around who march in parades all the time. Put turbans instead of Stetsons on the guys who ride them, we'll be all set. But they probably should ride ahead of the Holy Family instead of behind so Don Qui can see Heinzie. And that way, they can soften up the crowd."

So it was decided. I reluctantly agreed to line up the magi and Louise agreed to line up their wives to make their costumes and turbans.

"All right. Now, so far, we have the Mossy Creek marching band to start, followed by the drill team and the Shrine clowns and the Garden Club float."

"The youth groups at the churches are all going to do floats," Peggy Caldwell said. "Not big ones. They'll be pulled by pickup trucks."

"What we don't have is Santa Claus," Louise said. "With Ed Brady gone . . ."

A spontaneous silence hushed the group as everyone remembered the beloved icon who'd played Santa Claus in Mossy Creek for decades.

Always pragmatic, Peggy finally broke the quiet. "We also don't have any kind of float for Santa to ride. Amos has played Santa before, but he can't . . . or won't."

"He's too young and too skinny," Ida insisted.

Knowing looks around the table said, "*And she should know.*" The ladies kept their mouths shut, however. They preferred to down their mimosas through *all* their teeth. Ida could be prickly about her thing with Amos.

"What about the fire truck?" Eleanor Abercrombie asked. "Ed always rode on top."

Ida shook her head. "Unfortunately, those days are over. The State Fire Marshall's office has cracked down. They tried to insist several years ago, but Ed was dead set on tradition. It was one of those cases where we asked forgiveness instead of permission. Now that Ed's gone, we've got to toe the line or we'll lose state funding. So we definitely need a float."

"The Holy Horns brass quartet from the Baptist Church want to ride on Santa's float. They'll play all the way, then have a sing-along with the spectators at the Square to sing carols," Eustene Oscar said.

"It's a shame it's too hot for reindeer in Mossy Creek," said Mimsy Allen.

"We don't have a sleigh or snow either," Ida said dryly.

"But we have plenty of horses," Louise said.

Finally, I couldn't keep quiet any longer. I had what could be the perfect solution. "Let me work on a Santa float. I think I can get my hands on just the thing."

That afternoon I called my friend, Dick Fitzgibbons, a horse breeder from lower South Carolina who showed draft horses in horse shows and parades all over the South.

When he answered, I said, "Dick, I need you."

"Sweet thing, I been tellin' you that, but you don't listen."

"Not for that. I need your largest pair of Percherons to pull a big flat-bed hay wagon for Santa to use in the Christmas parade. I also need to borrow a wagon."

"Uh-huh. When?"

I game him dates and times.

"Why do you need a flatbed?" Dick asked. "How come Santa can't just ride in my big Victoria carriage?"

"The Holy Horns, the brass quartet from the First Baptist Church, is going to be seated on the float in front of Santa. They'll play carols along the parade route, then do a carol sing-along at the big crèche in the park. You don't care if we drill a few holes in the floor of the wagon, do you? We need to secure the orchestra chairs so that the musicians don't get knocked around, and Santa's throne behind them."

"Go right ahead. It's got plenty of nail and screw holes in it already."

• • •

Over the next few weeks, everyone on the parade committee brainstormed possible Santa Clauses. Just before Thanksgiving, we were still minus one Kris Kringle.

Ida was set against fake beards except as a last resort, which let out a number of clean-shaven jolly ol' elves. Of the remaining candidates, several had beards that had been treated to suspicious black rinses. The ones left were either too thin, too fat, or too sour.

The Tuesday before Thanksgiving, I happened to be talking with Ida as she waited to pick up a prescription at the drug store when a man walked up behind us. She turned to give him a mayorly smile but instead gasped and grabbed my arm.

I turned to look. He was *Miracle on 34th Street* come to life. The smile he turned on us was incandescent.

Ida recovered first and said, "I'm Ida Walker . . ."

"Ah. Her Honor the Mayor." He actually bent over her hand. "I am delighted to meet you. I'm Beauregard Hatcher. Call me Beau, everybody does."

Ida waved a hand at me. "This is Merry Abbott, who owns a horse training facility just outside of Mossy Creek."

The man beamed. "Ah, Mossy Creek. I'm thinking of moving to your charming town."

Ida and I exchanged glances. At that moment, all we cared about was that he remain in Mossy Creek until after the Christmas parade.

Five minutes later, after they both collected their prescriptions, Ida and I shuffled Beau off to the Naked Bean to seduce him into playing Santa.

Beau Hatcher said he was retired, but not from what or where. He was trying to find a place that was warm in the winter to settle down after a lifetime at work and remembered driving through Mossy Creek many years earlier and liking it. He'd decided to come to town, rent one of the studio apartments down the hill and spend six months or so deciding whether to buy a cottage and stay.

Half an hour later, Ida and I went straight to her office where she called as many of members of the parade committee as she could get on a conference call. "The man is straight out of Central Casting! But I couldn't walk up to a totally strange elderly man and ask him to play Santa Claus in our Christmas Parade."

"Why not?" Louise asked. "You're famous for giving people jobs and demanding they do them."

"I do not!" Ida glanced at me and my thoughts must've shown on my face because she reluctantly admitted, "Well, not often. All I'm saying is I've spotted the game. Someone else needs to bag him."

I could hear exasperation in Louise's voice as she said, "I guess it's up to me."

• • •

The next afternoon, Louise dragged me to town so we could "accidentally" run into Beau Hatcher. We caught him outside Town Hall. She switched her schmooze switch to "kill" and gave him the smile that never failed to straighten out unruly students.

After introductions and a few polite niceties, Louise said brightly, "Now that you're a Creekite, Mr. Hatcher, we think it's high time we welcomed you properly."

He turned a sunny smile on her. "Everybody has been great."

I noted that he waxed the ends of his white mustache and twisted them up. The effect was a permanent smile.

"Oh, you haven't begun to be integrated into Mossy Creek." Louise shook an admonitory finger at him. "We are very big on civic pride in our small town. When there's anything important going on, everyone pitches in to make it a success."

Beau looked a tad confused, but nodded.

"You do know our Ninety-Sixth Christmas Parade is coming up the Saturday after Thanksgiving weekend?"

"I've heard something about it."

Louise laughed and patted his arm. "We've encountered a tiny problem that I know you're going to fix for the entire town."

Now, he looked not only confused, but wary. "Um, I don't know . . ."

"Oh, it's a great honor and afterward you'll be the town hero."

Nervous ramped up to scared. He tried to pull away, but Louise held firm.

"It's right up your alley. You won't even have to leave town. Just ride from the high school by way of City Hall for the ceremony."

"You want me to *marry* somebody?" He turned ashen, while his warm brown eyes were the size of Mars.

Louise laughed. The tinkly one she used to mollify difficult students. "Of course not! We want you to be Santa Claus in the parade!"

He let out a long breath and grinned. "Is that all? Why, I played Santa for so many years in the Christmas party at the YMCA, I've got my own costumes." He patted his tummy. "Used to need padding. Not anymore." He turned toward the Square and barked, "Ho! Ho! Ho!"

All discernible activity on the Square halted immediately.

A small child's voice asked, "Mama, is that Santa Claus?"

With a wink at me, Louise checked off another box on her mental "to-do" list.

• • •

At the last committee meeting before the parade, Ida went over her personal punch list. "Your friend Dick Fitzgibbons, Merry, is no youngster. There's going to be a lot of fuss. You think he can drive those two giant horses the whole parade route by the churches and into the Square for the crèche ceremony?"

"They're his personal team," I told her. "He's driven them in a thousand draft horse shows and parades and fairs. This is nothing compared to what he normally does with them. We all know the route. From the staging area out by the high school, down Trailhead, Hamilton and Laurel to Church Street. It swings by each of the churches, then East Mossy Creek to Bigelow Rd., circles Town Square, then stops at the crèche by Town Hall so Kristin can lay the Baby Jesus in the manger. I'll be on the box beside Dick, in case he needs directions or an extra pair of hands on the reins."

"What precisely happens at the crèche?" Geraldine Matthews asked.

"It's the Unitarians' turn to say the opening prayer this year," Ida said. "Then I'll do the welcome and the parade begins."

Something hadn't occurred to me. "We'll be at the High

School, over a mile from Town Square. How will we know when it's time to start? Synchronize our watches?"

"That's what we used to do before cell phones," said Eleanor Abercrombie. "Since I'm not in the parade, I'll be in the crowd on Town Square. I'll call you or Louise or whoever I need to and let you know the minute Ida's done."

"That work for everyone?" Louise asked.

Everyone nodded.

Ida went on with her rundown of the program. "After the parade ends at Town Square, Kristin puts the baby in the manger, everybody sings *a few carols* to the accompaniment of the Holy Horns. They then lead Santa and the spectators into Town Hall with cocoa and cookies for everyone. After that, the parade circles back to the high school football field. Done for another year. Successful parade over for the—what it is, the ninety-third time?"

"Ninety-sixth," Peggy Caldwell corrected.

I continued Ida's list, "Dick Fitzgibbons and I unharness the horses and load them and the wagon back into his van. He and his crew leave to go back home."

"But the musicians need their music stands on Sunday morning," Eleanor said.

"And the chairs have to be unscrewed and put back in the Baptist sanctuary," Helen Overbury said. "They can take their time with Santa's throne, but not the chairs."

I ran fingers through my already messy hair, "Shoot, I didn't think of that."

"Dick will have a couple of his grooms with him, won't he?" Louise asked. "They can unscrew the chairs and put them away while everyone is in the Town Hall having refreshments. Shouldn't take more than twenty minutes. It's just a quartet, after all."

"How does that *jackass* get home?" Helen asked. She neither liked nor trusted Don Qui.

"I figured he could ride with Dick's horses and get dropped off at my place on the way," I said.

Louise shook her head. "If those two Percherons get antsy, they could stomp him to a pulp. Merry, I think we need to bring

Don Qui in our trailer and take him home ourselves. We have to bring Heinzie anyway to be a Magi horse."

"An even better idea," I said. "The closer Heinzie stays to Don Qui, the safer we'll be. No problem."

"Right," Ida said. "What could possibly go wrong?"

COUNTDOWN TO THE PARADE

The day before the parade, the Garden Club ladies brought the bags of pine, holly, fairy lights and Christmas balls they had been collecting out to my farm to decorate the hay wagon and organize the decorations for the horses. Those would have to be done early Saturday morning. If the horses were decked out on Friday, they'd un-deck themselves Friday night.

"No decorations on that donkey," Louise decreed.

By Friday evening, the hay wagon no longer resembled farm equipment.

The fairy lights glimmered with new battery packs. The horses' manes and tails were brushed and ready to be braided with Christmas baubles.

Pine and holly garlands festooned the sides of the wagon, fans of magnolia leaves sprayed gold and wreaths of greenery and berries decorated all sides. The chairs for the Baptist Church's quartet, the Holy Horns, had been carefully screwed to the bed of the wagon and the music stands bungeed to the chairs.

The senior advanced shop class at Mossy Creek High School had built a dais that was now screwed to the hay wagon behind where the musicians would sit. Louise had found an ornate chair in her attic that could be attached to the dais for Santa Claus to use as a throne. Five feet in the air, it was now covered by greenery and twinkling with lights.

When Louise asked me to pick up Beau's Santa suit at the cleaners Friday afternoon and drop it by his apartment, I agreed since I was planning to be in town anyway. One less thing to worry about.

When I knocked on his door, Beau answered it on crutches.

I dropped the suit and gaped. "What happened?"

He looked down at his wrapped ankle. "Twisted the heck

out of it this morning when I hit a patch of ice walking to the coffee shop. Just a sprain, but it hurts like heck."

"Oh no!" Visions of an empty Santa float danced in my head as I stepped into his room. "What are we going to do?"

He pulled himself up as straight as he could on crutches. "Don't you worry, pretty lady. Beau Hatcher never lets down the kiddies."

I laid the Santa suit on the bed, thinking through the whole Santa-loading scenario. I turned to him, shaking my head. "You don't understand. You'll have to climb up on a hay wagon. It would be tricky even if you had two good legs."

"I'll be there. You'll see."

With no other choice but to believe him, I left. A sick feeling accompanied me all the way home.

• • •

The morning of the parade turned out to be one of those perfect late-fall-nearly-winter days that were like fine wine in North Georgia.

"Perfect," I said as I ran my curry comb over Don Qui's newly-shampooed and conditioned pelt. I agreed with Louise that it would be a mistake to try to decorate him.

"This is a poor family running away to Egypt to save their lives," Louise said. "I do not think they want fairy lights all over their donkey. Might as well put a sign on his rump that says, 'Here we are, Herod. Chase us.'"

With all the decorating done, I led the procession of trucks and trailers to the staging area with my trailer carrying Don Qui and Heinzie. Next came Dick's horse van—massive enough to hold two Percheron horses and a hay wagon.

With no rain in a week, the big field by the high school where the parade would stage and end wouldn't mire everybody down in mud. It was perfect.

Set up went smoothly. Frighteningly so. Enough that I began to think maybe we could pull it off.

"You would think we have done this a thousand times," said Helen Overbury of the Garden Club.

"Only ninety-five," Louise said. "Now hush up about it. Talk about a jinx."

"Nonsense. Look at the weather. It's providence."

"It's terrifying, is what it is," I whispered. "Things never go smoothly in Mossy Creek."

• • •

The Garden Club ladies, the parade board and the people who were to be in the parade assembled in the football field by Mossy Creek High School for the ten o'clock start to the parade.

Earl Baron, trombone, tallest and heaviest of the Holy Horns, checked each musician's chair by sitting in it to make certain the chairs didn't wobble or the music stands fall.

Earl and the French horn player were to sit right behind the driver's bench. The trumpet and tuba players would be just in front of Santa's throne with plenty of room because of the tuba's size.

"Where does your leader stand?" Peggy asked.

"We don't have a leader because we play together all the time," Earl said. "We do church music, but we play a lot of jazz and zydeco outside of our church gig. All we need is a downbeat." He glanced around him. "And I swear to God, if any of y'all asks for *The Little Drummer Boy*, I'll jump right off the wagon, run over and slug you."

"Oh, Earl, y'all *got* to play some non-carols," said Eustene Oscar. "I like *Rudolph* and the kids love him."

"We have to do *I Saw Mommy Kissing Santa Claus*," Mimsy Allen said. "We can't go the whole parade playing *Away in a Manger*. *Silent Night* is too quiet for a parade. You'll have the marching band in front of you, don't forget. You'll have to play loud."

"Yeah, but the band leads off and we come last with Santa. There's plenty of parade between us and them. Folks'll hear us, don't you worry. We're doing non-carols too, Mimsy. Don't sweat it. We got to jazz it up some—make a joyful noise, y'all. Emphasis on the *noise*! Shoot, some of y'all would make us play Gregorian plain chant or madrigals or such like. *Bor-ing!* We could really swing *Good King Wenceslas*," Earl said.

"No, we could not," Louise said firmly. "No funny stuff."

"We got to finish with *Hark the Herald Angels Sing*," Earl said. "Really blow them off the sidewalk."

"Bite your tongue! We got to finish with *Joy to the World*," Eustene said. "Right when you haul up in front of the crèche in the Square."

"Okay, we'll finish with *Joy to the World*," Earl said. Everybody was starting to sound excited. "I'm gonna go check on my boys and make sure they've got their horns." He chortled. "Occasionally, they forget."

Several of the cheerleaders had asked if they could dress up in veils and do Bollywood dancing down the parade route. Louise had to explain to them the difference between dancing in Bethlehem and dancing in Calcutta two thousand years ago. She was determined to check them before they started marching to be certain they hadn't added a few extraneous bangles and scarves to their cheerleader costumes. They were perfectly capable of inserting a few Bollywood moves into the marching band's routines. Shamira's poor father would probably have a heart attack.

Heinzie had come with Don Qui, and both horses relaxed tied to my trailer and snacking on oats to keep them happy. Don Qui was a little antsy, but he usually minded his manners so long as he was close to his big buddy Heinzie.

The wise men's other two horses arrived with their riders, the grooms went to work getting the wagon hooked up, the Percherons were decorated, everything was checked and rechecked. The three wise men tacked up their horses and poked at their turbans.

Cheerleaders wandered around petting the horses until Louise confiscated their scarves and shooed them out of the parking lot.

The floats lined up in order. The marching band scurried into its ranks in front of them.

"It's starting to look like a parade," Ida whispered.

Don Qui brayed. Loud.

"I never really understood what ear-splitting mean until I heard that donkey bray," Louise said to me. "Have you seen Kristin and Meat?"

"Not this morning. I'll go find her."

I checked the high school parking lot for Kristin's car, a bright red convertible her parents had given her as an early graduation present. At first, I didn't spot it. Just when I was ready to give up and panic, I spotted it at the very back in the edge of the trees. Two heads close together showed over the back of the front seat.

I shouted, "Kristin, you and Meat need to come get ready. Love on Don Qui. Now! You can do *that* later."

I grinned as both heads disappeared below the back of the seat. They'd give themselves a couple of minutes to "reorganize," and then they'd come.

I walked back to the staging area and gave Louise a thumbs-up.

"Thank heaven," Louise said. "Now, who has seen Mr. Hatcher?"

Silence.

My heart sank to the pit of my stomach. I had told the committee about Beau's ankle.

"It's almost time to mount up on the wagon," said the French horn player. "Gentlemen, have you set up your music and your instruments?"

A chorus of yeses answered. The musicians climbed into the wagon and settled down on their chairs with their music.

"I can't find Mr. Hatcher anywhere," Louise said. "I called his cell phone and it's not answering. I left messages. Surely he would've called if he really couldn't make it. I hope nothing's happened to him. He's not a young man."

"I sent my boy to check on him a few minutes ago," Eustene said. "He lives right down there." She pointed to the new apartments. At that moment, her phone rang. "Bobby, is that you? Is he all right?" She turned away, put her finger in her other ear to cut the ambient noise.

A moment later her shoulders went rigid. "I do *not* believe it! No, of course I am not calling you a liar." She looked over at Ida. "Bobby said Beau's ankle made him take some pain-killers this morning and he's . . ." she lowered her voice to a whisper ". . . high as a kite."

Now *that*, I thought, was the real Mossy Creek.

"There's nobody to take his place," Louise said. "Ida, what—?"

"Anything I can do?"

We all whirled at the quiet question. A man had materialized behind us—a short man with a full white beard, round belly, twinkling eyes, even dimples.

Louise blinked, then quickly asked, "Can you play Santa for the parade?"

He smiled broadly and let go with a loud, merry, "Ho! Ho! Ho!"

Everyone around stopped and turned our way.

I broke the stunned silence. "Wow. A dead ringer. He looks even more authentic than Beau."

"Thank you," the man said, laughter in his whole demeanor.

"No, thank *you*," Louise said. "You've saved our butts. Eustene, can you have Bobby pick up Beau's costume? Maybe it'll fit—"

"I have my own," the new Santa said. "Give me five minutes to change."

Everyone heaved a sigh of relief. The tuba *ooompahed* in celebration. Don Qui brayed.

"I worried this would wind up being the year without a Santa Claus," I whispered to Louise.

"I was afraid we'd have to haul Dick off the driver's box, stuff him into that Santa costume . . ."

"And let the horses drive themselves?" I asked.

Four minutes later, Santa arrived in all his glory.

The entire parade committee stared in wonder.

Our Santa couldn't look more like the real Santa.

"How'd you get changed so quickly?" Ida asked.

The man just grinned. "A little Christmas magic."

"Or miracle," I said. "As in, it's a miracle we have a Santa."

Chuckling, the man spryly swung himself into the wagon and settled on Santa's throne. "Ready when you are."

Dick leaned over and whispered, "You don't know anything about this guy, right?"

I nodded. "Never laid eyes on him and as far as I know, nobody in Mossy Creek has ever laid eyes on him."

"Then maybe I better get up there with him. You know, in case he all of a sudden tries to flash the crowd."

I looked at him, horrified. "You don't think . . ."

"I think it's better to be safe than have to apologize to hundreds of kids later." Dick pointed at his Percherons. "Can you drive these guys?"

"I've driven them before at your place. They'll be okay with me on the box, won't they?"

"They're dead broke, Merry, but no horse is bomb-proof under these circumstances."

"The parade route is just under five miles. I see no alternative."

He looked me over as if to judge not only my competence, but my will. Obviously satisfied, he climbed into the wagon and slipped through the musicians to stand close by Santa's throne, ostensibly to hand him candy to toss to the crowd.

Santa winked at me as if he knew what we were doing and approved.

As prearranged, Eleanor Abercrombie was positioned right in front of the small reviewing stand in the Town Square with her cell phone. She called just as the microphone on the stand squawked.

I listened as the minister of the Unitarian Church give a very short prayer. Ida's threats to cut him off if he got long-winded must have worked. After the prayer, Ida declared the Ninety-Sixth Annual Mossy Creek Christmas Parade open.

As everybody on Town Square a mile away applauded and shouted, I waved at Louise who signaled the parade to begin.

The Mossy Creek High School band—best in the state two years running—stepped off with the Mossy Creek fight song, which raised a few eyebrows.

As they wended through town, those who lined the streets laughed at the Shrine clowns and pointed out the paper chains and other homemade decorations the children had used to decorate the youth groups' floats.

The church floats came next. The Presbyterians' replica of their church as it looked when it was built nearly a hundred-fifty years before had won first place and sported a big blue ribbon right on front.

Next, the fancy Garden Club float elicited oohs and aahs from everyone.

Heinzie, the largest of the three Magi horses, walked ahead of Don Qui; the other two smaller horses walked on either side of him—but not within kicking distance.

Breathless from sprinting back from the head of the parade, Louise climbed up next to me on the Santa wagon. "Here we go."

Meat stood on Don Qui's left side with the lead line snugged up to a few inches from his body. Kristin held the bucking strap with her right hand and cradled the Cabbage Patch Jesus in the crook of her left arm.

As though he had done it a thousand times, Don Qui stepped forward, head high, tail switching like a very small, proud parade horse.

And then came Santa and his quartet. Somebody gave a downbeat. The Holy Horns struck up their version of *Hark the Herald Angels Sing*.

At the first note, I felt the near horse, an eighteen-two-hand mare named Large Marge, stiffen and jerk her head in surprise. She might have been in parades and horse shows before, but she obviously wasn't used to the sound of horns right behind her playing at full volume.

I clucked to her. She relaxed a bit. The right-hand horse, Small Paul, who only stood seventeen three hands tall, didn't bobble. I clucked again and said, "Walk on."

They did.

I was beginning to feel we might actually make it. Don Qui amazed me. Maybe having Heinzie in front of him steadied him.

We made it all the way through town, past the churches and were just turning into Bigelow Road which bracketed Town Square when the horns really started letting loose. I wasn't certain where *When the Saints Go Marching In* ranked in the list of Christmas carols, but apparently close enough. The New Orleans funeral rendition rocked.

The noise was too much for Large Marge. She shook her head, laid her ears back and stomped her hind foot.

Unfortunately, at that moment Earl, the trombone player, seated just behind Louise, swiveled himself and his trombone around and shot the slide straight between Large Marge's back legs. High. And hard.

Large Marge jerked, squealed and kicked high and hard right back. As Marge's giant hooves connected with the dashboard, I gave thanks we'd added bucking straps to the harness. Marge couldn't kick high enough or hard enough to take Louise's or my head off or destroy the wagon.

Louise, however, yelped and slid as far to the left as she could—prepared to bail if necessary.

Balked at kicking, Marge chose instead to rear. In double harness, it was impossible for one horse to rear without hauling the other along. Small Paul was dragged off the ground beside her.

"Whoa! Whoa! Stand!" I shouted, hauling on the reins and reaching for the brake pedal.

There wasn't one. Not on a hay wagon. Marge and Paul didn't break into a canter—there wasn't enough space on the road for that—but they moved off at a fast trot, totally ignoring my commands.

When the horses bolted, the musicians were thrown out of their chairs and landed on hands and knees on the floor of the wagon. Their instruments squawked, the music stands fell over and got tangled in everyone's feet. They all grabbed for something to hang onto while they tried to keep their instruments from rolling off the side of the wagon.

Candy flew out of Santa's bucket, spraying onto the ground around the wagon. Kids ran out almost under the wheels to scoop it up while their parents screamed and dragged them back to the sidewalk.

His eyes laughing as if he were thrilled to be on this roller coaster, Santa continued waving and stayed on his throne. Dick clung to *him*.

Santa gave Dick a cheerful smile. "Ho, Ho, Ho!"

From her perch on the bench beside me, Louise waved madly and shouted, "Kristin! Get out of the way!"

Kristin glanced back, saw disaster trotting straight at her, yanked Don Qui toward the sidewalk and hopped off.

In midair, she tossed the Baby Jesus in a Hail Mary pass straight at Meat.

He dropped Don Qui's lead line, launched himself and caught the now-naked doll six feet from the ground in a catch reminiscent of his interception in the last Homecoming game.

Don Qui leapt onto the sidewalk and ran straight into the spectators.

"Somebody grab that ass!" Kristin yelled.

Recognizing hers as the voice of love and sanctuary, Don Qui wheeled and ran smack into her, braying at the top of his donkey lungs and knocking her flat on the sidewalk.

Meanwhile, I muscled the Percherons down to a fast walk. I stopped them just short of rear-ending the Magi.

For an instant, everyone and everything seemed frozen. And blessedly quiet.

From the crowd came the piercing voice of the lead boy soprano in the Methodist children's choir. "Mommy, that's not the Baby Jesus. He don't got no wee-wee!"

• • •

Everything after that was anticlimactic. The musicians unwound themselves and sorted out their sheet music. With Dick's assistance, Santa Claus regained his throne and tossed the remains of his candy to the crowd, smiling and waving as though this was the way parades always went.

Kristin's hijab hung off one side of her hard hat. Her blue robe looked as though it really had come through the Sinai on a donkey. She took the Baby Jesus from Meat, walked with dignity to the crèche, laid the baby in the manger and reclaimed Don Qui's lead line.

Everyone applauded.

Don Qui brayed and tried to kick her. She sidestepped him neatly, then nudged him hard with her hip. He hung his head and snorted.

The Magi horses, including Heinzie, behaved perfectly throughout the melee and afterward.

Other than a little hard breathing, Large Marge and Small Paul were perfect angels even during the Holy Horns' rendition of *Joy to the World*.

After we all had cocoa and cookies at the Town Hall—which gave the animals time to recover and calm down—we finished the parade.

Back at the staging ground, Large Marge and Small Paul walked into their trailer as though they could not wait to get home. The grooms took out the chairs and music stands, put them in the back of Earl's pickup and loaded the hay wagon inside the van. They made no attempt to sweep up the greenery strewn along the parade route.

Don Qui practically ran into his trailer.

Heinzie, not noted for his intelligence, was simply bemused.

The fairy lights continued to twinkle in the Percherons' manes.

With the exception of a few bruises and a split lip the trumpet player got when his lip connected with his music stand, there were no major injuries.

Everybody congratulated everybody else.

I felt like a prize idiot—as did Earl who'd smacked Large Marge in the rump. Still, everyone agreed that it was a memorable parade.

Ida said, "Just think how well we'll do next year."

Everyone was too startled to answer until Santa Claus boomed, "Ho, Ho, Ho! Merrrry Christmas! Y'all do know how to throw a parade!"

Then something occurred to me. "I'm sorry to say that we never even asked your name."

His eyes twinkled. "Why, Kris Kringle, of course."

"Uh huh."

"Merry Christmas, Merry!"

With that, he threw some sparkly stuff that looked like glitter into the air. My eyes followed it naturally. When I looked back, he was gone.

"Ho. Ho. Ho," Ida said, coming up behind me with Louise. "Another Mossy Creek Christmas Parade come and gone."

I sighed. "This was one for the record book."

Ida and Louise burst out laughing.

I grinned. "You're right. Who am I kidding? This was just another Christmas in Mossy Creek."

WMOS
R A D I O

"The Voice Of The Creek"

Hey, folks! It's your friendly Man-On-The-Air, Bert Lyman, here.

Whoooooeee! Did y'all see the commotion that went on at the Mossy Creek Christmas parade this morning? It was something out of *Wild Kingdom*, I swannee. There were horses going this way and donkeys going that way. Candy shooting everywhere with kids scrambling after it. Cabbage Patch Jesuses flying through the air. Mcat Reece's catch of Baby Jesus was nothing short of sublime, I must say. Hope there were a few scouts out there. If any are listening, I've got it on good authority that Rainey Cecil caught it all on her cell phone. Just give us a call here at WMOS radio and we'll hook you up.

I got the low-down about how it all happened from Louise Sawyer, coordinator of this year's parade. Give a listen—

Okay, wait a minute . . . just gotta push this here button. . . . Got it!

Louise Sawyer: "Yes, I saw it all—actually, I *felt* it all since I was sitting right behind the mare that threw the first punch. The trombone player in the Holy Horns got a little too rambunctious during—oh, I forget what song it was. Anyway, he turned and blew a long note right up the mare's tush. Can I say that on the air? Anyway, it terrified her and she took off. The rest was a chain reaction. Everyone's okay now, though. Nobody hurt. Thank goodness. All's well that ends well, and all that."

That's the scoop, folk. Now back to our Christmas carols. . . .

The main reason Santa is jolly is because
he knows where all the bad girls live.

—George Carlin

The Christmas Competition

The week before Thanksgiving, my grandma, Inez Hamilton Hilley and I were all set to break in a brand-new Korean-made industrial food processor for our chow-chow operation. The Christmas orders were coming in faster than we could fill them, and we needed to grind our signature chili peppers fast.

I read the directions while Grandma stood ready to assemble the parts. "Sure to make fingers not live in chopper hopper," I read.

"Sounds like sage advice." Grandma Inez pushed her glasses higher on her short, round nose and fit the food hopper into the grinder unit. "Now where's that catcher bowl?"

Just as Grandma stuffed a handful of trimmed peppers into the hopper, the door of our newly remodeled commercial kitchen flew open, ushering in a stout old woman on a gust of cold wind.

"Inez! Lucy Belle! I've got news," declared my great-aunt Addie Lou Hamilton Womack. Without a trace of irony—or a trace of a waistline—she wore the tackiest Christmas sweater I ever saw. She and her sister, Grandma Inez, were built like a couple of bowling balls. A leering, felt Rudolph was appliquéd to the front of the sweater with a garland of pompoms swinging from his antlers.

Addie Lou paused for dramatic effect, then—as if she were proclaiming the devil's name himself—said in a stage whisper, "It's Ardaleen."

Inez's snow-white eyebrow flew upward like a gull's wing.

She and her cousin Ardaleen had been mortal enemies since Ardaleen turned her back on Mossy Creek years ago. Theirs had been a battle of constant one-upmanship ever since. They clashed over everything from pickles and preserves competitions at the Bigelow County Fair to the County Extension Service's Top Master Gardener contest to the Georgia Needlework Guild's crochet-off. Ardaleen had proven she would resort to the most underhanded of tactics to prevail in their challenges. Truth to tell, Grandma wasn't much better, and there was a burned-out Mercedes sedan somewhere in the county junkyard to prove it.

"What has she done?" Grandma demanded.

Addie Lou took a deep breath. "She's started decorating Bigelow for Christmas."

Inez started so violently she somehow activated the foreign food processor, which roared to life beneath her hands.

"Watch your fingers!" I shouted.

Inez released the machine, but not before a torrent of chewed-up red chili peppers exploded from its maw and sprayed the kitchen like blood spatter.

Addie Lou pointed out, "You're supposed to have the catcher bowl under that spout."

"Ya think?" Inez dabbed red goo off her glasses with a dishtowel. She gave the mess not a glance; she had more important matters on her mind. Grandma and I were perennial chair and vice-chair, respectively, of the Mossy Creek Municipal Christmas Decorating Committee, and we took our responsibilities seriously. "How do you know she's started decorating?"

"I had to drive through Bigelow on my way back from my podiatrist appointment, and I seen the decorations with my own two eyes. You know my bunion acts up something fierce when the weather cools down. Anyway, them decorations was about to go up."

"Ardaleen couldn't," I stated. "Could she? It isn't even Thanksgiving yet." Breaking the longstanding agreement that neither side would begin their tinsel-tossing activities before December first was nothing short of an act of war.

Addie Lou crossed her heart, causing Rudolph's cottontail to wag. "Some workmen were unloading boxes onto the sidewalk in the middle of town. Ardaleen was there too. She had them break one open and take something out."

Grandma and I leaned forward. "What was it?" Grandma asked.

"I'm not sure, but . . ." Here, Addie Lou paused for effect and gestured into the distance with one QVC-jewel-encrusted finger. "As sure as God made little green apples, there, twinkling in the sun, I saw tinsel."

"Tinsel?" Grandma and I repeated in unison.

"Tinsel," Addie Lou intoned.

"Why this year—after all these years—is Ardaleen breaking the pact?" I asked. The agreement was struck before I was born. The two had agreed to a fair fight in the spirit of the season and for the sake of the blessed Baby Jesus.

"Something's not right," Grandma declared. "Something's different." Her beady, black eyes focused into space as if she could see into downtown Bigelow with only her mind's eye.

"What are you thinking, Grandma?" I asked with trepidation.

"We've got to go and see for ourselves," she declared.

"But what about all those chow-chow orders?" I insisted.

"Priorities, child," Grandma said firmly.

"Shotgun!" hollered Addie Lou.

• • •

Grandma had always wanted a Cadillac, so when our chow-chow business—which now included Mossy Creek Red-Hot Apple Rings—took off, she bought a big, black Escalade SUV with fancy rims. Our company logo (a red chili pepper with yellow flames shooting out of it) was emblazoned tastefully on each side.

Needless to say, there was nothing covert about our reconnaissance mission. Our driving down Bigelow's main drag was akin to one of Patton's Sherman tanks driving up to Rommel's headquarters and tweaking his nose.

Grandma, whose legs were so short her foot barely touched the pedals, insisted on driving. Her oxygen bottle was in its customary holster as she chomped her Nicorette gum. Inez in full nicotine withdrawal was not something you ever wanted to experience.

"There she is!" Addie Lou exclaimed. "There on the next block."

Grandma locked onto her target like an F-16 and stomped the accelerator.

"Get us through this block in one piece first!" I cried.

Grandma had already started into the traffic circle without yielding to the oncoming compact car on her left. The Georgia Department of Transportation had begun installing European-style roundabouts here and there, and this had been one of the first by virtue of the fact that this was the governor's hometown. It was meant to ease traffic. However, Grandma seemed to regard it as a specially engineered game of chicken.

In a maneuver worthy of an astronaut training exercise in G forces, Grandma slingshot us out of the circle and into the next block. Ardaleen was indeed standing on the sidewalk, clipboard in hand. Beside her, in a tiny shearling coat, was her ridiculous Shih Tzu, Pierre.

That dog detested me with the white-hot hatred of the truly wronged. Without meaning to, I had been the source of that pooch's pain and humiliation on a number of occasions. I had nearly drowned him by accident at a garden party and had inadvertently given the lining of his mouth first-degree burns from hot chili peppers.

"Look," Addie Lou pointed out, "fussy old Ardaleen made those city workers line up those crates as straight as a row of tin soldiers."

"Slow down," I urged Grandma.

"What?" replied the selectively hearing-impaired Inez.

Just as Ardaleen spied the Caddy with her elderly, elfin cousin at the wheel, the vehicle's front wheel hit a rut and the vehicle headed directly for Ardaleen and her cargo.

"Watch out!" I yelled.

"Mercy!" Addie Lou hollered.

Grandma stomped on the brakes and the SUV skidded to a long, screeching stop, but not before it connected with the first in the long row of crates with a loud crunch.

I was out of the backseat in a flash to inspect the damage, Grandma and Addie Lou close behind me. The Escalade was fine. There wasn't a scratch on the bumper. I couldn't say the same for the crate it struck, which teetered ominously for a moment before falling heavily onto the next crate. That one, in turn, began its own descent.

The three old women, the workmen, the dog and I all froze in unison watching the giant dominoes as they began to fall. By the time the third one started to totter, Ardaleen's mouth was working like a beached guppy's.

"Do something!" she screeched at the workmen.

The workers ran to the next falling domino, but seemed loath to put themselves in harm's way to save crates of teetering tinsel. And who could blame them? While the others fixed their gazes on the falling boxes, I noticed that the first one had burst open at the corner where the SUV's bumper had struck it. I stooped down and lifted the cracked piece of wood.

Garlands of blue-and-white tinsel and other reflective materials winked in the sun like giant, shiny snakes coiled and ready to strike. On top of the stacked loops nested a silver Mylar diamond.

A booted foot came down onto the top of the busted crate, closing it from further inspection. Ardaleen and Pierre both bared their teeth at me.

"How dare you try and sabotage Bigelow's Christmas decorating!" Ardaleen said, addressing Grandma, Addie Lou and me.

"How dare you break our agreement not to start before December first?" Grandma demanded.

Ardaleen waved a dismissive hand. "Bigelow has outgrown that musty old agreement. It was only your attempt to hold us back anyway. Li'l ol' Mossy Creek can't compete with us in anything. We're out of your league."

Grandma's eyes flashed with outrage. "Oh yeah? Mossy Creek's decorations will put Bigelow's to shame just like they do every year, just like my fudge pound cake put your apple cobbler to shame in the last county bake-off."

Ardaleen was so visibly shaken her big hair bobbed forward for a moment. "Well . . . I . . . never!"

"Never beat me in a cook-off, bake-off, county fair contest, county extension contest, and you never will."

"Oh, snap," Addie Lou put in.

"Burn," I observed.

The trash talk grew fast and furious, and I took advantage of the melee to sneak around behind Ardaleen. "Psst!" I tried to get the attention of the nearest city worker, but he was wearing ear buds. Then I saw Pierre. The Shih Tzu is a sweet-natured breed by all accounts, but not this tiny terror. As if sensing what I was up to, he advanced on me, growling as menacingly as he could manage.

"Nice coat," I said to him.

I heard one of the other workmen laugh. "He's got a better coat than the one I'm getting my wife for Christmas."

"Say," I said, "do you know what the, uh, theme of these Christmas decorations is?"

"Tacky?" he suggested.

"Probably, but what's the, you know, message?"

"I don't have a clue, lady, but I do know that you're about to have trouble." I followed the direction of his gaze and my feet got to moving as soon as I saw the black-and-white Crown Victoria easing toward us.

"Visit's over. Time to go," I said to Grandma and Addie Lou, catching each of them by one arm and steering them back toward the Escalade.

Fortunately, Grandma saw the cop car before Ardaleen did and got it in gear, but not before Ardaleen flung out one last salvo: "You just wait and see what Bigelow has in store for Mossy Creek. It's a Christmas present you won't soon forget!"

We were all buckled in by the time Ardaleen had a chance to approach the cruiser with her complaints against us. Grandma executed a sharp U-turn, taking advantage of the fact that the scattered crates blocked the police car's way. By the time the sputtering Ardaleen had made her accusations and the workmen had cleared the street, we were long gone.

• • •

Just after lunch the next day, Grandma stood in front of a whiteboard in the community room of the library, a dry-erase maker in her hand. She looked hopefully from one member of the Mossy Creek Historical Preservation Society to the next. That is to say, from the wizened and judgmental face of Adele Clearwater to the inquisitive face of jack-of-all-trades Dan McNeil.

The main goal of the Society was to preserve the ambience of Mossy Creek, so they were a more-or-less natural choice to help brainstorm a new theme for this year's decorations. I say more-or-less because their secondary goal was to mind other people's business, especially when it came to what they did with their own property. They might prove more hindrance than help, depending on how creative Grandma wanted to get. But if she could get them on board with a new-and-improved decorating theme, their buy-in could prove valuable.

"I thought we were using last year's decorations in order to save money," Dan stated.

"Last year's municipal decorations are perfectly good. They were very tasteful," Adele said, smoothing her skirt over her knobby knees.

"Thank you, Adele," Grandma said patiently. "But as I just explained, Bigelow is stepping up their game this year, and we must do the same. We used the Winter Wonderland theme already. We need to come up with something new, something that will make people sit up and take notice."

"Are the citizens of Mossy Creek expected to use the same theme in their own yard decorations for consistency's sake?" Adele wanted to know.

"Ideally, yes," Grandma said. "I think that would make the biggest impact."

Adele nodded in agreement, no doubt savoring the excuse to tell people how their front lawns ought to look.

"Wait a minute," I said. "We've never asked people to do that before. Doesn't expecting everyone to go with one theme violate the Mossy Creek spirit of independence and individualism?"

Adele and Dan looked at me as if I'd just suggested we all join up with the Taliban.

"They can be independent and individual, as long as they follow our rules," Grandma explained patiently. "Now, the theme itself has to be perfect. That's the key."

Dan looked at me. "What's our budget for this, Lucy Belle?"

"Uh," I began, but Grandma cut me off.

"Never mind that," she said.

"Are you underwriting the purchase of a whole new set of municipal decorations?" Adele challenged.

"Well, then . . ." Dan said, a twinkle forming in his eye, likely imagining all the lumber and nails he was going to buy with our chow-chow money.

"Wait a minute," I said, waving my hands. "We don't have a budget this year."

"That's what I figured," Adele said sourly. "It seems to me that it's too late and too expensive to devise another theme."

"Not at all!" Inez insisted. "All we need is a new direction, a creative spark, something that sizzles and pops, not something necessarily expensive."

"I've got it," Dan put in. "How about a down-home, country Christmas? I can take a couple of wagons from Ida's farm and make them look like sleighs."

"And do what with them? Hitch the dairy cows to them?" Adele harrumphed.

"We could make garlands out of popcorn and cranberries," Dan said, undeterred. "Just like in the old days."

"How long do you think it would take for the birds to eat that, you loon?" Adele asked.

"Yeah, no," Grandma said, stroking her chin. "That idea doesn't wow me."

"Me neither," Adele said.

"Okay, then, let's hear one of your bright ideas." Dan glared at Adele.

"I suggest a traditional-values Christmas," Adele said. "We at the Yonder Faith and Forgiveness Baptist Church feel . . ." She attempted to elaborate, but thank goodness Inez cut in quickly.

"Pass," Inez said. "Come on, people. Let's get with it."

Dan and Adele exchanged affronted glances.

"I'll tell you what," Dan said, standing. "I've got a business to run. Why don't you just decide what you want the decorating theme to be and let us know."

"And we'll let you know if we think the theme is appropriate for Mossy Creek," Adele said.

"I don't even know why we have to make this a competition with Bigelow anyway," Dan said. "Just let them have their display as we have ours. Who cares whose is the fanciest?"

The Mossy Creek Historical Society took their exit, muttering about having motorized bookcases to build and Bible studies to attend.

Inez capped the marker and threw it onto the floor in frustration. "They were no help at all," she declared.

I could have told her that going in, but when Grandma's on a mission, there's no telling her anything. "Grandma, December is just around the corner. What are the odds that we can pull off a town-wide, blockbuster Christmas display at this late date?" I asked.

"It's like Han Solo said in *Star Wars*," Grandma said cryptically.

"'Let the wookie win'?" I quoted, thinking of Ardaleen, the resources of the governor behind her, and the never-ending competition between the two cousins. "Grandma, have you ever thought that maybe, just maybe, it might be time to let Ardaleen grab the brass ring?"

Grandma gave me a defiant stare. "Not on your life!"

"Okay," I said. "What else did Han Solo say?"

"'Never tell me the odds, kid.'"

• • •

Two days later, Grandma and I still hadn't gotten the new food processor to give up its secrets. "This thing has got to be from *North* Korea," Inez said. "They sent it here to drive us crazy so they could launch an invasion."

"I doubt if it's weaponized," I said. "The chili peppers are certainly in no danger." The machine had tuckered out after its initial burst of energy. The motor now produced approximately the same number of revolutions per minute as an octogenarian figure skater.

While working over the chow-chow, Inez and I alternately pitched ideas for Christmas themes to each other, cussed at the food processor and argued about the advisability of taking on

Ardaleen and all of Bigelow over Christmas decorations again. "Can't you just give it a rest this year?" I asked. "Why don't you take joy in the fact that our business is thriving and Piggly Wiggly is considering a distribution deal for the chow-chow and red-hot apple rings?"

While the business was profitable enough for Inez to buy that new Escalade, she couldn't underwrite new city decorations and make those payments at the same time. And I certainly wasn't going to spend my hard-earned money on artificial Christmas trees and the like.

"Never!" she declared and launched into a harangue about Bigelows and old injustices.

I was thankful when a knock at the door interrupted her.

"Come in!" I called. It could be the Grinch himself at the door as long as something stopped Inez's ratchet jawing, at least temporarily.

Dan McNeil stepped into the kitchen and removed his Mossy Creek Lady Mustangs softball cap. "Ladies," he greeted. He carried a glossy brochure in one hand.

"Why, howdy, Dan," Grandma said. "What brings you by?"

"I think I've figured out why Bigelow is pulling out all the Christmas-decorating stops this year." He waved the publication he held.

Grandma nearly jumped the kitchen counter in her eagerness to find out what he'd discovered. She and I stood before him anxiously.

"I took a little drive to an auction up in Chattanooga and stopped at a rest station near the Tennessee state line. They were giving away these here Christmas travel brochures. It says on the back that it was produced and distributed by Governor Ham Bigelow's Travel and Tourism department."

Sensing trouble, Grandma fixed her sharp gaze on the publication's cover as Dan held up the brochure for our inspection.

"It's promoting a 'Spend Christmas in Georgia' campaign," I observed.

The cover depicted a Christmas tree with the most picturesque Georgia mountain cities shown as lights on the tree. Helen, Blairsville, Toccoa, Blue Ridge—all the prominent cities were shown—except Mossy Creek! And to add insult to injury,

Bigelow was at the apex of the tree, depicted not as a star but as a diamond. The text beside the diamond read "Bigelow, the jewel in North Georgia's Christmas crown. "

Grandma's face went rigid with fury. I exchanged worried glances with Dan. I was afraid Grandma would have a stroke. For his part, I expect Dan feared she would try to kill the messenger.

"This is what Ardaleen meant when she said Bigelow had a Christmas present for Mossy Creek we wouldn't soon forget!"

"This explains what those tacky Mylar diamonds signified," I added.

I could see competitive fire replace the rage in Inez's eyes, which was almost as scary. "Now," she railed. "Do you *still* want to let Bigelow win this year?"

I looked again at that wretched piece of art on the brochure's cover, and I had to admit it got my goat. "No, I don't."

Ever the tinkerer, Dan's eye had been caught by the shiny, North Korean food processor. "What is this thing?" he wanted to know.

"It's a red communist food processor that doesn't work worth a flip," Inez told him.

"You mind if I try to fix it?"

I waved a hand dismissively. "Knock yourself out."

He laid the brochure on the counter, put his ball cap back on his head and hoisted the food chopper under one arm. We bid him goodbye as he let himself out.

"So what are we going to do now?" I asked Grandma Inez.

"We take it to the town," she said. "This is war."

• • •

Inez prevailed on her cousin Ida to call a town meeting for the next day. Emails and texts were dispatched and the telephone "tree" was employed to reach citizens who eschewed computers and cell phones.

Grandma lured attendees by promising a weenie roast in the Town Square—complete with all the chow-chow you could dress your hotdog with, of course. I handed out sharp sticks for people to roast weenies and jumbo marshmallows while directing them to pick up one of the brochures we had spirited out of the giveaway racks from all the North Georgia retail establishments we could reach on short notice.

So that she could be better seen and heard, Dan helped Grandma climb up onto the base of the statue of General Augustus Brimberry Hamilton of Jefferson Davis's Third Confederate Division. Grandma held fast to the general's granite leg near the loose, bronze plaque where Millicent Abigail Hart Lavender hides her stolen loot. As people skewered their weenies and roasted their marshmallows, Grandma held forth.

"Fellow citizens of Mossy Creek," she sang out. "Many of you have seen the abject insult that has been dealt us by Governor Ham Bigelow's state Travel and Tourism department." She waved the Christmas brochure for effect. There were nods of assent, murmurs of agreement and belches of indifference from the crowd.

"There are a good number of us who rely on the tourist trade for at least part of our incomes. The omission of Mossy Creek from the Christmas campaign takes money from our pockets and food from our tables!"

I noticed some of the merchants in the crowd, like Pearl Quinlan and Eugenia Townsend, nodding in agreement.

"But this is not just an economic issue. Folks, this is about Mossy Creek pride! Our rivalry with Bigelow is legendary. A school was burned down, an elephant was lost, livestock was toasted and traumatized, and the list goes on. We can't let them and the governor get away with slighting Mossy Creek in this despicable way."

I shivered, put in mind of the angry mobs in the old monster movies.

"So fellow citizens, I propose that we not take this effrontery and economic terrorism lying down. I say we attract our own holiday tourists to Mossy Creek by decorating our town using the most meaningful, original, unifying Christmas theme we can come up with! We want a theme that will embody the blessed peace of the Christmas season—a theme that will kick Bigelow right in the butt."

I winced, wishing I'd been close enough to Grandma to stuff a hotdog in her mouth. Judging by the looks on the gathered faces, Grandma's discordant note seemed to have turned off some and fired up others. I sighed and popped a charred marshmallow in my mouth.

"So as chairwoman of the Mossy Creek Christmas Decorating committee, I'm announcing a contest for the best Christmas theme. Me and Lucy Belle, my vice chairwoman, will be the judges."

"Uh-oh," I muttered. I could see myself falling off of a slew of Christmas lists this year.

"Since time is short," Grandma continued, "we need you to bring your ideas, mockups and proofs of concept right here to the Town Square day after tomorrow at high noon. Then Lucy Belle and I will name a winner and the Christmas decorating will begin! Let's hear it for Mossy Creek Pride!"

A cheer went up from the crowd. Never let it be said that Inez Hamilton Hilley can't rouse the rabble. It only remained to be seen if the rabble could rise to the occasion and come up with an idea that Inez could get behind.

• • •

Two days later—what I was calling *Judgment Day*—full of hope and anticipation, Inez and I set up a folding table and chairs at the base of the statue in Town Square.

By half past noon, Grandma's blood pressure was rising and my heart was sinking. The suggestions the townspeople had come up with were, by turns, uninspiring, inappropriate, boring, tacky, ridiculous and downright appalling.

Rainey Cecil of Goldilocks Hair, Nail and Tanning Salon on Main, came up with a theme she called, "The Beauty of Christmas" which involved—as near as I could figure—local beauty queens in winter regalia (complete with expensive up-do's provided by Rainey herself, no doubt) posing in people's yards with a beauty contest to follow.

Orville Gene Simple had driven forth a faded plastic Christmas tree in the bed of his truck. The tree, like Orville's driveway, was decorated with hubcaps, as many as could be wired onto it. Grandma and I couldn't quite tell what theme he as trying to express, but we thanked him for his efforts.

Stone-deaf Lorna Bingham had suggested a "SpongeBob

Square Dance" Christmas because her pal, young John Wesley McCready, liked the program and she had surely loved a good square dance in her youth.

Foxer Atlas, denizen of the Mossy Creek library, proposed a "Historical" Mossy Creek Christmas, which might as well have been a "Hysterical" Christmas—as in hysterically funny. He had rendered a model of Richard Stanhope and his bride Isabella Salter in papier-mâché, complete with a Downton Abbey-like structure in the background, festooned with colored lights. The papier-mâché had a rough texture and looked as if it had been caught in the rain. It didn't look like a historical diorama as much as a giant dirt dauber nest.

"Of course, the final version will be life-sized," he assured us.

"God a'mighty," I muttered.

"What was that?" said Foxer.

"I said, 'that'll take a lot of Mod Podge, all righty.'"

Grandma gave me a withering look. "Thanks, Foxer. We'll let you know."

The old ladies' man gave her a wink and towed his creation away in a Radio Flyer.

"Grandma, that was our last contestant. What are we going to do?"

"I was about to ask you the same question." Restaurateur and cooking show host Win Allen had been standing behind us while we viewed Foxer's creation. As president of the Town Council, Win had to deal with one headache after another. I guessed he figured the Christmas decorating dilemma was his latest migraine.

"Do you ladies have the decoration situation under control?"

"Of course we do," Grandma said.

"We do?" I asked.

Grandma scowled at me for not backing her up.

Win regarded her doubtfully. "It doesn't look like you got two good ideas to rub together."

"I wouldn't say that," Inez said defensively. "I think some of the ideas have merit."

"Which ones would those be?" Win asked. "Flaviberto's Latin boogie Christmas or Del Jackson's martial arts Christmas?"

"We've got it covered," she insisted.

43

"Why don't you come by the city council meeting tomorrow and we'll all discuss it?"

Smelling a rat, Grandma's eyes narrowed and she scanned the small gathering of onlookers. Adele Clearwater gazed off at something in the distance to keep from making eye contact with Grandma.

"Why sure, Win. We'd be happy to."

Win thanked us and walked away.

"Adele must have complained to Win," I said.

"The old heifer," Grandma said. "So what are we going to tell the council?"

"Never mind that." I gestured at the small crowd. "What are we going to tell these people who are waiting for us to name a winner?"

Grandma grabbed my hand when they weren't looking. "Follow me."

Hunching over, she led me around behind Orville Gene Simple's pickup, which he'd just fired up to head back home. I eased down the tailgate and helped her scramble in, then climbed in beside her. We hunkered down behind the tree so nobody could see us, hubcaps knocking us in the head.

We rode as far as the end of our street before we knocked on the cab window for Orville to stop and let us out. For some reason, he didn't seem surprised that we were there. We hoofed it back home wondering what we were going to do next.

• • •

The next day, Win Allen pounded his gavel to bring the meeting to order and to silence the rumble of angry voices from the standing-room-only crowd. The citizenry were none too happy with Inez and me for bugging out of our own Christmas theme competition, and I couldn't rightly blame them.

When things were quiet, Win pointed his gavel at us. "Have you ladies made a decision as to who won the Christmas theme contest?"

"Uh, well, not exactly," Inez began.

A low buzz of voices started up, and Win pounded his gavel again, asking patiently, "Why not?"

"The, ah, the entries were so good, we just couldn't decide," Inez said.

"Are you kidding me?" I whispered.

Council member Albert "Egg" Egbert, a retired Georgia Tech professor, said, "Well, go ahead and name a winner and a theme right here and now. What's it going to be?"

Inez said, "The problem is, as good as the entries were, nothing was exactly . . . right."

The mob-like rabble from the assembled crowd increased in volume.

"As I understand it," Win said, "the original plan was to go with the same theme as last year for budgetary reasons. If you're not prepared to name a new theme and a plan to execute it, I think we should go ahead and do what was originally agreed to."

Inez began to repeat her spiel about the importance of outdoing Bigelow in the Christmas decoration arena, but Win held up a hand to silence her. "I know all about the competitive aspects of this situation. But the parade and tree-lighting ceremony is a week from Saturday, so the decorations should already be up."

Grandma gave him her best sweet-little-old-lady face and said, "Win, I'm an old woman and I just don't know which one of these years will be my last. I just want this year to be special."

"Here we go," I muttered under my breath.

Inez ignored me. "The Christmas decorating committee is what I live for."

This was Grandma's go-to argument with her family, when it was clear that her latest whim would not be indulged unless she played the card of last resort. The I-might-not-be-here-tomorrow card. When she was really on her game, she could even squeeze out a little tear. I watched her closely as she and Win stared each other down. She produced a delicately embroidered hanky from her cleavage and dabbed at bone-dry eyes with it. And then, there they came. Copious tears streamed down her face.

My nose twitched. The unmistakable aroma of hot chili pepper juice wafted from the hanky. "Seriously?" I hissed *sotto voce*. "You're unbelievable."

I could tell by the look of discomfort on Win's face that he would cave. "All right, Inez," he said. "I'll give you one more day and if you don't have a solution by then, come Monday morning, the city workers will begin putting up last year's decorations without committee supervision."

As people began to file out, I caught the eye of Adele Clearwater. She pointed to her eyes with two fingers and then pointed at us in the universal "I'm watching you" gesture. Grandma was about to hold up her hand with her own gesture in reply but I wrist-wrestled her arm down before anyone could see it.

"Why prolong this?" I demanded of her. "If you haven't thought up the perfect theme by this time, you're not going to."

"Have faith, child," she said. "My muse will arrive just in time. I know it." She squinted, her eyes red and rheumy.

"That makes one of us," I muttered.

• • •

The next morning, Inez and I were driving out South Bigelow road on the way to the big membership warehouse out on the interstate. We had run out of vinegar and sugar, so we had to make a quick run for an SUV load of the stuff. Plus, Inez was partial to their cranberry chicken salad with pecans, and I liked their huge bags of coffee.

We had barely made it out of Mossy Creek when Inez screeched on the brakes. There, right even with the *Leaving Mossy Creek* sign, was a highway sign proclaiming Bigelow as the Jewel in Georgia's Christmas crown. Inez swore and banged her fist on the steering wheel.

"Shake it off!" I urged, and Inez drove on. Unfortunately, the same sign had been erected every half mile or so from Mossy Creek to the interstate.

"This is like those Burma Shave signs," Inez fumed.

"What?"

"Never mind. That was before your time. This stunt has Ardaleen's fingerprints all over it."

"It's such a shame that she has to disrespect her own hometown," I said.

"If she could wipe it off the map, she probably would," Inez said bitterly.

"That reminds me of what Cousin Ida once said. 'We might make only a pinpoint on maps of the world, but that pinpoint is a jewel.' And now Ardaleen has twisted that lovely sentiment for her own ends."

"She probably put Ham up to making the Department of Transportation erect those signs. I'm surprised he hasn't hired skywriters."

"Don't put it past him."

I imagined governor Ham Bigelow hiring private planes to skywrite the dreaded slogan. I could also imagine Inez letting loose with an anti-aircraft barrage with her AR-15. I suspected that most general aviation pilots weren't used to incoming flak from the countryside. Thoughts of gunfire and Cousin Ida were beginning to give me inspiration, however.

Inez, simmering with impotent rage, went on another of her rants, threatening to erect decorations that featured all of Ardaleen's past misdeeds.

"That would hardly suit the spirit of the season," I said. "However, it does give me an idea."

"Do tell!" Inez perked up. "What kind of idea?"

"One that actually will remind people of one of the gravest insults that Ardaleen and Ham ever tried to dole out to Mossy Creek."

"That's my girl!"

"The stunt I have in mind will remind everyone that you can't push Mossy Creek around, at least not where highway signage is concerned. Besides it has a certain historical resonance."

"Sounds perfect. What do we do?"

"Stop at that auto parts store up ahead and I'll show you."

• • •

As soon as it got dark, Inez and I set out to make our statement. We donned black sweat suits and covered our faces with dark face paint. We enlisted Aunt Addie Lou as a co-conspirator and getaway driver since her Buick sedan was not painted with our logo.

The plan was to sneak up to each of the hated highway signs and plaster them with bullet-hole decals. The kind that young men with more testosterone than sense put on their pickup trucks to make it look to the world as if they led an edgier existence than living in their mom and dad's basement.

Certainly, my and Inez's gesture was childish; maybe it was even a little crazy. But in our hands, the decals became an homage to the awe-inspiring way in which Ida dealt with another one of Ham's offensive signs a few years back. He had state workers erect signs with a new town motto, the opposite of the real one.

Our beloved motto, welcoming visitors and newcomers for generations, had been painted on the Hamilton farm's silo as far back as anyone could remember:

Welcome to Mossy Creek, The Town You Can Count On.
Ain't Going Nowhere and Don't Want To.

The new welcome sign had said:

The Town That IS Going Somewhere,
And DOES Want To.
By Order of Hamilton Bigelow, Governor of Georgia

Ida's response was to pepper that sign with so many shells from her heirloom twelve-gauge shotgun the only letters that were left visible spelled "Ham to Go."

"This is what you might call poetic justice," Inez said as she peeled the backing off of a sticker.

"It's certainly punishment that fits the crime. That shotgun of Ida's is a nice piece. She took it out of the mahogany gun cabinet in her parlor office and showed it to me once."

"That the one with the silver-inlaid Hamilton crest?"

"That's the one."

"You know," Inez began. "We could always . . ."

"Don't even think about it," I said. "This lets us make our point without gunplay." Inez shot like she drove, and I didn't care to wind up with a backside full of accidental buckshot.

"You're no fun sometimes," Inez said with a sigh, but I could tell that the whole enterprise had raised her spirits.

In fact, I was mentally congratulating myself on the perfection of my stunt all the way up until the blue bubble lights topped the hill behind us.

"Run," Inez said, hugging her oxygen bottle. We both hightailed it for Addie Lou's sedan, but Grandma ran with the approximate speed and grace of a 'possum crossing the road, and I'm not much faster.

Before we could make it to the car, a huge state trooper was out of his cruiser, training a flashlight in our eyes and telling us to show him our hands. Next thing we knew, he was telling us to spread said hands onto the roof of his patrol car.

When the trooper felt Grandma's shoulders, her eyes opened wide. She began to speak, a note of disbelief in her voice. "Am I being frisked?"

"Yes, ma'am," the trooper said.

When his hands went from her waist to her hips, I saw an expression in her eyes I'd never seen before. I was afraid the indignity was about to cause her mind to snap.

I finally found my voice. "Uh, what seems to be the problem, officer?"

"I'm arresting you for defacing state property."

"Why, we're not doing any such thing. We-we're having car trouble," I insisted. "What would make you think we were defacing state property?"

"Mostly that," the trooper said, training his flashlight beam on the trail of decals that led, like Hansel and Gretel's bread-crumbs, from the highway sign all the way to the ones spilling out of Inez's back pocket.

At that, Inez snapped out of her funk and turned on me. "I told you we should have shot those signs, just like Ida! At least we would have had our bail money's worth of mischief."

I rolled my eyes at Inez, who'd just incriminated the both of us. I pointed a finger at her. "You have the right to remain silent!"

The trooper glared at the both of us. "I'm supposed to say that."

The state trooper turned out not to be completely heartless. He listened to aunt Addie Lou swear that she had no idea what Inez and I were up to and decided to let her go on back home.

When we got to the county jail in Bigelow, Grandma insisted on her phone call, the one they promise everybody who gets ar-rested in the movies. She called Teresa Hamilton Walker, wife of Ida's son Robert. I'd insisted to Inez that as a tax attorney, Teresa might not be the best choice to represent us even if she was kin. But of course, Grandma ignored me.

While Grandma was talking to Teresa, I thought about our situation. It seemed mighty strange to me that the State Patrol would be out of their usual jurisdiction on the interstate and on South Bigelow Road in the middle of the night. In fact, I wouldn't have put it past Ardaleen if she'd alerted the GSP to look for vandals in the proximity of the new signage. Entrapment! That's what this was.

I interrupted Grandma's conversation and urged her not to insist that Teresa come to the jailhouse in the middle of the night. She argued with me until I explained the advantages of waiting to be bailed out until the next day. She'd understood immediately and made herself comfortable on the cot in our cell with a smile on her cherubic face.

Then I asked the deputy for a phone call of my own. I contacted my old UGA college roommate, apologized for the hour and apprised her of the situation.

• • •

On cue, Ardaleen showed up at the county jail bright and early in the morning. Grandma and I were looking out our barred window when her car pulled into the parking lot.

It was pretty plain that she'd been tipped off to our arrest by the sheriff if not by the State Patrol itself. Just as I'd suspected.

"You smelled a rat, and here she is," Grandma observed.

In a few moments, Ardaleen came strutting down the aisle between the rows of cells, the vile Pierre tucked into the crook of her elbow.

"I should have known," she began, "that you have no more respect for your betters, or for authority itself, than you ever did."

"Betters!" Grandma sputtered. "Why I oughta—"

I elbowed her in the ribs and she hushed, although I could tell that it took every ounce of her inconsiderable self-control to do so.

Ardaleen went on an extended rant that insulted Mossy Creek in general and the Mossy Creek Hamiltons in particular. Dripping with venomous condescension and contempt, the diatribe was quite spectacular in its use of colorful language.

For his part, Pierre glared and growled at me the whole time, barking now and then as if to punctuate his mistress's barbs. For her part, Grandma had put on what I called her "Mrs. Santa face." With her little wire glasses, round face and button nose, all she needed was the little red cap and she could look like every Mrs. Santa Claus in any picture book. Add to that the guileless, hurt expression she feigned and she made you want to put your arms around her and pat her on the head.

"Poor little podunk Mossy Creek," Ardaleen sneered. "I was in the square that day you had your little contest and saw all those pitiful homemade Christmas decorations your towns-people paraded past. What a sorry display that was. Y'all have been in Bigelow's shadow for so long, it just drives you crazy, doesn't it?"

"You know what the definition of crazy is, cousin Ardaleen?" I asked.

"Enlighten me, Lucy Belle," she declared, looking down her nose.

"Doing the same thing over and over and expecting a different result."

"Cut!" called out Ginger Rude, my old college roommate and producer of the noon news on Channel 4 in Atlanta.

Ardaleen's eyes went wide and she whirled to face the camera crew. For good measure, Ginger had brought along a couple of the network flagship station's radio reporters as well.

"This is like déjà vu all over again," Inez said.

"Ida's arrest for sign shooting resulted in some awfully bad publicity for Governor Bigelow, didn't it?"

Ginger called out to me, "We've got all we need for a great piece. Thanks for the tip." She shook my hand through the bars. "Say, how soon can you get sprung from here? We've got plenty of time for a cup of coffee before our live standup in front of the courthouse for the noon news."

"Should be any minute now," I said. Ginger had studied for her degree from the University of Georgia's Henry W. Grady school of journalism while I studied computer science.

Ginger, signaling the cameraman to start shooting again, took advantage of the opportunity to get a quote. "Mrs. Bigelow, can you tell us what this feud with your family and Mossy Creek neighbors says about your son's ability to be statesmanlike if he ever decides to run for higher office? Does fractiousness run in your family?"

She has no idea.

Ardaleen looked as if she'd been slapped. Pierre responded by grabbing the microphone in his teeth and tearing away the spongy gray, wind-protecting cover.

After our coffee with Ginger, Inez and I made it to Bigelow's sports bar just in time to watch the noon news on the big screen.

Teresa hadn't had to bail us out after all, because the charges were quickly and mysteriously dropped. We'd caught her on her cell phone before she'd driven all the way to Bigelow, and then called Addie Lou to come and pick us up.

While we waited, Grandma put two fingers in her mouth and whistled for the bartender. "Two Irish coffees," she called.

"Isn't it a little early?" I asked.

"It's never too early to celebrate," she said.

Ardaleen's conniption fit was the lead story. The footage depicted her clearly as a vicious harpy who got her jollies from shaming elderly townspeople over homemade Christmas ornaments. It was a thing of beauty. I could just hear Ham reading his mother the riot act for the bad publicity.

"Ho, ho, ho. Merry Christmas," I said.

"She's a ho, all right," Grandma said.

When the bartender put two steaming mugs before us, I raised mine toward Inez. "Grandma, you have won the day no matter what happens with the Christmas decoration competition."

Inez clinked my glass with hers. "Child, I had plenty of time to think while we were in the pokey overnight."

"Oh?" I took a sip of the warming drink, just what the doctor ordered.

"Yep, I got to thinking about what you said when we first met with the historical society, and you were right."

"I was?" The alcohol surely wasn't making me loopy already. But I could have sworn I just heard Grandma say I was right about something.

"Yes, you were, and I've made a decision about the theme. It's time to get everyone to work."

• • •

So Bigelow would be the focus of media attention, Ardaleen had decided that their tree-lighting ceremony would be a week after all the other north Georgia towns included in the Christmas tourism campaign—the week after Thanksgiving weekend. Inez and I had selected the same night for the Mossy Creek pageant of Christmas displays for the opposite reason—so there would be fewer comparisons of the two towns' decorations.

It was finally time to end the decorating competition.

It helped us time-wise, as well, because it gave us time to bring Creekites around to Grandma's way of thinking about this year's theme.

Grandma Inez and I couldn't help ourselves, though. After attending the Mossy Creek Christmas parade, we just had to attend the Bigelow tree-lighting event if only for a few minutes before we beat it down the road to preside over our own. It was a big crowd. The Georgia Travel and Tourism Department had indeed attracted a good showing of tourists. We blended in with the crowd of visitors without attracting the attention of any native Bigelowans.

I helped Grandma up onto the bleachers so we had a good view of the proceedings. All the decorations leading to the Town Square had matched precisely. All were uniform in size, the same shade of blue and silver, and the same distance apart.

"Say, isn't that your friend the TV producer?"

"Yeah. Her jailhouse story caused such a sensation, she wanted to come back and cover the ceremony as a follow-up in case somebody says or does something interesting."

"Oh, I could tell her nobody's going to say anything interesting. Ham Bigelow is going to make a speech."

There were actually a number of TV news crews present, hoping to get in on the act. The footage of the hateful Georgia governor's mom had made the national news and gone viral on the Internet. Hamilton Bigelow had released a statement condemning his mother and denying any personal animosity between himself and anyone in Mossy Creek, most especially his own beloved Aunt Ida and cousins Inez and Lucy Belle. He asserted that the arrest of his cousins was all a big misunderstanding.

Of course, Ardaleen had been obliged to issue her own apology, and it was an abject one indeed. I could see in my mind's eye Ardaleen stomping about while she argued in vain over the wording with Ham's public relations handlers.

"Look. There's Ardaleen," I said. "There in the white fur ear muffs."

"I'll bet she's got 'em covered because they're still ringing with Ham accusing her of her ruining his chances for national office."

"I wouldn't be surprised. Look at that getup."

Ardaleen was decked out to match the decorations in an electric-blue lamé dress with white fur trim. Pierre wore a red velvet Santa suit, complete with hat and beard.

"There's the governor," Inez said, pointing.

Ham Bigelow took the podium, seized the microphone and issued the standard remarks about growing up in Bigelow at Christmas time.

"Blah, blah, blah," Inez whispered, making me giggle.

Finally, Ham pulled a cord unveiling the tacky blue Christmas tree. There were the requisite oohs, aahs and scattered applause. With a flourish, the governor flipped the switch on the tree's bright silver lights, their near-blinding wattage illuminating the surrounding area, including the crowd.

Pierre the surly, four-legged Santa wasn't impressed. Just as he lifted his leg to pee on the base of the tree, he made eye contact with me, the bane of his existence. Unpleasant memories of our painful, if inadvertent, run-ins threw off his aim. He growled menacingly and urinated directly onto the tree's main electrical connection.

The lights blinked on and off and the citizens looked at each other, wondering if a light show was part of the festivities. Poor Pierre ran right out of the smoking beard and hat, yelping in the direction of the North Pole as the tree finally shorted out and the tree lights went out completely. Only the regular streetlights remained lit.

Inez and I looked at each other for a moment of mutual inspiration. "Competition back on!" Inez whispered. Without another word, I raced to the nearby Escalade while Inez stood on her seat and shouted as loud as she could.

"Since the Bigelow tree lighting got hosed, follow me to Mossy Creek and we'll show you how it's done!"

I peeled the Escalade out of the primo parking place I'd staked out earlier while Ardaleen advanced on Grandma with violence in her eyes. Somebody helped Grandma down off the bleachers and she was in the passenger seat in moments, barely ahead of Ardaleen's reach. We roared out of town like the Pied Piper, followed by TV news vans, curious tourists and annoyed Bigelowans.

When we arrived in Mossy Creek, the Creekites were waiting to start the festivities with cold eggnog, hot cider, toasted marshmallows and plenty of music and carols.

As the visitors gathered, they were greeted as honored guests with food, drink, handshakes and hugs. A welcoming committee of old folks from the Magnolia Manor nursing home was there handing out candy canes. Their wheelchairs were all in a row, and each oldster was proudly showing off the lap quilt Clementine's home ec class made for them.

Grandma had said that she wanted a simple Christmas theme, but it had to be perfect and as it turned out, it was. Last year's city decorations were reworked slightly to represent the new theme: *The People of Mossy Creek.*

We'd gotten out the word that we wanted each citizen or family to depict their feelings about their town in their own individual ways. Nothing matched, nothing was forced, nothing was uniform or regimented, and everything was perfect.

Adele Clearwater had to admit that she loved it, even though she didn't get to boss anybody around. She had her traditional-values Christmas display with life-sized dolls she made herself depicting an Eve and a Steve and their two appropriate children gathered around a manger scene.

Raney Cecil had her "Beauty of Christmas" display in the front window of Goldilocks Hair Salon with live mannequins posing in the latest hairstyles. Five Christmas trees were visible in The Naked Bean, each depicting a different era in Mossy Creek. Pearl Quinlan's Mossy Creek Books and Whatnots' tree displayed Victorian-era antique ornaments.

The creativity and individuality that Creekites had always been proud of were on full display. Many scenes depicted events and personalities in the town's history. Foxer Atlas fulfilled his promise to depict Richard Stanhope and Isabella Salter in life-sized papier-mâché and for an extra special touch, Dan McNeil had used the broken food processor to animate the figures. The couple rotated on a gaily-decorated stand in front of their Downton-like estate. Maybe it was the spirit of the season, or maybe it was the spirits in the eggnog someone just handed me, but I had to admit that Dan and Foxer's creation wasn't awful.

Ardaleen appeared beside Grandma and me. She made a grand gesture with her blue-clad arms. "But—but there's no overarching theme, no common motifs to unify the display."

"There don't have to be," Inez assured her. "There's something I want you to see." She led her cousin to the front window of Hamilton's department store, the grand old three-story stone building that dominated Mossy Creek's Town Square. The window decorations—painstakingly created by a team of Mossy Creek Hamiltons—depicted major events and important people in the history of the town.

In one corner of the huge diorama were the figures of founders Benjamin Salter and Joshua Hamilton—the great-great-great grandfather shared by Ida, Ardaleen, Inez and Addie Lou—depicted planting the great white oak tree that stood proud and tall above Town Square.

A series of emotions crossed Ardaleen's face as she studied the history of the town of her birth, which eventually softened in the gentle glow of a nearby streetlamp. I got a glimpse of the girl she'd been, full of hope and promise. Snow, soft as a whisper, began to fall all around us. Ardaleen burst into tears and reached for Inez. The cousins embraced for the first time in years.

The television cameras pressed forward, capturing the special moment between the women as well as the essence of Christmas in Mossy Creek.

The crowd, as one, uttered a tender sigh, and the Methodist Church choir began to sing *Silent Night*.

Cousin Ham appeared at my side and put his arm around my shoulder. "I owe you one," he said.

"Nah," I said. "It's time to stop keeping score." He gave my shoulder a gentle squeeze and began working his way toward the cameras, shaking hands as he went.

Someone opened a car door nearby and Pierre—sans Santa suit—jumped out. Uncertain, he scanned the crowd for his mistress. I reached over to one of the refreshment tables, snagged a cocktail weenie and extended it to him as a peace offering. He gingerly accepted both the treat and a scratch behind his right ear.

"Merry Christmas, buddy," I said. Pierre licked my hand. "Say, your feet must be cold." With no small amount of trepidation, I lifted Pierre and cradled him against my chest. He nestled his fuzzy head under my chin as the Mossy Creek Christmas tree was lit.

The crowd applauded and cheered. The light refracting off the snowflakes made the hubcaps glitter like jewels.

Mossy Creek Gazette

Volume IX, No. One   Mossy Creek, Georgia

The Bellringer

Skydiving Mishap Leaves Bigelow Christmas Festivities With No Santa

by Katie Bell

Those of you who popped down to the Tree Lighting down in Bigelow might not have been aware of the to-do about their Santa Claus since you skedaddled back to Mossy Creek for ours.

Well, their grand finale was supposed to be Santa skydiving into Bigelow Park where the gala was being held. You already know that the lighting ceremony fizzled out, so to speak, due to a peeing incident by a certain holiday-dressed Shih Tzu.

Well, that caused the jump plane—a 1967 Cessna 182 Skylane out of Cherokee County—to miss the blacked-out town. Instead, he zeroed in on Mossy Creek's lights and let that Santa fly.

Santa (aka Harvey Cartwright from Ballground who had been hired by Gov. Ham Bigelow's staff) said, "Yep, I floated in pretty as you please. My first clue something was wrong was there was another Santa and there wasn't supposed to be. But ho, ho, ho, I decided to go with the flow, and so did the other Santa. He took kids' wish lists on the dais and I worked the crowd. I just hope I get paid the other half of what I'm owed. I did my part. Bigelow didn't do theirs."

I ask solemnly, Creekites . . . do they ever?

Gifts of time and love are surely the most basic ingredients of a truly merry Christmas.

—Peg Bracken

You Get What You Give

Pearl Quinlin

It was a want, not a need, and an expensive one at that. Christmas was slightly more than a month away, and I shouldn't be looking at a gift for myself—especially one that cost three hundred and ninety-five dollars plus tax and shipping.

With one last glance at the most gorgeous Victorian-inspired tree topper I'd ever seen with an authentic Dresden angel face, antique trims and aged blown glass, I clicked off the Dresden Star website that squandered my time worse than Pinterest.

I went back to threading a pretty red satin ribbon through the metal loop of one of my prized ornaments. One down, twenty-four more to go. I glanced up at the clock behind the register. It was a slow day at Mossy Creek Books and Whatnots, which always sent me into worry-mode about Books-A-Zillion in Bigelow stealing all my business. The bright spot in this otherwise dismal sale day? My sister Spiva would be here any minute with my non-fat, skinny, sugar-free hazelnut latte from The Naked Bean.

Sure enough, not two minutes later, the bells attached to the door chimed. Dressed in one of her many pantsuits, Spiva barreled into the store. Papers pinned to the cork community bulletin board fluttered in her wake. Josie wanted me to go digital and ditch the cluttered cork board when I remodeled, and I was weighing it as well as everything else she'd suggested.

Spiva placed the cardboard holder on the counter with a plate-sized brioche sandwiched between two cups embossed with the Naked Bean logo. Although I tried to resist its glossy golden crust, the pastry beckoned. I imagined the buttery bread melting on my tongue or, better yet, toasted and spread with some homemade strawberry jam.

My mouth watered, and I shook myself out of the brioche-inspired trance. A healthier alternative would be a thin slice of whole grain toast with fresh strawberries on top . . . if they were in season. And they weren't.

Spiva, who is three years older, thinks she's three times wiser when it comes to battling cholesterol because she takes a pill once a day. Only you obviously couldn't call what she was doing a battle since she still ate and drank everything she shouldn't. I, on the other hand, measured and substituted and worked out extra long if I fudged.

"Which one's mine?" I asked, knowing my sister loved her full fat lattes and that I couldn't afford those calories if I was going out to dinner and a movie with Allen.

"The one with the LF scrawled on it," Spiva said, her mountain twang very much in evidence. She leaned over the counter in a conspiratorial way. "Scuttlebutt around town is that not only did Ardaleen Bigelow go all-out with her tacky tinsel Christmas decorations and violate the pact by putting them up early, this whole *Spend Christmas in Georgia* campaign that excludes Mossy Creek has her prints all over it."

The news wasn't exactly as jaw-dropping as Spiva hoped it would be. Josie Rutherford had been the first to share the scoop when she came by this morning with her sketches of how she imagined my store renovation would go in January. I liked the better use of my existing space and how she'd incorporated the principles of feng shui. She'd even designed a play space for my ferret Twinkie with PVC tubing and a miniature slide, something that would probably cost more than what I'd set aside. By the time she'd left, though, she had a canvas tote filled with *What to Expect the First Year* and as many board books as she could carry while eight months pregnant.

Even earlier, I'd heard the very same gossip from Peggy Caldwell. She'd come in for the latest Karin Slaughter mystery as soon as I'd flipped the sign to open. Thank goodness for the people in this world who still liked to hold books in their hands.

Spiva crinkled her nose and sniffed twice. "I think you should probably change the litter box more than once a day during the holiday season, if you know what I mean."

Twinkie, who'd been sleeping in the hood of my sweater, poked her head out at mention of her litter box. I breathed in the delightful scent of paper bound with glue and thread. The store smelled fine to me, good even.

"Why such an interest in Twinkie's litter box habits?" I knew my sister. That gleam of mischief in her eye meant trouble—usually for me—and a whole lot of bossing.

"Well, it's Christmas and the store should smell . . . like it's the holidays," she said, shrugging. "I read somewhere that Abercrombie squirts one of their colognes in the air, and it has some sort of psychological effect that makes people buy more of their clothes."

"Do you do this at Hamilton's?" I might be game if I saw some definitive data and a cheaper way to achieve the same ends.

"No, but we should. I gotta remember to talk to Rob about it."

Spiva was an equal opportunity bosser. To be fair, her bossiness didn't always lead to irritation alone. Sometimes it led to good things. When we were little, her pushiness kept bullies at bay, ensured I did well in school, and she often challenged me to go after things I wanted, but thought I couldn't have. These days, she steered business my way by telling parents shopping in the children's department at Hamilton's about my store. She'd mention that I'd order anything that wasn't currently in stock, that I made a habit of filling the children's section with ALA winners and kept my prices reasonable. She even sealed the deal with talk of my pet ferret that didn't bite and loved to play with kids. Most recently, Spiva had nudged Allen Singleton to ask me out, and we were still seeing each other. So far, that had proven to be a *really* good thing.

Head cocked, Spiva focused her dark gaze on my sprinkler system. "It may be connected to the sprinklers. We're not the dullest knives in the drawer, Pearl. We could rig something up. What do you think?"

Rigging? I don't like that word. It derives from jury-rig and leads to things falling apart and costing me more money than I was trying to save. "In a word, no."

"Fine. Then use some scented candles. You've got a pile of them on your whatnots shelves in the back. Or get you one of those squirt thingies they show on the TV commercials. You just plug 'em in a couple of outlets."

Maybe she had a point. "If I were to do this, what scent would you suggest might influence people into buying more books?"

"I don't know, pumpkin spice, apple pie, sugar cookies... It would go with the theme I'm presenting to the committee. Holiday treats."

Yes, food. Not only would I smell treats all day if she had her way, I'd see them everywhere if she won the Christmas theme contest. I imagined the town decked out like Candy Land come to life. I'd be confronted literally at every turn by foods that would tempt me to fall off my low-fat, no sugar wagon. I wasn't convinced those scents and my sister's theme would do anything other than sabotage me.

She jabbed her brioche in the air. "And speaking of sugar cookies, *that man* bought every last one of the Christmas tree cookies Betty Halfacre made over at the Bean. Two dozen. What's he going to do with two dozen sugar cookies?"

That man was Derbert Koomer. In Spiva's mind, he was irritating because he got in the way of what Spiva wanted— be it a deep fryer at a garage sale or a specialty baked good. What stuck in her craw most of late was Derbert coming in here to read books without buying them. He had a favorite spot, too, and yes, it was the same mid-century modern chair Spiva liked to sit in to peruse her purchased material, usually a paperback romance or *Better Homes and Garden* magazine.

"Consider his greed a favor." Even though, in my choles-terol-fighting mind, the difference between brioche and sugar cookies, both made with real butter, was negligible when it came to fat, she had at least saved herself from the sugar.

Spiva glared at me for all of two seconds. "Item two. Do you happen to know anyone who might be willing to play Santa at Magnolia Manor's Christmas Party? Clementine Carlisle is looking. The student who was supposed to do it can't 'cause his family is heading out of town. Hayden can't do it, but won't say why. I suspect there's something fishy going on there. And obviously, we've got Kris Kringle—gotta love that name!—booked at Hamilton's."

"What you're really saying is that you want me to ask Allen?"

"No. Great gravy. We've got a few boomers at the manor who might've been Chinaberry Charmer fans. We don't want anyone having a heart attack."

She took another bite of brioche, swallowed, then said, "Just think about it, and if any ideas come to you, get on the horn to Tiny."

"Okay." I was a little worried there might be something else because whatever the gleam was about hadn't been broached yet. Gleams usually involved me more directly.

"Anyhoo, I was thinking . . ."

Here it comes. I braced myself. She'd led with the scent-squirter smelling like all the treats I tried to avoid, to serve as a gauge for my mood. The whole Santa thing had been a diversion, so she could screw up her courage before laying on me whatever this scheme was.

"You really should up your game decor-wise, and I don't just mean with the way this place smells. All the shops on the square are going all-out this year."

"All?" I questioned, certain she was exaggerating. Sure, I'd seen something about everyone needing to comply with whatever idea won the theme contest held by the decorating committee, but I wasn't interested in doing more than the usual. I didn't see what was wrong with last year's municipal decor either. And to be perfectly honest, it kind of bothered me that two people would have a say over what we all did. I mean, what happened to the sense of individuality that Mossy Creek was known for?

"Most. You want to know why?" she said in a secretive whisper even though the only being in the store, other than the two of us, was a ferret. "Those Bigelowans have basically declared war." She pulled one of the glossy brochures that had been making the rounds and placed it on the counter. The cover depicted a Christmas tree with the most picturesque Georgia mountain towns shown as lights. Helen, Blairsville, Toccoa, Blue Ridge. Of course, Bigelow was at the apex of the tree, depicted not as a star but as a diamond, their theme. With her readers set on the bridge of her short nose, she read, "Bigelow, the jewel in North Georgia's Christmas crown. Jewel, my hiney."

"Leaving out Mossy Creek isn't fair, but—"

Spiva's nostrils flared as she interrupted me. "Their mall has even bought in on this tacky diamond theme."

"Even Books-a-Zillion?" I asked, and took a sip of my skinny hazelnut latte for fortification.

"From what I hear, yes."

Even though I could beat them hands-down when it came to customer service, I couldn't dream of competing when it came to decorating. I was David, they were Goliath. I had no sling-shot, much less a rock. "As you well know, I don't have the money to go all-out."

Besides I preferred to keep it simple, one little tree and a fresh wreath on my door. I'd already cut back on a lot of extras I didn't need to start the much-needed upgrades to the shop come January. Refinishing hardwood floors and such didn't come cheap. Josie assured me that once we'd pulled up the carpet and padding, and we sanded off what was left of the old finish on the scratched hardwoods, we could do one of those dark stains that I liked that were so popular on some of my favorite HGTV shows. Who knew what surprises were in store renovating an old building? I needed to keep my credit card balance as low as possible for any emergency that could crop up, like finding below-code wiring, rotting subfloors and beams, plumbing leaks, foundation cracks, or, God forbid, termites.

Not to mention, I hadn't even bought a gift for Spiva yet. I'd wanted it to be something special until she came in here insisting I upgrade my holiday decorations.

Spiva engendered that look of a gypsy fortune teller that boded even less well than the mischievous gleam. "That's precisely what those Bigelowans want you to say. But you're a scrapper, Pearl. You're a short-nosed Quinlan, who takes a stacked deck and wins anyway."

"You sure your latte didn't get a little Irish added to it?" I asked, hoping against hope that the old bait-and-switch would deter my sister.

"You're upping your decorating, and Mossy Creek is gonna beat Bigelow at its own game." Spiva waved her arms so that her coffee nearly sloshed out of her lid and onto my circular rack of Cliff Notes. There was more going on here than simple bossing or spiked coffee.

I paused from carefully threading satin ribbon through another of my favorite antique ornaments. She wouldn't meet my gaze. She'd ignored my comment about the coffee being spiked, so I knew for sure now it wasn't.

Already on alert, I moved from DEFCON Four to Three. "How about if I promise to up my decorating game next year?"

"Next year is too late." Nervous sweat beaded on her currently hair-free upper lip.

I shrugged. "Then it's no big deal."

"No big deal? Where's your town spirit?" She bit off a hunk of buttery brioche, made sounds to let me know how much she was enjoying it as she chewed, then swallowed. "You *have* to do this."

"You make it sound like I have no choice in the matter." Which meant I probably didn't. DEFCON Two.

Spiva was focused on the sprinkler heads in the ceiling again.

"Look at me, Spiva. Did you tell someone the bookstore was going all-out with whatever this theme is without consulting me first?"

She offered me the rest of her brioche. "Here, I can't finish this, and it's really, really good. Just take an extra turn or two on my treadmill."

Or five or six. "Spiva?"

She rolled her beady brown eyes. "All right. Yes, I admit I said you'd do it. But it's not like I expect you to do *all* the work. I'll help you decorate. I'm pretty dang good at merchandising the children's department. It's what a Cheerful Cherub would do."

I pictured the paragraph devoted in Katie Bell's *Bellringer* gossip column to my pathetic decorating and how I let the town down. DEFCON One. Where was that rubber band Spiva'd told me she'd start wearing to remind herself not to be so bossy? She needed to snap it. Hard. Repeatedly.

"You realize it's wrong to say I'm doing something without consulting me." Yet one of many reasons we sold our shared childhood home and purchased the duplex. My sister had promised to stop trying to run my life. This latest line-crossing was a definite violation of our agreement. Apparently, separate living space wasn't the deterrent I'd hoped it would be.

Spiva cocked her ultra-short-haired head to the side. "It won't be wrong when you help us beat Ardaleen, and you will. All these people coming from Atlanta to spend time in the mountains don't want to go to shops you'd find in every cookie-cutter suburb. They don't want jewels and blue tinsel. They want quaint, small town. Unique. Even when it comes to buying books."

I looked out the big picture window where, during the holidays, I always displayed my Victorian ornament collection along with the latest bestsellers and children's books. The bright sunlight on the cold November day highlighted the shiny red satin bows on the fresh wreaths hanging from the police station's doors. Simple was pretty. Why did we have to all participate in some town-wide theme? That was the opposite of unique.

"If you don't want to do it, even though your shop *is* on the Town Square, just tell Inez you can't."

I'd given in last year to Inez Hamilton Hilley, guilt master extraordinaire, and consented to flock my tree and wreath to fulfill the municipal winter wonderland theme. However, I could stand up to the woman if I had to. I could see this contest was really all about her and Ardaleen's nearly lifelong feud. She wasn't dragging me and my hard-earned savings into it. "You know what, I think I *will* tell her no."

"Oh. Then, I guess, you should call Lucy Belle in the next five minutes. She said she'd be here after she went to the bank. She wants to go over all the rules with you." Spiva waved her hand in the air. "You know, the usual rigmarole. Having your idea cleared through her to make sure it relates to the overall theme."

"Good idea. I'll call her now." As I walked back to the computer behind the counter, to pick up the phone and get myself out of the bind my sister had tried to put me in, the sunlight coming through the picture window hit my sister's gold cross pendant.

"What happened?" I asked and pointed to the satin cording where her chain holding her gold cross used to be.

Spiva sighed. "The chain broke—*again*."

"You should replace it with something better."

Spiva raised both drawn-on eyebrows. "You seen what gold costs lately?"

Couldn't say that I had. But I'd had to brace myself against the old chipped counter when I priced materials for a new one after Josie's visit.

"Not to whine," Spiva added as she finished off the last bite of the half brioche she'd offered to me, "but I just had to replace the muffler and all four tires on my car."

"What about your Hamilton's employee discount?" I asked, thinking it and a sale could maybe make the price of a decent gold chain not so problematic.

"It sure helps to have twenty percent off retail, but I'm not making the commissions I did before the mall went in at Bigelow and people started buying cheap overseas-manufactured clothing for their kids. Luckily, we still have the market cornered on cute holiday outfits. And you should see the dresses we ordered for Easter. They're fabulous and made in the US of A."

I better than anyone knew how she cherished her gold cross. She'd saved all her babysitting money to buy it when we were teenagers. I felt guilty that I'd never thought before now that a new chain would make a lovely gift.

So that's what I would do—buy her a gold chain worthy of her cross.

I pictured Spiva's shriek of delight at such a thoughtful gift, and for the first time since my perfect bite of spicy sweet pumpkin filling, buttery crust and real whipped cream drizzled with honey and walnuts at Thanksgiving, my heart filled with the joy of the holiday season.

As aggravating as Spiva's bossy ways sometimes were, they ensured we kept all the Quinlin holiday traditions—our mother's pumpkin pie recipe that Spiva followed to a T for Thanksgiving, Christmas Eve reserved for family, and her unwavering insistence that we play board games after all our festive meals—just like we had when there were four of us. I couldn't imagine holidays, or any day really, without her in it. Her big personality couldn't help but fill the vacant spaces the loss of our parents left in my heart.

Even though I was still a bit peeved she'd told Inez I was on board with this town-wide decorating scheme when I wasn't, I could forgive her. I would call Lucy Belle, bow out and all would be well.

Then I'd have to figure out how to pay for the gold chain.

• • •

Somehow, some way, Inez had either manipulated or perhaps hypnotized me into agreeing to follow whatever theme won the town contest. The details were still fuzzy in my head. I said the word "no" about five times, but she wore me down with her promises of help from other Creekites, appeals to my town pride, a remark about Allen's ex-wife Bonnie having a real flare for decorating and the *coup de grace*—her tear-filled reminder that this could very well be her last Christmas. I had my suspicions that those were crocodile tears, but she'd dabbed at them quite convincingly with her embroidered hanky.

I had nothing much to offer Inez and Lucy Belle other than expanding on the fresh greenery and red ribbons like the wreath on my door. Traditional and somewhat lacking in imagination. At least it fulfilled the agreed-upon theme—the *People of Mossy Creek*. I was pretty sure no one else with the exception of the police station was doing anything as simple.

To make myself feel better about giving in, I indulged in my guilty pleasure—visiting the Dresden Star Ornament website. Obsessing over the gilded angel that someone else would buy to be the crowning glory of *their* rather than *my* Victorian tree didn't lift my spirits as I'd hoped it would.

If I had the money, I'd go all-out with Victorian decorations, but I didn't. In fact, by noon tomorrow, I would no longer have any Victorian Christmas decorations. At least, none of any value. None that I cherished.

After a visit to Hamilton's had revealed the cost of a fourteen-carat gold necklace—even one less than half-price on sale—I knew the only way to pay for my sister's Christmas present was to sell my ornaments. All my savings had been earmarked for the store renovations. There was nothing left in the tank.

I had to admit I panicked when the realization came to me, and the selfish side of me tried its best to talk me into a much less expensive chain. But I couldn't do that to my sister. Even though sometimes she irritated the stew out of me, I knew she would move heaven and earth to help me, and she deserved the best.

So I sucked it up, and yesterday I found someone who wanted my ornament collection on eBay. She'd already paid me. I just had to carefully pack and ship the blown glass.

With a smidge of irritation, I checked the clock, again. I needed to head over to Hamilton's in a couple of minutes, and Inez still hadn't arrived to approve my decor. Her perspective of the hours qualifying as morning were apparently different than mine. Spiva was due here any minute, and I didn't want her present when I told Inez how I planned to fulfill this year's

Christmas theme. My sister would interject herself into the process, and who knew what I'd end up having to do.

Spiva had agreed to man the store for about an hour before her afternoon shift. That gave me both the time to pick up the gold chain I'd special-ordered from Hamilton's jewelry department and the assurance I wouldn't run into her.

While at Hamilton's, I planned to take a gander at the Santa they hired this year. Word around town was Mr. Kris Kringle fit the Clement C. Moore description to a fare-thee-well. If so I might be tempted to ask if he was available to read the classic poem on Christmas Eve. Or maybe I'd sit on his lap and ask for my sister to be less overbearing in the new year.

The bells attached to the door jangled, and I quickly clicked off my favorite time-killing website.

"News alert," Spiva said, shaking her fingers in a very jazz hands kind of way as she approached the counter. "Guess who was buying some items in the lingerie department?"

I grabbed my purse. "And why is this news?"

"Because it was Ida." She batted her eyelashes at me.

"Mama always said, there's no such thing as too much underwear." She especially liked to say this after Spiva and I opened festively wrapped Christmas boxes filled with undergarments and socks and groaned in disappointment. Quite frankly, what Ida bought was her business.

"Yeah, right. It wasn't underwear." Spiva wiggled her eyebrows and an imaginary cigar a la Groucho Marx. "That's all Lila would say."

"For all you know, it could have been Spanx."

"Our esteemed mayor does not need Spanx," Spiva pointed out.

No, she didn't. She was living the dream, George Clooney look-a-like man friend who was younger and sexy. And she still had a great body even though she was a grandmother. I bet she had one of those metabolisms that let you eat whatever you wanted without gaining a pound.

"So? What did you come up with for Inez and Lucy Belle?" Spiva asked.

"Fresh greenery and red ribbons. Simple and old-fashioned."

"Funny," Spiva said with a snort. "I used an idea board to cement my plan for my side of the duplex. My giant hot chocolate mug built with scrap lumber, fluffy foam marshmallows and dry ice *steam* was particularly inspired. So really, what's your idea?"

"I'm not kidding."

Spiva blinked rapidly. "You gotta think of something else to fit the theme and pronto."

"I'm a person, and I don't like extravagant."

"Except when it comes to those Victorian ornaments on your tree," she pointed out, like only a sister could.

Something clever and cheap to fulfill the *People of Mossy Creek* theme was too much for my noggin today. Here I was, already lying to my sister so she'd watch my store so I could pick up the gold chain I'd purchased for her from people she worked with. Now that I had confirmation that the salespeople in Hamilton's talked, I was almost tempted to decline it, then drive into Atlanta on Sunday and go to some fancy jeweler that advertised on the radio and talked in a monotone voice.

"Pearl," Spiva said, in her I'm-exasperated-enough-to-walk-right-out-of-here tone. She slammed her hand on the counter as punctuation.

"What?"

"Fresh greens and red ribbon is B-O-R-I-N-G." She slammed her hand on the counter a second time, waking up the ferret who'd been sleeping peacefully in her hammock. Twinkie, who always picked up on agitation, squeaked her displeasure at being awakened and started dashing madly around the store, then scooted up the tree holding my expensive Victorian ornaments and hid among the branches. Correction—they were no longer mine.

"I swear, I've told you a million times not to do that when Twinkie's sleeping." Another reason we were living in our own spaces in a duplex.

One of the ball-shaped ornaments started to wiggle as Twinkie tried to knock it off the tree. Thank goodness I'd double-knotted the ribbon. "If she breaks it, you're going to owe me big time." Actually, not me, some lady in California.

"Hey," Spiva said, the all-too-familiar gleam lighting her eyes. "Why not decorate the whole store like your tree?"

Obviously, she didn't know what those puppies cost me. And those puppies wouldn't be here by the time the post office opened in the morning.

"Those Bigelowans won't know what hit them. It'll be so different from those oversized corporate decorations. These are one of a kind."

They were, but I would not dwell on what could not be. The ornaments now belonged to someone else.

With another jangle of bells, Inez, her mini oxygen tank, and her granddaughter walked in. The scent of hot chili pepper and sweet wafted in with them. I should have sped out of here rather than chat with Spiva. They weren't going to like my idea.

"Well?" Inez asked, chomping on her Nicorette gum and raising one snowy eyebrow above the rim of her wire-framed glasses.

Spiva grinned broadly. Time seemed to slow as the horror of what she was about to do dawned on me.

Before I could shout *No*, Spiva said, "Victorian. She's embracing the idea of Mossy Creek individuality. As you can see, Pearl has a small collection of antique Christmas ornaments. We'll just expand it to include the rest of the store . . ." She trailed off as Inez's face pinched in thought.

"Actually, *my plan* is to expand the fresh greenery and red satin ribbon over all the shelves, sort of like the wreath on the front door. I could even decorate the register area," I suggested, praying she liked my far less expensive idea.

Inez walked over to the picture window and assessed the tree that had even more of an authentic Victorian vibe thanks to the remote control electric candles I'd splurged on last year.

"You see how I used the fresh tree and red ribbon here to match the wreath on the front door? It'll all tie together nicely, and it'll smell great."

Twinkie tried to play peek-a-boo with her, but Inez ignored the ferret's attempts at play. Twinkie didn't seem to mind. She kept on chortling and clucking, what we ferret owners called dooking. The kids who came into the store loved it when she did this. Inez? Not so much. She was focused on her mission.

"Do you have anything other than these ornaments from the era?" Lucy Belle asked. "Like furniture, pillows? The red ribbons and bows are nice and all, but they're . . . expected."

"She means boring," Inez translated.

My sister nodded. "I told her as much."

"I really don't think I can do this whole place in Victoriana. I don't have the—"

"Stockings would be nice," Inez said, ignoring my protest and all the while tapping her index finger against her mouth.

"And maybe a tufted chair and stool in a rich velvet in front of a low fire," Spiva added.

"I don't have a fireplace," I pointed out. And I wasn't paying for a painted mural depicting the scene in her head.

"Well, we'll have to build one," Inez said as if that could happen with the snap of her gnarled fingers. Or as if I could pay for one.

I stayed firm. "I can't build a fireplace. I can't shut my doors. December is big for my bottom line."

"What about putting in one of those electric fireplaces you just plug in the wall?" Spiva suggested, then beamed at me because she must have thought she'd come up with a great solution.

Inez shook her head. "That wouldn't be authentic. We need masonry brick."

"Then let's find a different theme," I said. "How about me taking a Christmas story and decorating in that theme, like *The Grinch Who Stole Christmas?*" Or the sister.

"Or Dickens's *Christmas Carol*," Spiva offered, again with the broad grin. "Which happens to be Victorian."

Inez nodded her approval. "Perfect. Victorian and literary. Unique."

Something dinged, and Lucy Belle pulled her smart phone out of her coat pocket. "Sorry to cut our consultation short, ladies, but we've gotta get back. Love the Victorian Christmas, love the whole fireplace idea."

Which I hadn't agreed to.

"And I'm *really* going to love seeing Ardaleen's eyes blink in horror in her Botox-injected, Restalyne-filled face when all those tourists rave about your bookstore on Yelp."

Only that wouldn't be happening because I had no idea how to decorate this space and leave enough money for my renovations. I'd already hired contractors and ordered stain, polyurethane and shelving. And I no longer owned the Victorian ornaments that were supposed to be the centerpieces of this whole, big, fat mess.

"Oh," Inez said as she secured her scarf around her head and tied it under her chin, "I'll make a few phone calls and see if we can find some antiques to replace your furniture. Do you needlepoint?"

Dumbfounded, I shook my head.

"Too bad. *That* could have been great for the stockings and pillows. We may have to go Out-of-Creek to purchase a couple for your mantel. Or maybe—take a note here, Lucy Belle—we can have one of the church craft groups whip something up."

"You're not hearing me, Miss Inez," I said, raising my voice to a less-than-pleasant level. "I haven't agreed to build a fireplace, much less a mantel to hang needlepoint stockings on."

Lucy Belle shrugged at me like none of this was her fault. "Call Patty Campbell. She's always going to garage and estate sales, picking up this and that. I bet she has a mantel or two."

"And I bet," Inez said, "you can convince her to donate one to your cause."

My cause?

With that, the chow-chow queens of Mossy Creek swung out the door, the bells jangled, and I was left with an even bigger dilemma than I'd faced this morning. Even though there was no way I was going all-out and having a masonry brick fireplace installed, I would have to take away something else from the renovation budget for the mantel. There went the new bathroom tile, probably the cabinet and sink as well.

I'd been railroaded again, and the conductor was Spiva. Where the heck was I going to come up with the money if taking away the refurbished bathroom wasn't enough? I wasn't getting an equity loan since I hadn't built any in the duplex yet. I had nothing of value but a few sentimental antiques. The Victorian ornaments decorating the tree in the store window that had unfortunately prompted my sister's uniquely Mossy idea no longer belonged to me. Maybe I should have said something about selling them, but I didn't want to spoil her surprise.

"Pearl?" Spiva said loudly. "Don't you have to be somewhere?"

I blinked at the clock. I had about a half hour to jog over to Hamilton's and pick up the gold chain.

"Don't get your big-girl panties in a wad," she said. "I'll figure this out. You go run your errands, and I'll put a call out for anything Victorian in Mossy Creek on Facebook. You won't have to spend a cent."

Doubtful.

A part of me was grateful to have a big sister who felt it was her life's mission to help me out of jams, the other part was aggravated that I was only in this particular jam thanks to her bossing me around and being too free with *her* brilliant ideas about *my* store.

The phone behind the counter rang, and Spiva reached it first. She put her hand over the receiver for a sec and shooed me toward the coat rack. "Mossy Creek Books and Whatnots, Spiva speaking. May I help you?"

I hoped it was a big order.

As I slipped my arms through my coat sleeves, Spiva halted me. "It's Effie. Says she has a couple bolts of fabric and some discounted gold ball fringe for window treatments and pillows for your Victorian Christmas decorations. She can't give it to you outright, but she'll only charge you what it cost her. Oh, and she says they'll coordinate well with your ornaments and the ribbon already on the tree."

"How did she . . ." I stuttered more to myself than to Spiva.

We both looked at each other and said in unison, "Inez."

There may have been more, but I didn't hear it. I was calculating in my head what I'd do to come up with the money for the fabric. I looked at Spiva's cross hanging from the satin cording. I wasn't sacrificing her gift. But, oh, how I was tempted.

• • •

Spiva Quinlan

Going to run some errands, my hiney. My sister Pearl could no more lie than I could keep my nose out of her business. She was Christmas shopping—for me. And because I was a better-than-your-average older sister, I was going to take this opportunity to snoop my way into finding the perfect gift for her.

Not that I was feeling overly guilty about getting her to up her decorating game. Or at least I hadn't been until Inez took my idea, and we both kind of turned it into an extremely expensive proposition. But I would come to Pearl's rescue like I always did.

I also needed to figure out what authentic Victorian decorating would require. Between ringing up customers, I surfed and discovered that Victorians made some decorations with paper. That tidbit led to a genius idea. We could get parents and their kids into the store by offering free Victorian Christmas craft classes. Of course, I'd help Pearl, and I'd convince one of the teachers from the elementary school to contribute some time.

Kids could surely make some of these cornucopias and garlands. It didn't look all that complicated. And even though we didn't have ground glass for "diamond dust," we could buy glitter.

The kids could make one for themselves to bring home and one for Pearl to use in the store on the tree in her window. It could even become an annual tradition. Sometimes I amaze myself with my brilliance.

Pleased as a caroler offered a mug of wassail, I made a list of materials we'd need. Dried cherries or cranberries, popcorn. I could get all that from Piggly Wiggly. Cotton thread and needles? Effie's. Fancy craft paper? I'd ask Josie—our local origami guru. All very doable and fairly inexpensive. Some of it wasn't even food.

Before I'd clicked off this Victoriana crafting website,

two people strolled in, and a rush of chilly air entered with them. Dan McNeil from Mossy Creek Hardware nodded to me and promptly walked to the long wall in the back of the store where Pearl housed her whatnots. The other customer? My nemesis Derbert Koomer. He headed right for the thriller section, most likely to finish the next chapter of the book he'd been coming in here to read rather than buy.

"I believe you're on chapter three," I called out to Derbert, who ignored my sarcasm.

The distinct metallic slide of a measuring tape retracting pulled me away from the computer. I came out from behind the counter and found Dan eyeballing the back wall. "Whatcha doing?"

"Measuring for the fireplace," Dan said.

My heart literally stopped beating. I splayed myself in front of the candles and knickknacks. "My sister didn't okay that."

"That's not what I heard." Dan waved at the shelving units. "All this has to go."

The bells at the door chimed again, and Patty Campbell made her way back to me and Mr. Thinks-he-knows-every-thing. "Talked to Inez, she said you're in need of an authentic Victorian mantel. I have two."

"I'll need those dimensions to calculate the size of the firebox before I start swinging the sledgehammer."

My heart squeezed in my chest. I could very well be having a heart attack. Maybe Pearl was right about watching the fat I was ingesting. I had to live. I couldn't let Pearl come back to a big ol' hole in the wall of her store. "No one's swinging anything."

"What do you think?" Patty asked as Dan scrolled back and forth between the pictures on her smart phone. "I kind of like the 1880 quarter-sawn oak with the decorative top. But then again, the 1885 carved dark cherry with the beveled mirror is nice, too."

I nosed my way in between them. "Y'all need to have your hearing checked. Pearl did not agree to anybody building a fireplace."

At long last, Patty stopped discussing the merits of her finds and paid attention to me. "You want to see her text?"

Okay. Now I was really confused. Pearl wasn't a fly-by-the-seat-of-her-pants kind of gal. That was more my thing. She was the voice of reason and moderation. I was the idea girl who needed grounding on occasion. But here she was fully committing to what looked to me like a bigger renovation than the one she'd planned for . . . *after* Christmas. I'd seen the blueprints, and they didn't include a fireplace in the back of her store. "Are you sure that text is from Pearl?"

"Who else has access to her phone?" Patty asked.

I wouldn't put it past Inez to somehow convince Lucy Belle, who was a computer whiz, to find a way to hack into my sister's phone. I shook off the conspiracy theory forming in my head. "Let me call her, just to voice verify."

"When you do, tell her I need to check with some salvage yards to see if I can match the brick," Dan said. "And we'll need to see the stain Josie's picked for the floor before we decide on the mantel."

"Don't you need a permit from the county?" I asked, certain nothing could happen soon.

"Already submitted. Just made a few adjustments to what we originally applied for," Dan said, then measured the wall again. "Should be approved by the end of the day. I got friends."

In low places was the phrase that came to mind.

"Could y'all keep it down?" Derbert called out from the comfy chair I liked.

Patty and Dan eyeballed the boxy chair and the small table with sleek reading lamp that was between it and its match.

"Too modern," Patty said. "I'm thinking Tiffany style or a stand with a fringed shade."

I was thinking dollar signs. "Are you donating? 'Cause Pearl's not made of money."

"Don't worry," Patty said. "Someone in town probably has a couple of Victorian lamps and maybe even a few chairs in an attic that I could reupholster for Pearl."

"As long as they're free, or close to it," I threw out there, so cost might become more than a slight consideration. "You know Pearl's not rolling in the dough here."

"Seriously, people, I'm reading," Derbert said, waving the copy of *Kill or Be Killed* that he'd had the gall to dog ear. "Y'all need to pipe down."

"How 'bout I ring that book up for you, and you can take it to where we aren't all talking?" I suggested. "Maybe to the Naked Bean. You could see if Jayne has any of those Christmas tree sugar cookies in her pastry case. You know, the ones you're always hoarding so no one else can buy them."

He sniffed, put the book down on the chair and left.

Good riddance. I looked at the clock. Dadblameit! Time was a-wasting. I had a stealth mission to accomplish. I had to find Pearl a great, and I do mean great, present. The reno's expedited timeline coming during the Christmas rush was going to stress her to no end. And my mouth had gotten her into this mess. I ran behind the counter as Dan and Patty continued discussing what needed to be done to make the fireplace happen.

I quickly looked through the list of my sister's recent visits on her browser and found this one page popping up again and again in her history—Dresden Star Ornaments. I clicked on the site and saw the beautiful Victorian angel tree topper she'd fixated on. Holy guacamole. The blasted thing cost three hundred and ninety-five bucks. I hadn't really wanted to spend that kind of money. But I could see it atop her tree filled with similar ornaments and the paper ones. The shop completely decked out in Victorian garb danced in my head. I should buy it.

After years of getting my sister nice things like pajamas that Pearl liked okay, I knew all the way to the marrow in my bones that this gift would engender an affection almost as big as my bossy, overprotective love. It's something no one, including Pearl's man friend Allen, would ever dream of giving her. Mostly because I wasn't going to tell him.

My only problem was how I would pay for it. My credit card was maxed out thanks to car repairs and the furniture I'd bought for the duplex. And I'd never been all that good about saving for a rainy day.

Fingering my gold cross, I sighed. I would have had to start saving over a year ago to come up with that kind of dough. There had to be another way to get cash fast.

And that's when I noticed the ad on the side of the computer screen.

We buy gold.

• • •

Pearl Quinlan

Christmas Eve arrived crisp and clear. Kris Kringle's reading of *'Twas the Night Before Christmas* was winding down, so I took a moment to let the whirlwind of December sink in while the children and Twinkie listened to Kris in rapt joy. Their parents and a few regulars, including Derbert, filled the space to capacity. Some were snapping pictures. Some were browsing. Some, thank goodness, were buying. Derbert was standing in a corner desperately trying to finish the thriller he'd started in November.

I had to admit, reluctantly, that the renovation with a nod to Victoriana that Spiva pushed me into was a good thing—as was the fact that my storefront wasn't damaged by the runaway horses during the Christmas parade. Jayne's offer to bring cookies and hot chocolate for the event tonight along with her son, Matt, were also good things. Probably another reason why Derbert was here.

"And to all a good night," Mr. Kringle finished with a twinkle in his merry eyes. "Now before you all go, our lovely Miss Quinlan has asked me to gift all the children with a copy of this most special poem originally titled *A Visit from St. Nicholas.*"

Interesting that he knew that fact. I'd snagged paperbacks at a huge discount because I bought them in bulk. It was the least I could do since this December's sales were looking to be the best I'd had in years, even with the store closed during the renovation.

The children crowded around Kris, and, I kid you not, he knew every one of their names. Even the child whose parents had rented a mountain chalet for the week. My heart sang with joy at the happiness contained in this store. Allen had come, too, with his teenage daughter—even though she'd complained she was too old for story time.

Mr. Kringle sought her out and handed her a new YA I thought she'd prefer to the classic poem. Allison turned it over to read the back-cover copy, and a slow smile spread across her face. Baby steps, I reminded myself.

"Thank you, Miss Pearl," Matt Reynolds said as he raced around the counter to give me a hug after he'd handed his book to his mom. Clay Campbell did the same.

Mr. Kringle made his way past the parents and children. "I must take my leave shortly, Miss Quinlan. As you know, I have a busy night ahead. Before I go, however, I must ask if anyone has seen Derbert Koomer?"

As I rang up a book about quilting for Patty Campbell, the children who hadn't left pointed to Derbert now sitting in the wingback vacated by Kris. I could see he was a few pages shy of the end of that book he'd been desperate to finish.

Mr. Kringle walked back to where Derbert was hurriedly reading and handed him the new thriller *Deadly Deceit*. "From the proprietor," he said. "Merry Christmas."

Derbert looked shocked, then pleased. "Thanks, Mr. Kringle. And you, too, Pearl."

Pleasing me to no end, Allen came around the counter to help me bag the last-minute purchases. I felt as giddy as a girl in high school having a guy carry her books. "I thought it irritated you that he never buys," he said in a near whisper and leaned close.

"It does, but it's Christmas."

He looked at me then in a way I'd never seen before. Kind of confused with a side of awe. "You want to come by tonight after you close shop?"

"Thank you," I said to the vacationers who bought the historical preservation society's holiday cookbook, three bestsellers and the Crayon series I'd recommended. I turned to Allen. "I'm sorry, I can't."

The fact that I wasn't jumping up and down over the invitation put me on the receiving end of another confused look. Allison tried to hide her happiness, but I noted it.

"For Quinlans, Christmas Eve is family time," I explained.

"But we're dating, so . . ." His words trailed off into something I wasn't dissecting tonight.

"I have plans with Spiva," I reminded him, and I wasn't leaving my sister in the lurch. He should know that about me.

With a sigh, he shrugged on his coat. "If you change your mind . . ."

"I won't." My tone edged toward annoyance. My good will toward men in general and him in particular was definitely being tested.

Luckily, Allen's daughter chose that moment to do something that surprised us both—she half-hugged me before leaving with her dad. And I swear I heard a mumbled Merry Christmas out of her, right after her thank you for the book.

No surprise that Derbert was the last to leave. I was glad he was done with the book before Spiva showed up. I didn't want anything to spoil the seasonal joy I was feeling, and her laying in to Derbert for treating the store like his personal library would have.

I checked the time again. Sales must have been better than good at Hamilton's for Spiva to be so late. She'd texted me this afternoon and said they'd moved her over to home goods, then women's sportswear as a floater because there were a lot of last-minute shoppers.

Deciding to wait a little longer, I turned the sign to closed and clicked the remote to turn off the fireplace. The Victorian mantel and masonry fireplace somehow looked like they'd always been here. Shaking my head with pride, I surveyed the beauty of my little bookstore that could *beat* Books-a-Zillion.

Since business was going to be interrupted anyway, I'd decided to go ahead with all the renovations.

Swagged and expensively trimmed window treatments, thanks to Effie, now framed the picture window along with a tufted stool next to the tree. Victorian parlor chairs from Ida's attic sat in a small reading nook. Potted palms and refurbished wing chairs from my house framed the gas-log fireplace, boasting needlepoint stockings gifted to me by Derbert of all people. A fringed scarf, greenery with red ribbons and a Victorian-era crèche graced the sawn-oak mantel Patty Campbell donated to my cause. The beautiful oak floors that Dan McNeil sanded, stained and finished. The shelving system so many friends pitched in to help me hammer together—all of it made me smile. Even the cinnamon scent drifting from a couple of those plug-in dispersers Spiva suggested. Repeatedly.

I couldn't have created this vision without the town's help, my sister's prodding and Inez's crazy feuding with her cousin. Best of all, I now had a theme to expand on during the rest of the year. Patty was already on the lookout for Victorian Easter items.

Not only were the renovations beautiful, they were a business expense and, as such, tax deductible.

The only pinch of sadness I felt was over losing the blown glass ornaments that had inspired the decorating theme. I'd carefully packed and mailed all twenty-five several weeks ago. Of course, Spiva had noticed the ornaments missing right after I'd mailed them, but I'd told her I had to make room for all the paper ones the kids made. Thankfully, she'd bought it.

My eye caught on the gilded angel figurine displayed with the antique crèche, and I clicked the switch to extinguish most of the pot lights in the shop, with the exception of the one shining on the reason for the season. I decided to keep the electric tree candles lit, too.

Ready to head home since Spiva said if she wasn't here by eight-thirty she'd meet me at the duplex, I bent to grab my purse and saw the small box wrapped in paper in one of the compartments. I kept her gift with me, so she wouldn't find it. Sometimes Spiva's bossiness extended to snoopiness.

The door swung open with a draft of air that not only felt but also smelled cold. The bells jangled. I looked up, a little fearful I'd spend the next half hour helping a frenzied holiday shopper find the perfect last-minute gift when I should be spending what was left of the evening with my sister.

"It's just me, silly," Spiva called out as she flipped on the switches, brightening the whole store and nearly blinded me.

My heart kicked up to treadmill speed. I didn't want her

asking about the missing ornaments again. I wasn't the best liar. "Turn those back off, and we'll head home. I was thinking the walk will be extra pretty tonight. Who knows? We might even see Kris flying in his sleigh."

"After we celebrate," Spiva insisted. "Sales were through the roof at Hamilton's today."

I was glad I wasn't the only one benefitting from Ham and Ardaleen's backfired campaign.

Spiva placed a tray from the Naked Bean on the counter, then locked the deadbolt and draped her overcoat on the antique credenza that had replaced my battered coat rack, thanks to Patty's bargain-hunting skills.

"We're celebrating Mossy Creek's win right here with sugar and fat in the form of Christmas tree cookies and hot chocolate with a ton o' marshmallow fluff," she said. "I don't want to hear any objections. It's Christmas Eve, and a little indulgence once in a while won't kill you."

I knew she wasn't just referring to the treats. She was also talking about the Victoriana surrounding us.

Wanting to savor this warm goodness like I'd savor my sister's reaction to her gift when we opened them tomorrow, I took a tentative sip. Something about the rich hot chocolate made me feel even more guilty about lying when she'd asked about the missing ornaments. If sales went as well in the new year as they'd gone the past few weeks, I'd start buying replacement ornaments. She might never notice or ask where I got the money to buy her necklace.

"Let's not wait 'til morning," Spiva said, gleam locked and loaded.

My heart revved to running speed. "Not wait for what?"

"Gift giving." She rolled her eyes. "Turn on that fireplace, so we can have some ambiance."

I thought about lying and saying I didn't happen to have her present with me. But I didn't. I took the fireplace remote, pressed the button and the gas logs came to life, flames dancing.

Spiva made her way to the wing chairs with her cup and the cookies as well as a shirt-sized box. Surprisingly, it wasn't wrapped in the usual Hamilton holiday paper, but instead in red foil and tied with a fancy gold tapestry ribbon.

"You go first," I said as we settled into the wing chairs. I hoped against all hope she'd love my gift to her as much as I'd imagined she would. Especially since her prodding and pushing had brought my store so much success.

She took a big slurp of her hot chocolate. "Fine by me. That'll make watching you open mine all the sweeter."

Once she tugged the satin ribbon, tore the paper and lifted the small box lid, she stared. Just stared.

"It's fourteen carat," I said, thinking maybe she hated it. "Thick enough that it won't ever break. You'll never lose your cross."

Tears shone in Spiva's eyes when she at long last looked at me, making me mist up, too. She did like it. The gesture meant as much to her as I'd hoped. The loss of my collection was so worth it. This gift had to be the best I'd ever given her.

"Do you like it, Spiva?" I asked, needing to hear it.

"Of course. And I don't just like it, I love it. How in the world did you pay for it with all this going on?" She waved her blazer-covered arms to encompass the newly renovated store and its Victorian Christmas decor.

I shrugged. "Where there's a will, there's a way."

Not another lie, per se. Merely an avoidance of details, for which I felt marginally guilty. But I didn't want her to feel badly about me selling my ornaments, so my skirting the truth was justified.

"Your turn," she said.

Careful not to tear the pretty paper, so I could use it again, I eventually got the lid off the box I figured held a sweater. I separated the layers of tissue and my jaw dropped. It was the tree topper I'd lamented being sold.

How pretty this Dresden angel would have been with the rest of my antique ornaments that were now part of someone else's collection. The angel blurred. My throat knotted with tears. In trying to give her something special, I'd managed to spoil her gift to me.

"Are you surprised?" she blurted. "I admit I snooped on your browser. I knew when I saw it, it was perfect for your tree. See?" She pointed to the angel's skirt. "It even has a similar trim as those two gold blown glass ornaments that you like to face out on the square."

It *was* perfect. I bit my lip, tried to smile and failed miserably.

Spiva's grin faded. "What? I can tell something's wrong when your forehead creases up like that."

My throat worked. My voice weakened to a whisper. "I sold the ornaments."

"Sold them? Why?"

"To pay for your gold chain, so you'd have something worthy to hang that cross pendant from. You know me, I can't stand being in debt."

After looking up at the ceiling, then swiping at her eyes, Spiva took a ragged breath and unbound her fashionable scarf. She pointed to her bare neck. "I sold my cross to buy you the tree topper."

She gazed down at the gold chain resting on cotton. "I don't know of another person who'd do something so nice for me, and after I got you involved in this grand Victorian decorating scheme. You must really love me."

"And I always will," I said, my voice gaining strength. I stood up to hug her. Spiva might be aggravating as all get out at times, but she was my sister, the *yes* to my ever-ready *no*. Giving her the gold necklace filled me with so much more joy than those Victorian ornaments ever had.

"Let's see how your angel looks on the tree," Spiva said and stepped over, cookie in hand, to the picture window to place it at the tippy top.

"Only if you wear your gold necklace."

I helped her and if I do say so myself, I was dead on with the length. I'd start saving to replace her cross. My Victorian blown glass could wait.

"You know those paper ornaments the kids made don't look half bad," Spiva said, then her eyes widened and lit with excitement. "Hey, I got an idea. You should do something similar with kids crafts for Valentine's Day and Easter and every other holiday. You could even do Victorian Fourth of July. And we could change out the scent in your squirters for each holiday. Valentine's could be chocolate, Easter could be marshmallow, Fourth of July could be watermelon, Back-to-School apple pie, Halloween pumpkin spice, Thanksgiving gingerbread, and of course—" she paused for a breath and a bite of her sugar cookie "—Christmas is sugar cookie."

I shook my head. Spiva would never change and when it came right down to it, that was okay with me. Her pushing and prodding usually worked out in the end. It was just a lot of aggravation getting there.

Some people like to say you get what you give. I sold cherished items to give Spiva a wonderful gift.

She did the same.

Funny thing was our true gift wasn't what we gave to each other, it was the sisterly bond we shared that shone brighter than gold.

Mossy Creek Gazette

Volume IX, No. Two   Mossy Creek, Georgia

Church Christmas Bazaars

compiled by Jess Crane

Mount Gilead Methodist Church Ladies Auxiliary on Church Street invite one and all to shop at their annual Holiday Bazaar the first Saturday in December from 9 a.m.–2 p.m. You know the drill, folks. All the usual handmade ornaments, quilts, baked goodies and holiday flower arrangements. I heard tell that Maggie Hart has figured out a way to use all those broken communion cups she's collected over the years since she washes them after church on Sunday. Nope. Not going to give away the secret. You'll just have to come out and see . . . although I will confide that in the right light, her artwork sparkles like the angels!

Yonder Faith and Forgiveness Baptist Church on Main Street in Yonder is also holding a Christmas Flea Market. Near as I can tell, it's the same thing as a bazaar because it's got all the usual handmade ornaments, quilts, baked goodies and holiday flower arrangements. Conveniently though, it's the second Saturday in December so if you didn't do all your Christmas shopping and decorating by then, swing on by! Time is 9 a.m.–2 p.m. Rhonda Clifton, Ms. Bigelow County several years back, will entertain the crowd at noon with her single-handed performance of the *Hallelujah Chorus* from Handel's *Messiah*. Bet she's out of breath after that! Adele Clearwater swears she sounds like an angel.

On the first Sunday at 2 p.m., **Mossy Creek First Baptist Church** on Church Street will present their annual Christmas Chorale featuring the Glory Hallelujah Choir accompanied by the Holy Horns. Selections include such favorites as *Joy to the World, Silent Night, O Holy Night, Oh Come All Ye Faithful* and *Angels We Have Heard on High*. Two highlights of the musical afternoon are an audience sing-along for several numbers, and as a special treat, Georgia and Burt Stroud along with Georgia's granddaughter, Therese, will perform their own rendition of *Hark! The Herald Angels Sing*.

(continued on page 89)

Church Christmas Bazaars

continued from page 88

Mossy Creek Presbyterian Church's Annual Christmas Pageant. This year's title is "Angel Wings and Donkeys Sing." Curious about that last part? All I can say is . . . only in Mossy Creek! You gotta see it to believe it. Not only that but Yours Truly will be playing one of the wise men—or should I say wise *people*? Hey, it could've happened! Anyway, this year's extravaganza will run all three nights at 6 p.m. the second weekend in December. Free tickets available at the *Mossy Creek Gazette*, the Naked Bean, or catch Josie Rutherford as she runs around town decorating for folks.

Mossy Creek Unitarian Church on Church Street wants to bring Christmas back to nature this year with a crafty morning of birdseed. They'll help all the children who show up make birdseed ornaments to hang on their outside trees. This happens the third Saturday in December from 9 a.m.–noon. Participants are advised to bring large cookie cutters. That's not to cut the birdseed apparently, but to shape the ornaments. Should be a hoot and a holler for kids of all ages. I sure plan to attend. See y'all there!

We are better throughout the year for having, in spirit, become a child again at Christmastime.

—Laura Ingalls Wilder

Miracle on Main Street

Jayne

"Well, bless my stockings."

Hearing the wonder in Ingrid's voice, I glanced up and followed her astonished gaze across the room. "Whoa. Wha— Is that guy for real?" I was as amazed as Ingrid at the sight across the room.

A small, rotund man sat in a chair beside Matt's play area, deep in conversation with my son. What made that remarkable was that the man was a dead ringer for Santa Claus—the only difference being he wore a ratty tweed jacket with suede elbow patches instead of a red fur suit.

"Looks pretty real to me," Patty Campbell said from across the counter. Mac's wife waited at the cash register for her low-fat cinnamon latte. "He's the guy who showed up at the last minute to be Santa in the Christmas Parade this morning. Mac and I took Clay. Quite an exciting parade, even by Mossy Creek standards."

"Yes, I heard. We were slammed this morning, as you can imagine, with all the people on the Square, so I missed the excitement. Win took Matt and told me all about the ruckus . . . and *him*." I stared across the dining room to where Matt talked to the rather small man with great animation. "Matt was very excited about *him*."

"New friends are always exciting," Ingrid said. "Especially imaginary friends like Santa."

"My son? Imaginary friend? And Santa Claus to boot? No way. He's got his engineer father's soul." But even as I scoffed, images of Christmases Past scurried through my mind. For all of Matthew Reynolds's deep-rooted practicality, he'd been like a kid in a candy store during Christmas. Every year he decorated our house as if we already had the six kids we'd planned on having—which had seemed further beyond our reach every Christmas—until all hope was gone during Matthew's last one. I hadn't known I was pregnant with Matt until after I'd moved to Mossy Creek a month after I put my husband in the ground.

Patty recited the most famous description of the legendary elf:

"His eyes—how they twinkled! His dimples how merry!"

Ingrid nodded. "Check."

"His cheeks were like roses, his nose like a cherry!

"His droll little mouth was drawn up like a bow,

"And the beard of his chin was as white as the snow."

"Check, check and check some more," Ingrid added, a bit of awe in her voice.

"Oh, come on!" I slid the door of the cookie counter closed and handed a Gingerbread Man across to Clay Campbell, Mac and Patty's adopted son. "Y'all don't really believe that man is . . ." I stopped as I realized I didn't know if ten-year-old Clay still believed.

Ingrid's chin came up—a sure sign she was turning ornery. "Sure looks like him."

I threw her a hard look, which she ignored, so I tossed it over to Patty, who tossed it right back. They both knew I was anti-Santa, and they both heartily disapproved.

"Oh, grow up." I grabbed my order pad and headed out from behind the counter.

It was a busy day in early December. Late enough in the month that nearly everything behind the counter related to the holidays in some way, but early enough that people were still coming in to place orders for holiday parties. Okay, yes, I refused to call them "Christmas" parties. "Holiday" was so much more universal.

As I reached the table where our unusual visitor sat, I pasted on my best proprietor smile. "Good afternoon. I'm pretty certain

I'm right in welcoming you to The Naked Bean for the first time. Can I assume you're new to Mossy Creek, as well?"

The man chuckled and yes, his belly did shake a little bit, but it was hardly a bowlful of jelly. "You'd be absolutely correct, Ms. Reynolds."

"Jayne, please," I insisted. "Mr. . . . ?"

"Kringle," he answered. "Kristopher Kringle."

My eyebrow shot up before I could stop it. "Uh huh."

He ignored my obvious skepticism. "Call me Kris, please. I've just secured a job at Hamilton's Department Store."

"He's Santa Claus!" Matt exclaimed.

"He is, is he?" I did not try to hide my frown. I'd worked hard keeping the Santa Claus myth from Matt's attention. It was getting harder every year.

"I start tomorrow," Kris said.

"Congratulations," I said. "I'm sure you'll do well. You certainly look the part. I hear you did a . . . credible job in the parade this morning."

"Thank you."

His gracious reply made me feel how *un*gracious my deliberate understatement had been. From what I'd heard, he'd saved the parade. At least, the Santa part.

"Can I get you some coffee?" I asked in an attempt to make myself feel better.

"Well, I'd love some. However, I'm a bit short of cash until my first paycheck. Could I owe you?"

Ahhh, a deadbeat Santa. A *real* Santa would be able to conjure cash when he needed it, right? Santa is a *magic* elf, after all.

Normally, I would give someone with a hard luck story a cup of coffee. It was a friendly thing to do and it didn't cost much. But this man pushed buttons I hadn't felt in years, freezing my charity right up. "I'm sorry. If I gave a cup to every—"

"I'll pay for it."

The familiar voice made me turn. "Win."

He smiled and leaned in for a kiss.

I turned slightly so it landed on my cheek. "You're here early."

"Win!" Matt's arms reached up.

Win plucked Matt from the play area and tossed him into the air. It had become a ritual between them whenever they'd been apart for even a few hours.

As Matt squealed his delight, it was clear that Win hadn't been phased by my rebuff. He probably chalked it up to the crowd of people in the shop. Everyone in town knew we were a couple, but no one—not even Josie Rutherford who I would trust with my darkest secrets—knew we were engaged. Win also knew I wasn't all that comfortable with public displays of affection, especially in our places of business.

"I'm avoiding the city office," he said. "Inez Hilley is on the rampage again, and I wanted to fortify myself with a cup of coffee before I went in."

"Why not just bring one from Bubba's?" I glanced at the clock. Win's restaurant—Bubba Rice Lunch & Catering, open only for breakfast and lunch—would've shut down over an hour ago. He'd spent the time since, no doubt, supervising the daily cleanup.

He shrugged after setting Matt down. "I wanted an excuse to stop in and, to tell the truth, it didn't occur to me until after we'd cleaned the coffee pots."

I understood that and turned back to the counter. "I'll get you a tall one to go."

"And one for my friend here," he called.

Ingrid was the only one who commented on my frown. "Does every mention of Christmas have to put a bee in your bonnet?"

"Don't start."

"It isn't like you to be rude to a Mossy Creek newcomer." There was real concern in her voice.

I knew it wasn't, but I couldn't help my pique. "I guess it is today."

• • •

Win

"Thank you," the short, rotund stranger said. "My name is Kris, and I'm much obliged."

I pulled my gaze away from Jayne—I loved watching her

walk away, even if it was in a snit. Seeing Kris's proffered hand, I shook it. "Nice to meet you. I'm—"

"Win Allen," he filled in quickly. "Proprietor of Bubba Rice Lunch & Catering and President of the Mossy Creek Town Council. Everyone knows you."

I sat opposite him at the little table. "Everyone in Mossy Creek knows me. So you must live fairly close."

He hesitated half a second. "Up the road a piece."

Feeling a tad rude by prying, I decided to ignore his enigmatic answer. He seemed harmless enough. "I apologize for Jayne. Usually she's much friendlier. I can't understand why she's—"

"Don't worry about it," Kris said. "I *do* understand."

"You do?"

"She doesn't like my profession." Kris didn't seem bothered by this possibility.

That took me aback. I'd never known Jayne to be prejudiced against anyone in any way. "What *is* your profession, if you don't mind me asking?"

"He's Santa Claus," Matt said, proud that he knew.

It was only then that I noticed the uncanny resemblance. I felt out of it for not noticing before. "Of course you are. Hamilton's?"

Kris nodded. "I start tomorrow."

"That's good," I answered absently. What was I missing? I knew some people had a debilitative fear of clowns. Was Jayne the same way about Santas?

Ingrid was the one who brought the two coffees to our table. "Yours is the way you like it, Win. Mr. Kringle, we have sugar and cream at the table, or you can doctor it up just about any ol' way over at the condiment bar."

"Kringle?" I asked, startled. "*Kris Kringle?*"

"That's right." Kris took a sip of coffee. "Thank you, Ingrid. It's perfect the way it is."

Now I couldn't help but pry. "Is that your real name?"

He grinned at me, looking every bit like he belonged in a Norman Rockwell drawing. Before he could answer me, Matt pulled his attention away.

"Santa? Do you really bring kids like me presents on Christmas Eve?"

As "Santa" replied, Ingrid started to move away. I quickly rose and stopped her with a hand on her arm. "Ingrid."

"Yes?"

I lowered my voice and nodded toward Kris. "What's up with this guy?"

Ingrid drew herself up as if she resented the question. "I like him. I think he's adorable. You feel like Jayne does? Are you going to be as rude as she was to that nice old man whose only crime is wanting to make a few bucks as a Christmas Santa?"

Her vehemence surprised me. "Hold on a minute. I'm the one who's paying for his coffee. But while we're on that subject, what's up with Jayne? Why is she being like that? Is she afraid of Santa? I've never seen her act like . . ."

"Like Scrooge?" Ingrid supplied when I hesitated. She glanced back over her shoulder. Jayne was deep in a conversation with Betty Halfacre, the Bean's taciturn half-Cherokee baking assistant. Ingrid turned back. "I don't know why she's got her mind set against Christmas, but she's been this way ever since moving to Mossy Creek. Although, now that you mention fear, a reaction so against character is almost always born out of fear of some kind."

"What do you mean by 'her mind set against Christmas?'"

Ingrid seemed uncomfortable, and I wondered if she would answer. Ingrid adored Jayne and Matt, and I knew her allegiance would always lie with them. Finally she said, "Jayne hates Christmas."

I was floored. "She hates Christmas? *Who* hates Christmas?"

Ingrid pulled me further away from the counter. Her voice lowered. "I wouldn't say anything, mind you. Lord knows I'm not one to gossip."

I wanted to laugh at the blatant lie, but even more, I wanted to know what was going on with the woman I'd fallen in love with. "Of course not."

She nodded grimly. "It's just that . . . well . . . she won't let Matt believe in Christmas, either. She tells him there's no Santa Claus. No reindeer. No presents under the tree. No nothing. And that's just wrong. Kids should be allowed to be kids. They're the only ones capable of believing in magic, and it's downright criminal to take that away from one, especially your own flesh and blood. I can't help thinking that. I just do."

She huffed, obviously winding down. "I'm sorry to vent like this, Win. But I love that little boy like he was my own grandson. You know that. Not believing in Santa makes him different from all the other kids. He's young enough now that it doesn't matter too much, but the older he gets, the more it will matter. That's gotta be damaging something in his soul. It's just gotta be."

I didn't know about damaging Matt's soul, but I agreed with Ingrid on the principle. Matt should be allowed to believe. It was a kid's rite of passage. I turned to watch him interact with Kris, remembering his eager question: *"Do you really bring kids like me presents on Christmas Eve?"* It was obvious he *wanted* to believe.

"Do you know why Jayne hates Christmas?" I asked Ingrid.

She shook her head. "She won't discuss it. And believe you me, I've tried."

"Thanks, Ingrid." I sighed. "There's still so much about Jayne I don't know. It helps to get information from someone who knows her so well."

Ingrid seemed pleased and moved on toward the counter. Not seeing Jayne there, I walked over as well, to say goodbye. As I neared, I saw that she and Betty Halfacre had moved into the back room where the baking ovens resided. It was there that Ingrid and Betty created the scrumptious baked goods sold in The Naked Bean.

Seeing Ingrid return, Jayne called her over. There being a lull in customer demand at the moment, Ingrid joined them. Their hushed, worried tones were unmistakable. Something must've happened to a piece of equipment. As a restaurant owner, I knew the awful feeling. And this was the Christmas season.

A moment later, Amanda Phillips wandered in and Jayne came out to wait on her. The wife of the minister at Mount Gilead Methodist Church ordered a low-fat caramel latte for herself plus a black coffee for her husband. At the last minute, she added half a dozen peppermint meringue cookies.

When she left, Jayne smiled at me for the first time. "Sorry if I was snippy. It's been one of those days."

I nodded toward the back. "Equipment problems?"

She sighed. "Our big oven. No heat. None. We've called the repair service in Bigelow, but it will be at least tomorrow."

"That's rough," I said. "You're welcome to use the oven at Bubba's. I'll need it by 4 a.m. for morning biscuits, but you could use it tonight."

"I think we're okay for a day, except for a few custom orders which we've divvied up among us to take care of at home."

"Okay. I was going to grab Matt, go up and get Glinda and make shrimp scampi at my place. How about we do the opposite? Matt and I will go get Cherry, and I'll rustle something up for us upstairs. Sound good?"

She was obviously relieved. "That'd be great, Win. I am so *not* going to feel up to cooking supper with six pans of brownies to make. I appreciate it."

I smiled. Before Jayne, it had been a long time since it felt better to please someone else than to please myself. "No problem."

We smiled across the counter, enjoying the intimacy of extended eye contact shared only by people who trust each other. Then the moment was shattered.

"Win, I'd like to thank you for the coffee before I go."

Just before I turned, I saw Jayne's face change. It went from being warm and open to closed and hard.

"If you'll let me know how much it is, I'll happily repay you when I get my first paycheck from Hamilton's," Kris added.

I turned and smiled. "Oh, no, you won't. Consider this a 'Welcome to Mossy Creek' cup of coffee."

"Much obliged." He turned to Jayne, and I would swear his eyes were twinkling. "Sorry to hear about your oven. Perhaps there will be a Christmas miracle."

Jayne smiled tightly. "If the repairman shows up tomorrow, I'll count that as miracle enough."

Kris nodded. "Well, I've got a big day tomorrow. See you later."

"Good luck," I called after him, then I turned to Jayne. Her narrowed eyes watched him leave her shop, as if she expected him to steal one of her mismatched chairs on the way out.

"How much do I owe you for the coffee?"

Her gaze snapped back to me and narrowed even further. "Don't start."

"But you made it clear—"

"Like I would make you pay. And you know as well as I do that it only cost about twelve cents for that coffee."

"Then why were you . . . ?"

She huffed. "I don't know. That man makes my skin crawl."

I stared at her lovely face, usually so calm and open. "Do you really have a problem with Santa Claus? Or is it all of Christmas?"

She looked startled. "Who told you that?"

Not wanting to give Ingrid away, I pointed toward the door. "Kris told me you don't like his profession. And from your behavior, that was fairly obvious."

Her chin lifted. "Christmas is a lie we tell our children. I want Matt to trust me not to lie to him . . . about anything."

"I see." The last thing I wanted was for Jayne to be angry with me, or to think I in any way thought she was a bad mother. "That *is* a conundrum. The whole world is telling Matt there is a Santa Claus—his friends, teachers, television, stores—but the one person he trusts most is telling him there isn't. No wonder he seems confused."

"Confused? What makes you think that?"

"The questions he was asking Mr. Kringle."

She snorted. "Like that's his real name."

"Jayne, I agree that telling the truth is a good thing. But . . . Matt's not even four years old."

"Your point?"

I shrugged. "I don't know. This is new information. I never would've pegged you as a Christmas cynic."

Just then, two teenaged couples entered the shop on a boisterous wind.

"I have to work," she said, and turned away.

• • •

Jayne

"No Christmas at the Reynolds's house, I hear."

I looked up from the cash register after ringing up the teenagers. Mossy Creek Librarian Hannah Longstreet stood on the other side of the counter, sliding into her coat. LuLynn McClure, Josie's mother, stood beside her. They'd met here an hour before and had sat at the farthest window table, catching up with each other's weeks. They had a standing appointment, every Saturday afternoon.

I slid the register drawer closed. "That didn't take long."

"What didn't?" LuLynn asked.

"For my personal information to carry across the shop."

Hannah smiled apologetically. "You know Mossy Creek."

"You don't believe in Christmas?" LuLynn exclaimed.

"Do you?"

"Absolutely!" she said. "It's one of the main decorating holidays of the year."

Somehow, I stopped my eyes from rolling. Josie's decorating knack had come naturally, although Josie had much better training and taste than her mother. That's why I had her decorate the shop for Christmas. I had no heart for it, and it had to be done . . . for business. For camouflage. So Creekites didn't ask *these* kinds of questions.

"To me, what Christmas means is making gingerbread men instead of Valentine hearts. See y'all next week."

Hannah, bless her intuitive heart, got the message and pulled LuLynn out of the shop.

My gaze followed them out and rested on Hamilton's Department Store, just across the Square. The reminder that this all started when Mr. Kringle walked into my shop made my low opinion of him plummet to hellfire depths.

Before today, only my closest friends knew about my aversion for Christmas. I'd known I'd probably have to tell Win at some point, but until now, it hadn't been foremost in my mind. I was too busy with the business that the Christmas season brought. Since I'd moved to Mossy Creek, every December night I'd blessed the good souls of Mossy Creek who believed wholeheartedly in Christmas. Their quaint decorations and shops brought droves of visitors to Mossy Creek, many of whom stopped for refreshment in The Naked Bean. As was the case with most retailers, Christmas was a large part of my yearly income. For that reason alone, I *should* believe in Christmas.

I did appreciate the business. If nothing else, it made me too tired every night to think. And for the last few years, the not-thinking had been important.

Oh, yes, I, too, had once upon a time believed in Santa and other fairy tales. At various points, I believed in the Tooth Fairy, the Easter Bunny and Milli Vanilli.

But the most painful fairy tale ending had been my belief that Matthew Reynolds was my Knight in Shining Armor. My belief that he was invincible. My belief that he told the truth when he kept insisting that he was just tired because his job was so stressful. I believed him when he insisted his cough was from allergies. I believed until the day he was diagnosed with stage four lung cancer.

That was the Tuesday before Thanksgiving. He died the day after New Year. I barely had time to wrap my mind around the disease before he was gone.

Yet, as sick as he was, he'd insisted we decorate for Christmas. And to keep his spirits up, I agreed. He loved Christmas so much. I had to do most of the work, of course. He was incredibly weak. But by the time we finished, every room in our moderate house shone with lights, tinsel and glitter.

On Christmas Day, he was so sick I took him to the hospital. He never came home.

I stayed with him the whole time, except for one quick trip home to pack a bag. I fed him, bathed him and held his hand as he took his last breath.

Then I went home and ripped down every ornament, every cross, every sprig of mistletoe. I shoved every stuffed Santa and elf and reindeer into boxes and dragged them out to the street. I had a small bonfire with the two live Christmas trees in the fire pit on our patio.

The day after Matthew's funeral, I put our house on the market. It sold a week later, so I quit my job, took the life insurance money and bought an empty storefront on Mossy Creek Town Square and transformed it into The Naked Bean.

When I learned I was pregnant, I swore that my child would never know the heartbreak of having their fairy tales ripped out from under them. Far better to never believe in the first place.

"Are you *Jewish?*"

The whisper brought my mind back to the shop. Reverend Hollingsworth stood across the counter.

I shook off the sad memories. "Reverend, I sing in the choir at your church. I'm there every Sunday. Alto? Second row, third from the left?"

"I know, but . . ."

"No, Reverend, I'm not Jewish. I've been a card-carrying Presbyterian my whole life."

"Then what do you—"

"What can I get you today, Reverend?" I asked brightly. "Our special today is Pumpkin Chai Tea."

• • •

Jayne

That evening, as soon as the supper dishes were in the dishwasher, I reached for the supplies I'd brought up from the shop below.

"Need my help?" Win asked.

"Nope. I got it covered."

"How about I get Matt ready for bed, then get out of your hair?"

I smiled at him, reminded of all the reasons I loved him. Not only did we have a lot in common, but he was amazingly sensitive to my needs. And he was going to make a fantastic father. Though Christmas brought Matthew vividly to my mind, for the first time since his death, I wasn't wracked with grief. I had someone else to think about. I had the possibility of a loving partner, if not for the rest of my life, at least for now. That's all I could count on. I'd learned that lesson well.

"Thanks," I said warmly. "And thanks for supper. And many thanks for not bringing up you-know-who again."

"No problem."

He turned his attention to Matt, but the tone of "No problem" let me know that we weren't through discussing it. I groaned inwardly, but knew I had no options. To be a worthy wife for Win, I had to open myself completely. I wasn't looking forward to explaining my feelings about Christmas, but I would. Surely he would understand after that.

I had a reprieve at least for tonight. Win was leaving before Matt went to bed, and Matt did *not* need to hear this conversation.

"Hey, cowboy. How certain are you that you're about to have a bath?"

Glinda's and Cherry's heads perked up from where they lay tangled together in a red and blonde furry ball. My Cairn Terrier and Win's Irish Setter had taken to each other like long-lost siblings, once Glinda established she was the alpha female. It was amusing to see my eighteen-pound scruffy-coated dog boss around Win's sixty pounds of auburn elegance.

Matt, however, did not perk up. He was busy constructing what looked like a castle with his Legos and did not want to be disturbed. "No cookie."

Percentages was a game Win had taken to playing with Matt, once he'd figured out what an analytical mind my son had. He'd started out with pieces of cookies, but had recently graduated to a more conceptual form of the game where Matt sometimes had to *think* about pieces of a cookie, rather than have one in front of him.

I'd begun using it, too, often saying, "I love you one whole cookie." Or when Glinda was barking too much, "I like Glinda only half a cookie right now."

"Think again, little man." Win scooped Matt off the floor. "Chances are one *whole* cookie."

"You can play with your Legos for a little while afterward," I called after them as they disappeared down the hall. Glinda and Cherry trotted after them, now they were certain the bath wasn't for them. They'd settle down in the hall outside the bathroom in their customary vantage point.

By the time Matt ran back into the open living space right before the dogs and then Win, I had the brownies mixed and the first two trays in the oven. Because it was a home-size oven, it would take several more hours to get them all done. I was just grateful that Betty had insisted on baking the cookies necessary for tomorrow. They had to be rolled and cut with cookie cutters, then baked and some of them iced, so they would take much longer. Betty, however, had a large extended family she would call on for help. I was happy to pay the extra wages to be able to get in bed at a halfway decent hour.

I met Win at the door as he pulled on his leather bomber jacket. I slid my arms around his neck and lifted my head for a kiss.

Win obliged with gusto, pulling me close.

"Thanks again for everything," I said. "I *could* do it all without you, but it's so much easier and so much more fun with you."

His face softened. "Well put. I feel the same, and I appreciate the appreciation."

All of a sudden, we were body slammed by a small boy. "Me too! Me too!"

Laughing, Win lifted him. Matt wrapped a tiny arm around each of our necks and we all shared a hug.

"Night, Win," Matt called as he raced back to his Legos.

"G'night, cowboy," Win called. He turned to me, his eyes sparkling, "Merry Christmas, sweet Jayne."

Knowing he was teasing me, I stuck my tongue out at him in the same spirit. He chuckled, called Cherry, walked down the stairs and left through the back entrance.

A few minutes later, I slipped another two trays of brownies into the oven and turned to Matt. "It's time for a bedtime story."

"Bob the Builder?" he asked hopefully.

I smiled at his predictability and followed him into his room. "Okay, yes, for the two hundredth night in a row. Which one this time?"

Glinda beat us both, jumping onto Matt's bed and settling into her spot at the bottom where she would stay all night. I was glad she'd chosen Matt's bed instead of mine. Though I'd come to love Glinda, I was a cat person at heart and preferred to share my bed with Emma, my calico.

"Skyscrapers!" Matt called, sliding his feet under the covers that Win had already turned down.

I located the book on the shelf and settled beside Matt.

Before I could even open the book, he turned to look up at me. "Mom?"

"Yes, baby?"

"Are you *sure* there's no Santa Claus?"

I sighed. "Yes, baby, I am. What makes you think there is?"

"Ever'body says so," he insisted.

"Who is 'everybody?'"

"Ever'body. All the kids at play school—Maybelle, Travis, Randy. Lots of people ask what Santa's gonna bring me Christmas Eve. Even Ingie says he's real. She says he's gonna bring me a real tool set. With a hammer and ever'thing!"

Ingie was the best Matt could do with "Ingrid" when he learned to talk and it had stuck. "She did, did she? Do you want to read this book or not?"

My hard-headed son refused to be distracted, insisting, "I met him today. Santa Claus. At the Bean."

"You met a man who looked like pictures you've seen of Santa," I corrected.

Matt's soft chin got the same stubbornly set look his father used to get. "It was him. It was Santa."

I laid the book on the bedside table and turned Matt in my arms so he could see me. "How certain are you?"

His cute little face screwed up with the effort that took. I could see the wheels of his young mind turning. Finally, he said, "Half a cookie, I reckon."

"Matt, Santa doesn't exist," I told him softly. "I'm a whole cookie sure about that. There is *no* magic. There's scientific fact behind everything and one day, when you're old enough to understand, I'll explain it to you."

"'K, Mama." Though his words said he agreed with me, his tone was begrudging.

"Since you don't seem to want a story tonight, I'll say goodnight." I kissed his cheek, then rose and tucked him in.

With a pat on Glinda's furry head, I turned out the light and closed the door.

It was obvious that Matt didn't quite believe me. This was the first time he'd questioned what I told him. He was beginning to develop independence, to become his own special person—and I didn't like it. I knew it was inevitable. A good sign, even. But I wanted my sweet, trusting baby.

To distract myself, I checked on the brownies, then turned

to the National Geographic channel on TV. I brightened when I saw that a rerun of *Brain Games* was on.

This episode was about creativity. It talked about how children's brains were so much more creative and open than adults'. How they can think outside the box more freely because they're not hampered by knowing what isn't possible.

As I baked, I couldn't help but apply what they said to the comments made today by Win and Ingrid and Patty and all the other Creekites in the Bean who felt free to comment on my life. Was I depriving Matt of a rite of childhood by taking away the possibility of magic? Of Santa Claus? Was I hampering his creativity?

That was hard to believe. How could saving him from future pain be hurting him? I was doing just the opposite.

No. I'd rather err on the side of not having him crushed the day he realized there is no Santa Claus.

But for the first time, I wasn't a whole cookie comfortable with my decision.

• • •

Jayne

When I woke the next morning, the first thing I noticed was the same wonderful aroma usually present on the mornings that Ingrid and Betty were downstairs baking. I dismissed it as phantom smells, left over from the past few days.

Instead of weakening as I showered and dressed, however, the scent grew stronger.

What was going on? We'd tried everything we knew how yesterday to revive the oven. It was broken. Absolutely, unequivocally broken.

I hurriedly dressed Matt and carried him downstairs. Glinda followed us down and I realized she needed to go out.

"Why can't you learn to use a litter box?" I asked her.

I grabbed one of the doggie bags I kept by the back door, then braved the cold. Luckily, she hurriedly completed her business and headed for the door. Setting Matt down, I cleaned up, then followed them both back in.

Glinda headed up the stairs to the apartment and Matt preceded me through the other door, the one that led into the shop.

The powerful, scrumptious smells of cookies, pastries and pies hit my senses like a wall of delectability.

How was this possible?

I heard Betty Halfacre humming in the kitchen. She always hummed when she was lost in her favorite occupation.

I waved at Matt with a vague, "Go play," and rounded the counter to see both Ingrid and Betty busy at their usual tasks.

Ingrid was concentrating on measuring flour into the mixer. "Morning, Jayne," she said absently, as if this were just another day.

Betty, as usual, only nodded.

"What's going on?" I asked. "The oven was broken."

"I know," Ingrid said happily. "I was sleeping in when Betty called me. Said the oven was working, and we'd best get to work. So I toddled on over."

"But...how?"

"Maybe a Christmas miracle."

I gaped at Betty, for two reasons. One was that she'd spoken at all. The middle-aged half-Cherokee woman was taciturn to the point of muteness. The second because Betty's words echoed what Kris Kringle had said just yesterday after hearing about the ovens.

Perhaps there will be a Christmas miracle.

The way he'd said it, it had seemed like a prediction. Was he a secret commercial oven repairman? Did he sneak into the shop last night and fix it like some . . . DIY elf?

I shook my head. "It was probably a short in the wiring that came back on. Ovens *do not* spontaneously heal. I'm going to let the repairman come on so he can check it out."

"Good idea," Ingrid said. "Did you get those brownies made?"

"Yes. I'll bring them down after I feed Matt and get him to daycare."

I turned to leave, but stopped at the kitchen door. "Betty?"

"Yes?"

I turned back to face her. "What made you come and check the oven? Since we determined yesterday that it needed a

106

repairman, you could've slept in. Did you think of something last night to try? Did you do something this morning that fixed it? Turn a knob a little harder? Kick it in the side? Anything?"

Betty was famous for her stony, assessing perusals. She gave me one now, and it felt as if she were wondering if I could handle the truth. Finally, she said simply, "I forgot it was broken."

I didn't believe that any more than I believed that Santa had sent in an elf last night. But I knew from experience that questioning Betty further would be an exercise in futility.

"I'll see y'all in about an hour," I said and left.

• • •

Win

After the bulk of the cooking was done for the lunch rush, I went to the dining room to greet the customers there, as usual.

Again, as was usual around Christmas, the lunch crowd at Bubba's consisted of about half Creekites and half visitors. New customers were never a bad thing.

The main topic of conversation among Creekites that day was the escalation of the Yuletide Feud with our nemesis town, Bigelow.

When I got to Table Fourteen, however, Tom Anglin asked, "Hey, Win. What's this I hear about Jayne bad-mouthing Santa Claus?"

I turned fully toward his table. The owner of Mossy Creek Hardware ate with his cousin, Mitty. "Hey, Tom, Mitty. How's that Trout Po'boy treating you?"

"Dee-lish as always, Win."

"How do you get these corn fritters so crisp?" Mitty asked above her vegetable plate.

I shook my head with a smile. "Trade secret. Got to have you comin' back, now, don't I?"

"Maybe I'll just bribe Sugar Jean to tell me."

I glanced back at Bubba Rice's star waitress. "I reckon you could *try*, Mitty. But Sugar Jean knows who signs her paycheck."

Mitty laughed. "Oh, go on with you. I won't take your livelihood away. You might be needing it for your new family, if rumors are true. Sure you want a wife who's a card-carrying member of MAFT?"

"MAFT?" Tom and I echoed.

Pleased she'd stumped us, Mitty said, "Mothers Against Fairy Tales."

"Cute," I said. "You can take the newspaperwoman away from the newspaper . . ." I let the comment slide. Mitty had sold *The Mossy Creek Gazette* to Sue Ora Bigelow several years back.

I started to move away, but a thought occurred to me. "Mitty, Tom, may I ask y'all a question?"

"Sure."

I glanced around to make sure no children were present. None were. School had not yet let out for the holidays. "When did each of you learn Santa wasn't real? Do you remember?"

"Who don't remember that?" Tom asked. "I reckon I was seven or thereabout. My older brother, Sam, dee-lighted in telling me. Truth be told, I think he'd just found out. Since I was counting on a Red Ryder BB Gun that year, it sho' nuff broke my heart. But you know what? I got that BB gun anyways."

"I was nearly twelve," Mitty said. "But things were diff'runt in my day. We didn't have an Internet to tell us what to think."

Seeing that Mossy Creek lawyer Mac Campbell and veterinarian Hank Blackshear had tuned into our conversation, I asked, "What about y'all? Feel like sharing? Traumatic or not?"

Being a lawyer, Mac had his answer ready. "I reckon I was about ten when I finally admitted it. A couple of my cousins had told me a few years before that, but I figured I'd ride the toy tide as long as I could. When it got so embarrassing that my friends thought I believed, I gave it up."

I chuckled. "Always a lawyer, huh? Working every angle."

He nodded. "Dang right. I got a couple more years of presents out of it."

"How about you, Hank?"

"I figured it out myself," Hank said. "I was about eight, I guess. It was right around the same time I figured out that babies don't come from storks. They come from human mothers the same way puppies come from dogs and calves from cows. Oh, and that Easter Bunnies are incapable of laying eggs."

The laughter that drew enveloped the whole dining room,

it seemed. Everyone wanted to share their story. Postal Carrier Jamie Green saw the Santa at Hamilton's kissing the women's lingerie clerk in a hidden corner of the store's loading dock. She'd watched, hidden, until the woman finally pushed him away, smoothed her hair, then went back to work. Santa had pulled down his beard and lit a cigarette, never knowing he was traumatizing a little girl.

Del Jackson saw Santa kissing *his mother* behind a door at his third grade Christmas party. When he realized that "Santa" was actually his father, the jig was up.

Maggie Hart insisted she *still* believed.

"How about you, Dwight?"

Mitty's question stopped the buzz cold. Dwight Truman had that effect on people.

Dwight sat at a table in the center of the melee, calmly, methodically cutting his chicken-fried steak. Dwight ate at my restaurant nearly every day. I suspected it was just to vex me—which it didn't. I'd taken the presidential seat on the Town Council away from him in August, and he just couldn't forgive me.

Dwight looked around the dining room, enjoying being the center of attention once again. Finally, he waved his fork in the air dismissively. "I never believed in Santa Claus. My father was *honest* with me, letting me know from the get-go that Santa isn't real."

"Explains a lot," someone muttered under their breath, raising a chuckle from those around him.

I stared at Dwight—the only person in the room I considered maladjusted. The words of his father had come from Jayne's lips just last night. She felt compelled to be *honest* with Matt.

It was like landing headfirst into a hill of snow. I had to save Matt. Somehow, I had to find a way.

"You didn't get no Christmas presents?" a visitor to Mossy Creek asked Dwight.

"I received gifts from my parents and grandparents," he said with a sniff. "That was adequate."

"I have one more question for everyone," I shouted above the din that had begun again. Every face turned toward me. "Does anyone *regret* believing in Santa Claus?"

The crowd looked among themselves, most of them shaking their heads.

"Thanks!"

I had work to do.

• • •

Win

That night after we'd put Matt to bed, I took Jayne's hand and led her into the family room. I set her down on the sofa and told her about the lively discussion at Bubba's during lunch. I ended with Dwight's remarks.

From the growing pinched look on Jayne's face, I could tell she did not want to talk about this.

"So?" she asked.

"So? Did you hear what I just said? Dwight Truman is socially impaired. Do you want Matt to end up like him? He's one of the most disliked people in town."

"There could be a million other reasons for that," she said. "I'm sure he didn't get to be so . . . dysfunctional just because his parents told him there was no Santa Claus. That's ludicrous."

"No, it's the principle. He's dysfunctional because he *had* parents who told him there was no Santa Claus. They robbed him of wonder-filled childhood memories. They robbed him of the magic of presents just showing up under the Christmas tree. They robbed him of *possibility*. That's what childhood is all about—possibility."

She glared at him. "So what you're really saying here is that I'm a terrible mother."

"No, Jayne, don't go—"

"You're comparing me to Dwight's parents. Ingrid told me they wouldn't let him play with other children, kept him busy all the time with science projects and community service. Do I do that to Matt?"

I started to panic. "Okay, that may be what it sounds like I'm saying, but you know it's not. It's just this one thing."

She sat forward on the sofa, her spine straight. "Matt is *my son*, and I'll raise him as I see fit."

"He'll be my son, too, when we get married."

Her eyes widened, as if she'd never considered the implications of that.

Knowing what the next thing coming out her mouth was going to be, I tried logic. "You decorate the shop for Christmas. Isn't that the same thing as a lie?"

"Josie decorates it." She obviously realized the weakness of that argument, because she added, "That's for business. And I've told Josie to never use Santa or elves or presents. It's only greenery and reindeer."

"Reindeer come from the Santa story," I pointed out. I knew I was pushing it, but she needed to see the possible consequences of her actions. "And you have Christmas trees. Not just one, but five. Don't they imply that there is a Santa who brings presents to put under those trees?"

She stared at me a long moment, then said, "I think you should leave."

"Jayne, I know this upsets you, but—"

"Oh, you do? Then why do you keep bringing it up? You claim to love me, but you keep trying to change me."

"Jayne, please—"

She stood and pointed at the door. "Winfield Jefferson Allen, this is *still* my house and Matt is still *my* son. Please leave."

I stood and faced her. "I do love you, and I love Matt. That's why I'm being so pushy." I stepped close to her, invading her space, but I didn't touch her. "What do you think being in a new relationship is but change? You're changing me, too, you know. You're not the only one going through growing pains."

"I . . ." She wrapped her sweater closer. "Go. Please."

I reached out and briefly squeezed her hands. "I'll see you tomorrow."

• • •

Win

"Win!"

Hearing the call on the icy wind blowing through the Town

Square, I twisted to see Josie Rutherford cross West Bigelow Road into the Square.

Extremely pregnant, it took her an awkward moment to join me on the bench with the best view of the official Mossy Creek Christmas Tree which had been lit Saturday evening at the culmination of the Christmas Parade and Festival.

The only help I could give her was to take the Naked Bean coffee cup in her hands. I handed it back to her when she settled beside me. She rested it on her enormous baby bump.

"When are you due?" He knew he should know, but he kept forgetting the exact day.

"January seventh. Can't come too soon."

I couldn't help but stare at her stomach. Looked like she was ready to pop. "I bet. Still don't know if it's a—?"

"No!" she insisted vehemently. "We're waiting. We want to be surprised."

It seemed to me that finding out whether you were having a boy or girl was a surprise no matter when you found out about it, but I'm a little more practical than old-fashioned.

"A cold day to be out here," she observed, though she didn't seem bothered by it. Josie was a mountain girl, through and through, for all of her mother's beauty queen aspirations for her. "Sittin' and thinkin'? Or just sittin'?"

My smile was as weak as her joke.

After a moment, Josie said, "It'll be okay, Win. Jayne loves you."

I was in awe, as usual, of Josie's intuitiveness. "As much as she loves Santa Claus?"

"That's not fair," Josie said softly.

"I know." I sighed. "It's just so frustrating. She won't tell me why. She wouldn't talk to me at all when I went in the Bean a little while ago."

Josie took a sip of her coffee, then leaned back against the bench. "There are reasons, you know."

"What reasons?" I cried, then brought my voice down. "Will you tell me? She won't. She just scowls and arches her back like an angry cat whenever Kris Kringle is mentioned or comes into the Bean."

Josie lifted her gaze to Colchik Mountain, clearly visible

above the Mossy Creek shops to the southwest. She'd met her husband, Harry Rutherford, on that mountain, and I wondered if she were thinking about that now.

"Yes, I will," she said. "I wouldn't if I thought it would hurt Jayne in any way, you understand. But even though she knows she has to tell you, she's being pig-headed and that's no way to treat someone you love. I'm going to tell her that I've told you. So promise."

"Promise what? That I won't hurt Jayne? How could I? I love her."

"Those are the ones we can hurt the most, and worst, but I'm going to believe you. I sincerely trust in your feelings for her." She searched my face, then nodded as if giving herself permission. "Jayne's husband died at Christmastime . . ."

As Josie explained, I went through a range of emotions. At first, my heart ached for Jayne. I wanted to rush into her shop and gather her into my arms and tell her that I would never leave her. But that's exactly what her first husband did. Then my logic kicked in and I could see exactly why she was acting the way she was. I vowed to stand beside her and deflect all the Christmas bugaboos away from her.

Then I thought about Matt. Poor little tyke. He never even knew his father.

"Do you understand now?"

I pulled my thoughts back to the Town Square. "Yes, I understand."

"But do you *understand*?"

I knew what she meant, and my gaze returned to the thirty-foot Christmas tree that had been grown on the Brady Farm and had been donated by Eddie Brady in honor of his father, Ed Sr., the town's Santa for decades.

Finally, I said, "If you're asking if I'm going to let it go, then no. It's no longer about Jayne. She has to think about Matt."

"Are you sure you're not speaking from jealousy?"

Her soft question surprised me, but I understood. Was I jealous that Jayne still grieved so much for her dead husband that she let one little man who looked like Santa push all her buttons? "Maybe a little. But that's not what's important. What's at stake here is a little boy's development. And no, I'm not more in love with Matt than Jayne. She's the most important thing to me, but he's important, too."

Josie smiled brilliantly. She was not in any sense a beautiful woman, but when she smiled, she was radiant. "That's what I was hoping you would say. Jayne needs to work through this. It's turning her aura a funky brown, not a good color on anyone."

"I can't do this alone," I told her. "I need your help."

She nodded. "You're going to need the whole town's help. The good news is, Mossy Creek *loves* this kind of project."

• • •

Jayne

"Ingrid, are you getting those two mocha lattes?"

"Just finishing them up now," she called back.

I looked up to help the next person, relieved to see there was just one more. We'd been slammed by a tour bus that had come from Atlanta. They came to see the "Jewel in North Georgia's Crown" that Ham Bigelow's administration had been touting, meaning Bigelow. But from the comments I'd been overhearing, they liked Mossy Creek's homier Christmas decorations much better. They weren't the first tourists who'd said so.

After I served the older man a half-skimmed-milk coffee and Candy Cane Cookies, I paused to survey the dining room. It was full as an August tick, and it was easy to spot the tourists among the Creekites. Maybe it was just that I knew them now. Maybe it was because they looked more at home.

My eyes lighted on the corner where my son played every afternoon after I picked him up from daycare. When I'd first glanced up a moment ago, he'd been playing by himself. But now I could see that he was holding out one of his toy trucks to a shy little boy about his age. The boy glanced up at his mother, who nodded permission, then he slowly joined Matt in his play area. This was nothing new. A gregarious boy, Matt wanted to play with any kid who came into the shop. Adults, too. Matt did not discriminate because of age.

Satisfied that my son was safe and happy, my gaze took in the boy's parents. Now that I looked closely, they didn't seem to be tourists. They sat at the table right next to the door, and weren't eating or drinking anything. Thinking back, I couldn't remember them coming up to the counter to order anything. Occasionally, either Ingrid or myself would go to a table to take an order. But it wasn't the norm. Not that it mattered. It was cold outside. Perhaps they'd just stopped in to warm up.

Looking even closer, I noticed their clothing was a bit rough around the edges, and though they didn't look starved, they didn't reek of opulence, either.

"Back in a sec," I said to Ingrid, then I made my way over to their table.

"Hi. I'm Jayne, the owner of The Naked Bean. That's my son, Matt. Can I get you folks something?"

The young mother slid her gaze to her husband, slightly flushed. He nodded at her, then said, "I'm J.D. Henley. This here's my wife Aileen. Our boy Cody. I'm afraid we can't afford fancy coffee. We been up and down the Square, looking for work. Just stopped in a spell to warm up, if you don't mind."

"Of course I don't mind."

"Would you . . ." Aileen swallowed hard. "Would you possibly have a job for me? I'm a hard worker. I can cook or clean or wait tables. Whatever you need."

"I . . ."

"J.D. lost his job at the tool and die shop down in Toccoa. We're living with his mother out Yonder way until we can get back on our feet."

I looked around the shop. Need help? We'd been slammed just about every afternoon since the Christmas parade on Saturday. I'd been so busy I hadn't had time to look for a temporary worker. "You're a godsend, that's what you are. I *do* have a job for you. But it's just a seasonal one. Just through New Year. After that, we slow way down."

They brightened in unison. Aileen squeezed J.D.'s hands in relief.

"I can start right now," she said.

"I'm not sure . . ." Glancing down the street, I spied another tour bus emptying onto the Mossy Creek Town Square. "Actually, if you really mean that, right now is perfect. Come on. I'll introduce you to Ingrid and Betty and get you an apron. Your first job is to bring your husband some coffee and your son a hot chocolate. And cookies—don't forget a couple of cookies."

J.D. put a hand on my arm as I shooed Aileen toward the counter. I stopped and looked into his grateful face.

"Thank you," he said.

I know my face was beaming. Nothing felt better than helping people in need. "You're very welcome. And welcome to Mossy Creek. I'll put out the word that you need a job, too. I'll bet you have one before Christmas."

The look on his face was thanks enough. Smiling, I turned toward the counter, only to stop short when I saw Kris Kringle within earshot.

He beamed at me, like he'd heard it all and was vastly amused.

I was not. As open as I'd been just a few seconds before, I felt my whole being snap shut. My smile vanished, my eyes narrowed and my face flushed.

He came in every afternoon, bought a cup of coffee and a cookie, which he consumed as he talked with my son and any other kids who happened to be there at that time.

He was taunting me. And I hated it.

I lifted my chin way too far in the air and sauntered past him with a stiff, "Good afternoon, Mr. Kringle."

He just smiled his knowing smile. "It *is* a good afternoon, Jayne."

The derelict.

• • •

Kris

"Good afternoon, Matt," I said as I settled into my customary seat by the young boy's play area. "Who's your new friend?"

"This here's Cody," Matt said with pride. "Cody, this here's Santa Claus."

Cody, nearly a year older than Matt, smiled shyly. "Are you *really* Santa Claus?"

I leaned closer. "Didn't I bring that G.I. Joe to you last year at Christmas?"

Cody began to nod, then realizing the implications of my question, his eyes grew bigger and he said with a touch of awe, "Yeah."

Matt was awed, as well, and reached for the action figure Cody had abandoned in favor of a dump truck. They both studied the doll as if it glowed with sparklers.

I sat back and took a sip of my coffee.

"And here I thought my mother bought it for him."

I twisted in my chair and met the amused gaze of Cody's father. "Oops. My secret's out!"

With a smile, he extended his hand. "J.D. Henley."

I shook his hand with my customary enthusiasm. "Kris Kringle."

"No. Seriously?"

"Serious as a full moon," I said, then explained, "I think heart attacks are *too* serious."

He chuckled. "May I join you?"

"Please do."

He settled in across from me just as his wife set three cups and cookies on the table. J.D. introduced his wife, then handed a cup of warm chocolate to each of the boys.

"How's the job hunt going?" I asked when he straightened.

He seemed surprised and a little embarrassed. "How did you know? Is there a vibe I'm giving off?"

"Not at all." I gave a sweeping wave around the room and gave the most believable explanation. "News travels fast in a small town."

"Aileen got one. Just today. Here."

"Did she now?" I sipped my coffee. "Jayne Reynolds is a wonderful woman and she needs the help."

He beamed. "Well, I don't know her well, since we just met, but I have to say that I think she's an angel."

I chuckled. "Not quite an angel, but some day."

"What's your line of work?" he asked, leading into a discussion that lasted almost half an hour.

Finally, Aileen came back. "I'm sorry to interrupt, honey, but why don't you take Cody on home? Jayne wants me to work until closing." She leaned closer. "I'm getting twice minimum wage, plus tips."

"Wow, sweetie, that's great," J.D. said. "It's sure going to help. What time's closing?"

"Seven o'clock. Jayne said that even at Christmas, people don't need caffeine after seven."

"I'll be here, sweetie. Cody, give your Mom a kiss. We've got to go check on Grannie."

Both Matt and Cody protested, but J.D. soon had Cody's coat buttoned securely and was shrugging into his own.

"Have you looked for a job at the Mossy Creek Candle Factory out on Trailhead Road?" I asked J.D., going for offhand.

"No, I haven't," J.D. said with surprise. "I thought their Christmas season would've been long over."

"True, but word is that they're about to get a big Valentine's candle order from a semi-major box store. If I were you, I'd go put in an application."

J.D. looked sincerely grateful and reached for my hand, "Thanks, Mr. Kringle. It's been a treat meeting you."

I shook his hand, then offered my own to Cody, who shook it with a shy smile.

"'Bye, Santa."

"See you later, Cody," I said. "Have your Dad or Grannie bring you around to see me at Hamilton's. We need to discuss your Christmas wish list for this year."

I loved seeing excitement in shy children. It was like they were about to burst, but didn't dare. Made you want to tickle them until they did. I refrained, however, and smiled at J.D.'s assurances that they'd see me soon.

Then I turned back to Matt. He studied me as if I were a Frank Gehry building whose construction methods he couldn't quite figure out.

"I have to say I'm impressed with your manners, Matt," I said.

That shook him out of his thoughts. "Huh?"

"You made introductions for me and your friend like a gallant gentleman. It wasn't quite out of Emily Post, but a darn good job."

Matt's face scrunched. "Who's Emily?"

I smiled. "A lady who lived a long time ago. What I mean

to say is that your mother is doing an excellent job raising you. You must love her very much."

He nodded with enthusiasm, his eyes seeking out his mother across the shop.

"If you were to come in and see me at Hamilton's, what would be on your Christmas wish list?"

"My what?"

"What would you tell Santa you want for Christmas?"

"I don't know. Mama says she brings me toys. She says Santa isn't real. *There is no magic.*"

"I know." I couldn't keep the sadness from my voice. "Do you believe in magic?"

Matt glanced at his mother, then crept closer to me and whispered with obvious guilt, "Sometimes I do."

His simple, childish admission tugged at my heart. "As well you should."

"Win!" Matt stood and held up his arms.

His strong cry made me turn, startled. "Win! We didn't see you come in."

Win tossed Matt into the air, as usual, then carefully set him into the play area and shook my hand. "Anybody need anything? I'm going to grab a cup. No? I'll be back in a sec."

As Win joined the line at the counter, my gaze returned to Matt. The boy watched Win worshipfully, like any boy would watch his father.

"I believe I know what you want for Christmas."

Matt turned back to me. "You do?"

"You want a daddy."

His eyes grew even wider than Cody's had. He looked a little bit afraid. "You really are Santa Claus, aren't you?"

I just smiled. "So I'm right."

Matt nodded. "All the other boys have daddies. But when I tell Mama I want one, too, she seems hurts and asks isn't she and Glinda enough."

I was a little surprised. "Aren't you getting a daddy soon? Isn't your Mama going to marry Win?"

Though I didn't think it possible, Matt's eyes got even wider. "She is? Win's going to be my daddy?"

Uh oh. "Sssshhh, Matt," I said. "It's a secret for now."

"Ooohhh. Okay."

Both Matt and I glanced toward the counter where Win still waited patiently in line. Instead of helping him quickly as she usually did, Jayne found a reason to be at the other end of the counter, but sent more than one annoyed look Win's way.

I pulled at my beard as I considered the situation. Looked like everything wasn't rosy in the Reynolds/Allen relationship. I'd have to think more about that. But for now . . .

"Matt?"

"Yeah, Santa?"

"Please call me Kris, Matt, like I asked before."

"But you're Santa."

I chuckled. "It's the same thing. You know, like your Mama is 'Mama' to you, but Jayne to her friends."

"Oh. Yeah. Okay, Kris."

"Isn't there something else Santa can bring to you? Something that only he knows about?" *To prove I'm real, at least to you, my young friend.*

Matt considered that a few seconds, then brightened. "A G.I. Joe!"

"Ahhh. Like the one I brought for Cody?"

"Yes, please. Mama doesn't know about G.I. Joe."

"Okay, then. Promise me that you won't tell her about it, okay?"

"Why?"

"I know it's going to be hard because you tell your mama everything. But if you don't tell her and you get a G.I. Joe on Christmas morning, that means that Santa is real, doesn't it?"

"Yeeeaaahh." Matt drew out the word, obviously considering my logic from several angles.

"Okay, then, so you're promising not to tell anyone else at all—not even Glinda—about wanting a G.I. Joe. Pinkie swear." I showed him how to link pinkie fingers for our solemn promise.

"Done."

Two seconds later, Win set his tall cup of coffee on the table. "I'm back."

"Win!" Matt jumped up and grabbed Win around one thigh.

"Hey, buddy. We already said hello, didn't we?"

Matt took a step back so he could peer excitedly up at Win. "Are you going to be my daddy, Win?"

Matt said it so loud, a hush fell over the shop.

Looking like a cornered deer, Win swallowed hard and looked at Jayne, who had the same shocked, fearful expression on her face.

Oh dear. They really hadn't told anyone.

Jayne's gaze fell on me and hardened.

Sometimes the better part of valor is retreat. *I'd better skedaddle.* My lunch break was about over, anyway.

• • •

Jayne

I caught Win at the door to the Bean as he was leaving a few minutes later. Though I didn't intend it, my hurt feelings came out in a hiss. "How could you?"

Win glanced around the shop at the Creekites who watched them closely. Taking my arm gently but firmly, he guided me outside.

I yanked my arm away. "How could you tell *that man* that we're engaged?"

"I didn't," he said calmly, sending a puzzled glance across the Square at Hamilton's department store.

"Then how does he know? We haven't told anyone. Not even Ingrid or Matt. Or Josie."

"I know that, Jayne. My opinion has been as strong as yours that we should wait a while. I didn't tell Kris anything. You have to believe me."

Win's baffled frustration made me realize I *did* believe him, and the pique flew away like a puff of smoke.

Studying his face, I was struck once again that Win Allen was an incredibly good-looking man, with his green eyes flashing and his slightly graying dark hair mussed from having sent a hand or two through it during all the questions he'd fielded in the last few minutes. All the reasons I loved him came flooding back, wiping away the last vestiges of anger I'd nursed for several days.

I slipped my hand into his.

Startled, his head swung around and his eyes searched mine.

"I'm sorry for the way I've been acting, Win," I said. "I need to tell you why."

He squeezed my hand. "I know why. Josie told me this morning. She told me she was going to tell you that she told me and why, but I guess she hasn't had a chance."

I was surprised at Josie's interference for just a second. Josie was a vault with information . . . unless she felt strongly that divulging said information would help someone, not hurt them.

I sighed. "She was right to. Although I would've . . . eventually."

"I know, love. And I would like to hear your version of it. But later . . ." He glanced around, then pulled me into the indented entryway of the old bakery Ingrid sold to me last year. Curtains inside blocked the view from the shop and from most of the street. Leaning me back against the cold window, Win shielded me with his body and bent his head to mine.

"Win, we . . ." But I gave in to the kiss. Everyone in town knew we were dating. A kiss in a doorway isn't an admission of being engaged. Realizing that, I wrapped my arms around his neck and threw myself into the embrace.

A moment later, he pulled back and leaned his forehead heavily against mine. "Wow."

"Yeah."

"I take it this means we're still engaged."

I breathed deeply, trying to recover my equilibrium. "Yeah."

"Get a room!" someone shouted from across the street.

I looked over Win's shoulder to see Mac Campbell grinning at us. But he hurried on toward Town Hall at the other end of the Square.

"Should we let the cat all the way out of the bag?" Win asked quietly. "Our concern that Matt wouldn't cotton to sharing his mother seems to be moot."

That certainly seemed to be true. Matt had been thrilled at the idea of Win becoming his father. "Can we wait until after Christmas? Or maybe Christmas Day. That can be one of our presents to him."

Win nodded. "Okay. If you can keep answering all their questions, so can I."

"'Do you see a ring on this finger?' seems to work for me," I said with a smile. "Although I didn't appreciate your 'When you've got the milk . . .' innuendo. Especially since you haven't had any milk."

"I know." Win eased away with a rueful smile. "I saw your frown when I came up with that one. That's why I quickly switched to the truth: 'We've only been dating a few months.' I guess that'll work for a few more weeks."

I straightened, shivering in the frigid mountain air as I pulled away from the cold, thick pane of glass.

Noticing, Win had his jacket off and around my shoulders in a heartbeat.

I guess my grateful smile was imbued with the warmth that enveloped me, because his face tightened. "Any more of that and we *will* need to get a room."

I nodded, though sorely tempted. But we'd decided from the beginning to wait to share intimacy for as long as we could stand it. Not only to get to know each other better as we became accustomed to this new possibility, but because we had a little boy close by most of the time and a town that seemed to have eyes everywhere. "I need to get back inside, I guess."

Grabbing my hand, he pulled me back onto the sidewalk. "Want me to take Matt upstairs?"

"Is it that time already?"

"I locked up Mama's forty-five minutes ago."

"It's amazing how time flies when you're so busy. I would've said it was about ten-thirty." I chuckled. "If I had been thinking clearly, I'm sure I would've wondered why you weren't still at the café."

He opened the door to the Bean and followed me inside. I relinquished his jacket, then went to grab Matt's.

I laid it over Win's coat on his arm. He took Matt's hand with the other. "Let's go, cowboy. I'm sure Glinda needs an outing."

He turned to me. "We'll go over to my place and grab Cherry, then swing back by and make supper. Eight, as usual?"

As I nodded, Win leaned down and kissed me full on the mouth.

I could feel my cheeks flush and a catcall whistled above the din.

"Yes, we're dating," Win announced loudly to the whole shop. "When, and if, we do become engaged, we'll let everyone know. Until then, deal with it."

Everyone turned back to their tables, disappointed, but buzzing with gossip anyway.

"Creekites," I said as we walked to the door that led upstairs. "Ya gotta love 'em."

His eyes shone with double meaning. "Yes, I do."

Feeling as if my whole being was lit from within, I turned toward the counter, only to be met with Ingrid's pursed lips. "Ingrid, as soon as Win puts a ring on my finger, you'll be the next person to know. I promise."

She sniffed. "I'd better."

A customer drew her attention, and I surveyed the shop. It looked as if everything was under control. As my gaze swept the Square to ascertain if more tour buses were regurgitating tourists, it settled on Hamilton's Department Store. The source of all my recent agitation was over there, indoctrinating little children into his cult.

How did Kris Kringle know Win and I were engaged? Just a good guess?

Knowing I wouldn't have a peaceful mind until I knew, I reached for my coat. "Ingrid, I'm taking a break."

"Got it covered," she returned absently as she whipped up a latte.

I made a beeline for Hamilton's, which sat cattycornered across the Square from The Naked Bean. On the way up to the third-floor Children's Department, I shared the elevator with Sandy Crane and her baby daughter, Faith. Faith looked so cute, dressed up in her red stretchy velvet onesie with a candy cane appliqué, that I had to pick her up. As the ancient elevator churned us upward, she chortled happily at me and kicked her legs and arms in excitement.

"Going to visit Santa," Sandy announced proudly. "Jess is probably already up there."

I blinked hard. "Santa? Seriously? Faith is only, what, seven months old? I know you probably think she's precocious, but still . . ."

"She's seven months next week," Sandy said proudly. "And we know she doesn't have a wish list or anything, but Kris Kringle makes such a cute Santa, he'll be perfect as the Santa in Faith's first Christmas picture."

I murmured something noncommittal and set Faith back in the stroller after we'd exited on the third floor.

I stopped for a moment to enjoy the ambiance. The brick columns of the hundred-year-old-plus building made perfect frames for the Christmas decorations that hung on every wall and from every heart-pine beam in the ceiling. Christmas smells of cinnamon and dried Georgia apples mingled with the slight mustiness of age.

Hamilton's was a dying breed. How many department stores were left anywhere in the USA that weren't connected to a national chain? Most had been either bought up or run out of business by the buying power of Macy's, Belk and the like. But Creekites were loyal customers, and Rob Hamilton knew how to keep his customers happy. That combination equaled success. It was one of my favorite buildings in Mossy Creek. I bought most of Matt's clothes and toys right here—both to support the Hamiltons and because I just loved coming inside.

Spying the sign to Santa's workshop, I waved to a number of Creekites in the middle of their Christmas shopping. Seeing the "enter" line on the right, I opted to go left, hoping to catch my faux Santa in a lull.

There were several families in line, however, so I half-hid behind a green velvet curtain to the side and slightly behind Santa's throne to watch.

The child sitting on Santa's lap was the youngest child who had been adopted by Opal Suggs a few years ago—Inez. To my surprise, and by the looks of it, to the surprise of everyone within earshot, Kris was speaking Spanish with Inez. He chatted like a native Mexican, or at least, what sounded like a native. I only spoke a few words, but I'd been around enough Mexicans in Atlanta to recognize the fluidity and ease Kris displayed with the language.

For a moment, I was impressed. Then I realized that Spanish was second only to Mandarin in the numbers of people who spoke it. Kris could easily be one of those people.

So chalk one up for Kris for learning another language. Bully for him.

The next child was escorted in by Orville and Roy Simple, two of the poorest, dirtiest and most unkempt bachelors in the area. These two probably met every one of Jeff Foxworthy's criteria for "You might be a redneck if . . ."

They introduced their nephew, Leon, visiting from up in Union County. Since the only Santa they had there was at the Walmart, Orville and Roy wanted to bring him over and show him a "real" Santa.

To my astonishment, Kris conversed easily with all three in another language altogether—Southern Mountain Redneck. He matched their cadence and used words I'd never heard, but were obviously perfectly clear to all three Simples.

At first, I thought he was making fun of them, but it soon became obvious that they loved having their own dialect spoken by Santa. It seemed as if all three of them left his presence believing they would get everything on their wish list come Christmas morning.

I nodded at Orville's friendly, "Howdy," on their way out and saw that the next child was Cody Henley. His father waved at me as he walked his shy son up to Kris's lap.

I was touched when the only thing Cody asked Santa for was that his father get a job. Less than a minute later, my jaw dropped. Did Kris really have the gall to promise Cody that his father would have a job by the end of the week and that he would be attending kindergarten in Mossy Creek the next school year?

I was so appalled that I didn't listen to the rest of the conversation. The obligatory picture flashed and J.D. brought Cody out my way. J.D. thanked me again, profusely, but I was in a hurry to get to Kris, who seemed to have a break in the action. As he reached for a bottle of water by his chair, I bid a firm goodbye to the Henleys and rounded the Santa throne.

"How could you?" I asked, hands on my hips.

Kris held up his hands defensively. "I'm sorry, Jayne. I didn't know you and Win were keeping your engagement a secret even from Matt. I apologize."

"We'll get to that in a minute. First, I want to know how you could promise Cody Henley that his father would have a job by the end of the week. You can't possibly know such a thing. How could you get his little hopes up like that? Trying to be the big baaaad Santa? Trying to sink him so deep in your Christmas cult that he'll never stop believing? Isn't the Peter Pan complex bad enough already?"

Kris didn't seem the least bit upset by my tirade. "Jayne, if J.D. doesn't get a job by Friday, I'll eat my Santa boots."

"Literally?" I asked.

"Yes, literally."

"Huh. Fine thing to promise when there are no witnesses."

"Do you want me to write it out and sign it? I've got a pot of Christmas Tree sap over here that—"

"What makes you think Win and I are engaged?"

He didn't even blink in the sudden change of subject. "It's common knowledge, isn't it? I heard it from several people."

"Who?"

"I don't remember."

"Oh, come on."

"Frankly, Jayne, after your reaction, I'd rather not get any more people into trouble."

I took a deep breath. I had not come over here to confront him in such a snit. He just pushed every button I had concerning Christmas. I hated the way I was acting, knew it wasn't like me at all. I just couldn't seem to help myself.

Kris pointed behind me. "If you're finished, it looks as if I've got more potential members for my Christmas cult; love that name, by the way."

I looked over my shoulder to see Jess and Sandy strolling Faith through the velvet rope lines. They must've gotten side-tracked on their way in.

My nails dug into my palms. I knew I should apologize, but he just made me so darn mad. "From now on, stay out of The Naked Bean."

One thick white eyebrow lifted. "Isn't your establishment a public place, and doesn't your business license demand you not discriminate against people who are different? Don't you think I fit that description?"

I lowered my voice, so the Cranes couldn't hear. "Are you saying you would sue me for discrimination? Is that a jolly old elf kind of thing to do?"

He sighed heavily. "Jayne, please. You need to relax. Breathe. No one is trying to sabotage you, especially me. I'm on your side."

"Ooohhhh!" Furious, I turned to leave but hadn't gotten three steps before his question stopped me short.

"How's your oven treating you?"

Slowly, I turned to face him. He gazed patiently back. He didn't look smug. There was no "nah-nah-nah-nah-nah" in his demeanor. He just smiled his elfish little smile.

Finally, he turned away and gestured to the Cranes to come forward.

I was rooted to the spot. Was he saying what I thought he was saying? The oven *had* seemed to spontaneously heal, and the repairman that had come that morning said he couldn't find anything wrong with the oven. No bad wiring. No busted parts. He said it looked as if it could go another twenty years.

Almost as if it were . . .

Magic.

"Isn't he amazing?"

My own amazement was still on my face, I knew, as I turned to find Ellen Stancil standing beside me.

Ellen used to work as a breakfast waitress at Mama's All You Can Eat Café. Then she'd been given a shopping spree at Hamilton's after her son, Billy Paul, fell down a well. Soon after, she went to work for Hamilton's as a sales clerk. A year later, she took over as manager for the children's department.

I admired the way Ellen had improved herself and her family's circumstances. She must be the one who'd hired Kris.

"He's just marvelous. So good with the kids," Ellen said.

"Who is he?" I had to ask.

"I thought you'd met him," she said in surprise. "I'll have to introduce you after—"

"No, I *have* met him," I said. "I just . . . I mean, really. Who *is* he?"

Ellen finally understood my question. "We don't know. He showed up out of the blue and looked so much like Santa that we'd have been idiots *not* to hire him."

As a businesswoman, I had to concede her point. "Where does he live?"

"I don't know. The address we have on file is the Hamilton House Inn. That's where he was staying when we first hired him. But I believe he's moved. I guess he found a room or apartment. I really should ask him to update his personnel file."

Talking with Ellen calmed me, and I couldn't help but smile. "That Hamilton's still calls its people 'personnel' instead of 'human resources' is one of the things I love about it."

Ellen smiled back. "Just like Mossy Creek, we 'ain't goin' nowhere, and don't want to.'"

"I know," I said fervently. "Don't ya just love it?"

• • •

Jayne

That evening, Matt, Win and I sat down to a mouth-watering supper featuring tuna steaks with mango salsa. A lovely broccoli risotto complemented it.

"Mama?" Matt regarded me thoughtfully. He'd not yet taken a bite of his tuna sandwich. Though not a picky eater, Matt's tastes were not as sophisticated as Win liked to cook, so Win usually "dumbed down" the entrée for Matt.

"Yes, my beautiful son?" I asked. I'd been in a much better mood since my trip to Hamilton's, though I couldn't have said why.

"Are you really, truly sure there is no Santa?"

Win went still, but I answered patiently, "Yes, Matt, I am."

"How sure?"

I wanted to lie. I really did. But wasn't honesty the point here? "Oh, about eighty percent. Seventy-five or eighty."

"Want to try sixty or maybe even fifty?" Win asked, clearly amused.

I lifted my chin. "I'll stick with seventy-five percent, thankyouverymuch."

Win raised his eyebrow.

"How much is that again?" Matt asked. "I forgot."

Win reached back and pulled one of the oatmeal cranberry cookies he'd made that afternoon from the cookie jar. He broke the cookie in half, then broke one half into half again. He put the half down in front of Matt, then added another quarter.

"Oh." Matt studied it a moment, then said, "That's most of a cookie."

"That's right, it is," I said, relieved to see in a concrete way that I still didn't believe in magic.

Win sighed and pushed the half cookie in front of my plate. "We'll give Mama the big piece," he told Matt, dividing the remaining half between them. "We need to feed her brain."

• • •

Jayne

When Matt was tucked in bed, fast asleep, Win and I spooned on the sofa.

"I hear you went to Hamilton's this afternoon."

I rolled my eyes, but since I was sitting back in his embrace, he couldn't see it. "The Mossy Creek grapevine is still working, I see. Who was it? Sandy Crane?"

"Probably the first to report, since she was there. That's not who I heard it from, though. Doesn't matter. You know Mossy Creek."

"Yes, I do."

"Did you get any answers from Kris?"

"No."

"So that visit isn't where the twenty-five percent of doubt came from?"

I sat up and turned to face him. "Why is this so important?"

"Because it is." Win searched my face, then asked softly, "How sure are you that I love you?"

I was shocked at his question.

"In percentages," he insisted.

"I can't put a number to that!"

"AAAANNNHHHHHH." He mimicked the harsh tones of

a buzzer. "That's the wrong answer. The right answer is a very quick one hundred percent."

"I . . ."

"Okay, let's start with an easy one. How sure are you that the sun will rise tomorrow?"

"One hundred percent."

"How certain are you that you moved to the right town?"

"One hundred and ten percent."

"How sure are you that I will never willingly leave you?"

I paused. "I have faith that you . . ."

"I'm asking you to go beyond faith, Jayne. I want absolute belief."

"There's a difference?"

"An enormous one. Belief is one hundred percent certainty. Faith involves hope, which gives that ol' hundred percent a fudge factor."

I panicked. "Are we back to this? I thought that discussion was over."

"It isn't."

"You know why I can't . . . won't believe in Santa Claus."

"I don't care what *you* believe. Of course you don't believe in Santa Claus. What matters in this instance is Matt."

I sat back, appalled at the thought that just occurred to me.

He saw it in my face. "No, I'm not in this relationship to gain a son. Matt is a bonus. I love him to pieces, but I love you more. But this is just as important for you as it is for him."

Not knowing what to say, I fell back on, "If you loved me, you'd let it go."

Win shook his head. "It's because I love you that I can't let it go. There *is* magic in the world. There is magic in love. Unless you can admit there is magic, even see the magic, how can you truly love?"

Shocked, devastated, I stared at him. "Are you breaking up with me?"

He sighed. "No, of course not. Because I *believe* that you not only are capable of believing in magic, I believe you are capable of phenomenal magic."

• • •

Jayne

Two afternoons later, Clive Tackett, owner of the Mossy Creek Candle Factory, strode excitedly into The Naked Bean. It was a rare occurrence, because he lived northwest of town, almost to Chinaberry—out the same road as his factory.

Though I'd met Mr. Tackett, I didn't know him well. But Ingrid had graduated Mossy Creek High School with him.

"Hey, Clive," she said. "You look as excited as a pig in a peach orchard."

"Hey, Ingrid," Clive said, grinning. "Give me a extra-large, extra-sweet, extra-whipped cream latte."

"Happy to," Ingrid told him. "You just happy it's Christmas, or did a rich uncle die?"

"Nope. Just a few hours ago—out of the blue!—I got a huge order for Valentine's Day candles for . . . well, I shouldn't say until the ink is dry, but it's a big chain and it's gonna be scads of candles. And if that goes well, we'll be doing Mother's Day candles, then the Fourth of July candles, then. . . .Well, pretty much all the major holidays."

"Well, ain't that grand." Ingrid gave Clive his change and turned to make his latte.

Clive seemed as if he couldn't stop talking. "Business is usually slower a herd of snails through peanut butter during the Christmas holidays. You know that, but now I got to hire two dozen new workers. More Creekites going to work!"

"Congratulations," Ingrid said sincerely. "We always like hearing Mossy Creek success stories. You mind if we spread the word?"

"Not a bit. That's why I came in. Figured this place was so busy, it's as good as a want ad. Please tell every able-bodied worker that I'm hiring. As a matter of fact, another reason I came was to—"

"Mr. Tackett?" Aileen Henley appeared at his elbow.

Clive turned and smiled. "Yes! You're Mrs. Henley, right? J.D. Henley's wife?"

"Yes sir."

"Excellent. That's one reason I'm here. He told me you were working at The Naked Bean when he applied yesterday for work.

I told him I wouldn't have any until early spring. But now I do. Yessir, I do! So you tell him to report for work at seven tomorrow morning, all right? I'm desperate for a new machinist, and he got a glowing report from his previous boss."

Aileen's face lit up like a Christmas tree topper. She grabbed Clive's hand and shook it vehemently. "Oh, thank you, Mr. Tackett. He'll be there on time, I promise you! Thank you soooo much!"

"You're welcome." Clive took his latte and sipped. "Mmmm. You do make a mean cuppa joe, Ingrid. You'll spread the word, right?"

"You betcha, Clive. This is great news for the whole town."

As Clive left, Aileen just stood there, beaming.

"Congratulations, Aileen," I said. "I'm happy things turned out so well."

I *was* happy. I really was. Aileen had turned out to be a godsend. She was a fabulous worker, and I was already trying to figure out how I could keep her on after the holidays. I really liked her husband, too. He seemed like a fine young man.

"Ditto from me," Ingrid echoed.

"This is so exciting!" Aileen said.

"Yep."

"No, you don't understand. Kris Kringle—the old man who's playing Santa Claus at Hamilton's Department store? He told J.D. the day you hired me to apply at the Candle Factory. J.D. went yesterday, and today he has a job! Do you think Mr. Kringle knew about the order coming to the Candle Factory?"

I felt as if someone had grabbed my feet and glued them to the floor.

Jayne, if J.D. doesn't get a job by Friday, I'll eat my Santa boots.

"Well if that don't beat all." Ingrid shook her head in wonder. "Clive didn't even know anything about it until today. He said the contract came out of the clear, blue sky."

"Then how did Mr. Kringle know?" Aileen asked in wonder.

How indeed?

"Why don't you ask him?" Ingrid pointed to the back corner of the shop. "He's right over there."

As Aileen hurried over, I met Kris's eyes across the room.

He didn't seem triumphant, just . . . knowing.

How *did* he know? How?

I could almost hear Win's whisper. *Magic.*

• • •

Jayne

On the next Saturday night, Win, Matt and I were invited to the Rutherfords' for supper. I'd tried to insist they come to my house instead, since Josie was eight months pregnant, but Josie wouldn't hear of it.

"Win cooks for us so much," she'd said when she came into the shop to invite us. "We just want to pay y'all back a little. Besides, it's easier to cook than to get up your stairs."

Though no chef, Josie was a good cook and we enjoyed a hearty roast beef with Yorkshire pudding and green peas. I'd brought one of Ingrid's red velvet cakes for dessert.

With Matt settled in front of the TV for *How the Grinch Stole Christmas*—Win had insisted Matt not miss the classic—the adults lingered over coffee.

We discussed the strange and funny things that had happened in town. Inez Hilley's ongoing feud with her cousin, Ardaleen Bigelow, the horses that had run amok at the Christmas parade the Saturday before, and the new jobs at the Candle Factory were just a few of the topics of conversation.

"I'll tell you something strange," Harry said during a lull in the conversation.

"Can you beat the 'possum that tore down Almira Olsen's Christmas lights and spelled out 'Noel' in her yard?"

"You really had to squint to read Noel in that mess," Josie insisted. "I saw it first-hand. Besides, I have it on good authority that Almira—shall we say *encouraged* the lights a tad."

Harry stroked his clean-shaven chin. He'd once sported a beard to hide the burn scars from a car accident on his face, but Josie loved the rough yin-yang appearance of the scars and begged him to wear them proudly. Since he would do anything for Josie, he shaved every morning.

"This just might top that," Harry said.

Both Win and I straightened in anticipation.

"Do tell," I said.

"Have I told you that the strange little man playing Santa Claus at Hamilton's . . ."

"Kris Kringle," Josie supplied when he paused. "Ooohhh, this is good."

I shifted in my seat, uncertain I wanted to hear anything else "weird" about Kris Kringle. And if Josie thought the story was good, there was a high percentage chance it was weird.

"Did I tell you that he's been staying in my cabin up on Colchik Mountain?"

"I think I heard that," Win said at the same time I said, "No."

I gave Win a "Why didn't you tell me?" look, but his attention was on Harry. I let it go because I knew why he hadn't told me.

Then I glanced at Josie.

She shrugged. "You seemed as if you didn't care to hear anything about Mr. Kringle."

That was true. Then the logistics hit me. "How does he get up and down the mountain every day? That's at least an hour coming down and twice that going up."

"That's not the strange part," Harry said.

"I think he flies!" Josie said with a giggle.

I rolled my eyes.

"You know how it kept threatening to snow all day Thursday," Harry said.

We nodded.

"I was up on Colchik, checking my instruments. I smelled smoke and knew it came from the cabin, so I decided to check on Kris. It was getting dark. You know that time of day when it's neither light nor dark. The time of day when your eyes can play tricks on you?"

I nodded along with Win, but suddenly, I did *not* want to hear the rest of this story.

"As I came into the clearing, I swear I saw small critters scurrying into hiding all around the cabin. But I didn't think anything much of that. Critters run around all over the mountains. Seemed like more than usual, but hey, critters are critters, right?"

"Right." Win leaned forward in anticipation.

"Well, when I got closer, those tracks didn't look like any tracks I've ever seen on that mountain. Some of them looked more like weird tiny footprints."

I leaned back.

"Even then, I put it down to overlapping bird or paw prints seen in dim light. So I knocked and went in," Harry continued. "It was the darnedest thing."

"Tell them!" Josie was grinning.

"It was filled with unfinished toys."

I blinked. With Harry's build-up, toys were the last thing I was expecting. Reindeer, elves, Mrs. Santa . . . even monsters. But toys?

"Toys?" Win echoed as if his thoughts were aligned with mine.

"Toys," Harry repeated, nodding. "It looked like a microcosm of Santa's Workshop, minus the elves."

"Wow!" Win glanced into the living room to see if Matt had heard, then whispered, "He's asleep."

All I could do was stare first at Harry, then Josie. "What . . ." I cleared my throat. "What were they?"

"When I asked, Kris told me he'd taken a part-time job as a toy repairman. But . . ." Harry shook his head. "I'm not an expert on toys, but those did not look like toys that needed repair. They looked like toys under construction."

I sat all the way back in my chair. "No. You're not saying . . . You can't possibly think . . ."

"Yes!" Josie exclaimed. "Isn't it fun?"

"No!" I repeated. "It can't be. Harry, you're a scientist. Surely you don't believe that man is Santa Claus and that he's moved the North Pole to Colchik Mountain."

Harry leaned back, his large frame making the dining room chair squeak. "Logic is against it, I know. But first-hand observation is one of the basic tenets of empirical study. I know what I saw. True, there was nothing magical about it. There were toys, yes, and it *looked* like Santa's Workshop, but he had everyday tools, no elves and there was no fairy dust floating around. You know I am not a fanciful man. Josie is fanciful enough for both of us. Still . . ."

Win sat back in his chair and pushed a hand through his hair. "Yeah. Still . . ."

Harry's attention was diverted when Josie squeezed his hand. He smiled down at her.

I stood. "One Christmas toy we could use in here is a nutcracker, because you're all nuts. Win, it's time to take—" I stopped when my eyes fell on Matt. "Oh, yes, indeed it *is* time to go home. Matt's already asleep."

• • •

Jayne

"Mama?"

I glanced across the kitchen island at Matt, who sat in a stool next to Win. They watched as I "cooked," for once. Just sandwiches for a light supper on Sunday night. There'd been a Holiday "dinner-on-the-grounds" after morning church services. Though we always ate in the large social room instead of on the "grounds," many Southern churches kept the old-timey name.

"Yes, baby?"

Matt stared at the cookie jar. "Mama, how much do you believe that Santa is real today?"

I looked at Win. "Did you tell him Harry's story?"

Win shrugged. "Yes, but he didn't seem to understand the reference. Because you've . . . well, shielded him, he hasn't heard enough Christmas stories to know that Santa has a toy workshop at the North Pole."

Trying to distract my son, I said, "Matt, why don't you go get your map book and we can find where the North Pole is located?"

"In a minute, Mama." Ever since he'd been born, Matt had had a one-track mind. It was getting harder and harder to distract him. "How much cookie?"

I struggled with the same feelings I'd had a few days ago. I wanted to lie and tell Matt zero percent, but my whole point from the beginning was honesty. I thought back over the last few weeks.

It wasn't zero percent.

Oh, I *knew* that Santa wasn't real. Every person past the age of ten knew that. But it was as if the universe was conspiring to convince me to leave my fearful hatred of Christmas behind. First Win, then Kris Kringle. *Kris Kringle*, for goodness' sake. Even logical, forthright Harry Rutherford seemed in on the conspiracy.

It was all so crazy. The universe doesn't teach lessons about something as commercial as Christmas.

The universe is full of magical things, patiently waiting for our wits to grow sharper.

The quote from Eden Philpots—whoever the heck he was— drifted back over time. It had been Matthew Reynolds's favorite. My dear, sweet husband, even with his engineer's love of logical function, believed in magic.

He believed in Christmas. He believed in Santa Claus and elves and toy workshops at the North Pole.

Oh, he didn't *really* believe, but he adored the magic of it, the possibilities. He would've loved sharing it with Matt. All the Nativity scenes. All the lights. All the handmade ornaments we'd collected over the years—which I'd thrown into boxes and given to the first thrift store I came across.

Suddenly, I was appalled. What was wrong with me? How could I disrespect my husband's memory so completely?

For the first time since Matthew died, I could see past my grief. I could see that, for all my talk about honesty, I wasn't being honest with myself. My grief had made me selfish. I hadn't wanted any part of Christmas because it reminded me of everything Matthew had loved. And I was angry at Matthew for leaving me.

Matthew would've hated what I was doing to our son. He would've hated what I was doing to myself.

All of a sudden, I saw that my reluctance to let Matt believe in Christmas was my idea of punishment for Matthew for leaving me.

I sucked in a breath as another realization hit me. My reluctance to fully commit to Win by questioning his motives at every turn was my way of holding onto a dearly loved husband, even though my subconscious wanted to punish him for dying.

How sick and warped was that?

But Matthew was dead. He was gone. There was nothing to hold onto but memories.

"Mama?"

I cleared my throat and raised tearful eyes to the two males sitting across from me.

Win saw immediately and his smug satisfaction vanished. "Jayne? Oh, my love, I'm sorry. Matt, let's not bother Mama right n—"

"No, I'm okay." I reached for the cookie jar and took out an iced Star of David. I stared down at it. "What was the question again? How much I believe or don't believe?"

Win watched me closely. "Matt asked how much you believe."

I met his eyes and smiled, then handed the entire cookie to Matt.

His eyes wide, Win stared at the cookie, then at me.

Matt stared down at the cookie, too. "That's a whole cookie."

"Yep."

Matt's happy eyes rose to mine, then he whooped and jumped up in his chair.

Win held my gaze across the granite, searching, silently asking why I had changed my mind. All I could do was smile— widely, brilliantly, feeling as if all of Bob Marley's chains had been wrapped around me for years, then suddenly disappeared.

Matt's happy jumps made his chair tip. Win grabbed him, then turned the protective gesture into celebration, throwing my giggling son into the air.

Glinda and Cherry joined in, jumping, barking and howling.

"Does this mean we can get a Christmas tree?" Matt asked when Win finally set him down between the dogs.

I hadn't thought through the ramifications of sudden belief. "Oh dear. We have no ornaments."

"Ornaments can be bought." Win slid his arms around my waist and kissed me.

I shook my head. "The best ones are homemade. If not by us, then a craftsperson or a little old lady for her church bazaar. And all the Christmas bazaars are over."

"We'll find ornaments. Don't worry. We'll string popcorn and cranberries if we have to. " Then Win turned to Matt. "Shall we go pick out a tree out at the Christmas Tree Farm tomorrow?"

"Hooray! Can we take Glinda?"

"Absolutely. Cherry can go, too. First tree one of them pees on, we'll buy."

I couldn't help laughing. "They're girl dogs. They don't pee on trees."

Matt giggled.

"We'll find one, don't worry."

"A good one."

"The best tree in Mossy Creek."

• • •

Jayne

I took the next day off from the Bean.

I'd never taken one, especially during the holidays, but Ingrid assured me that she, Betty and Aileen could handle any crowd that came through the door. When I told her what I was going to do and why, she stared at me in disbelief, then wrapped her wiry arms around me and twirled with me around the kitchen.

Aileen looked confused, but I'd swear I saw a smile on Betty Halfacre's face.

I kept Matt out of daycare and as soon as Hamilton's opened, we were first in line at Santa's workshop.

Kris's face beamed with pleasure when he spotted us. "Well, bless my soul. Jayne and Matt Reynolds. Come on up here, please."

Matt didn't quite know what to do, so Kris reached down and pulled him onto his lap. "I'm delighted to see you both. What brought this about?"

"Mama believes in Santa Claus now," Matt announced proudly. "I mean you."

"She does, does she?" Kris chuckled and said in a loud whisper to Matt, "It's about time, isn't it?"

Matt giggled and nodded.

"And do you believe, too?" Kris asked him.

"Yes, sir." Matt nodded solemnly, then asked, "Will you really slide down our chimney?"

"Absolutely."

Matt considered that, then my engineer son demanded, "How?"

Kris chuckled. "Magic."

"Ooohhh."

"Now, what would you like me to bring you on Christmas Eve?"

Matt named seven toys, all of which I'd already purchased. Then Matt whispered, "And you-know-what."

Kris smiled. "I do indeed."

"What?" I asked.

Matt nodded as Kris put his finger to his lips, then told me, "Just a secret between us guys."

I looked hard at Kris, trying to communicate my frustration at having to buy something when I didn't know what it was.

Kris grinned. "Don't worry about it, Jayne."

"Win's taking us to get a Christmas tree," Matt told him.

"Very good!"

"But we don't have ornalments."

I smiled at Matt's mangled word.

Kris winked at me over Matt's head. "Don't worry, son. No doubt the perfect ones will show up."

• • •

Jayne, Christmas Eve

"Look, Daddy, it's snowing!" Matt cried from the window of our apartment.

Win and I looked at each other in rueful resignation. We'd told Matt at supper that we were getting married in June. Ever since, he'd been calling Win "Daddy." Somehow, the whole town would know by morning.

"A little to the left," I told Win. We were decorating the Christmas tree. "No, that's too far. Back just a hair. Perfect!"

Win climbed down from the stool and surveyed his handi-work.

The crochet-skirted angel perched on top of our eight-foot tree, her crown of tiny lights shining.

"Wow!" Matt exclaimed.

The twelve-foot ceilings in the newly renovated apartment above The Naked Bean allowed us to get the tallest Christmas tree I'd ever seen in a real home. I was happy that Matt's first Christmas—even though he was four years old—was going to be special.

And it was—thanks to all my wonderful friends in Mossy Creek. Just a few minutes after we arrived home with the tree, Ingrid had climbed the stairs with a box she set on the kitchen table. It was filled with ornaments she'd used in the bakery, when she still owned it. Some of them were broken, but it was a start.

Then others began to arrive. Ingrid had spread the word and Creekites responded.

Betty had supplied the angel and a dozen crocheted stars. Josie had pine cones which she'd spray-painted silver and dusted with glitter. Spiva Quinlan had made bright bows from Christmas ribbon. Ladies from the Garden Club brought clear glass ornaments filled with perfectly preserved flowers from their gardens. Members of the Mossy Creek Presbyterian Church brought leftover ornaments from the Christmas Bazaar.

With all of that, plus the popcorn and holly berries Matt had helped me string, the tree was glittering and gorgeous.

"I have one more box," Win said, heading for the door. "I'll be right back."

He brought up an old, beat-up box and set it on the table.

"Where'd you get that?" I asked. Something about it looked familiar.

"I found it in the back room of an old thrift store down in Atlanta a couple of years ago. I'd forgotten about it until you mentioned handmade ornaments. It's been in my basement."

My hand went to my throat as I recognized the box. I moved to open it.

Unaware of the emotions flooding through me, Win pulled

off his sweater and sat hard on the sofa. "Whew! Tree trimming's hard work."

"Yeah!" Matt cried, jumping up and down.

Pulling back the flaps of the box, I looked down into my past. Matthew Reynolds stared up at me in the form of Christmas decorations. There were all kinds: crocheted snowflakes of many shapes, clay wise men, felt snowmen, sequined foam balls and trees and reindeer. Each one had a memory—either of when we'd purchased it together or when he'd brought it home from a trip, acting like a kid with a new toy.

"Mind if I turn off the fire?" Win asked. "It's a bit stuffy in here."

"That's fine," I murmured absently. "I guess I shouldn't have lit it. It just seemed like a Christmas thing to do."

"No problem," he said. "All I have to do is . . ." He pushed a button on the remote and the fire safely behind glass disappeared.

Matt climbed onto Win's lap and handed a him book to read.

"Everything okay over there?" he called, settling Matt more comfortably. "You're quiet all of a sudden. Are those ornaments that awful? It doesn't matter if you don't want to use them. I think I paid five dollars for the whole box."

I debated whether to tell him the treasure he'd given me, but finally said only, "They're perfect."

"I thought they would be." He opened the book. "They seemed to be handmade."

"They are. Thanks. I love them." I bent over the back of the sofa and placed a soft kiss on his lips. "And I love you."

"Me, too!"

I smiled and kissed my son's cheek.

Then he and Win concentrated on the book.

I turned back to the box. My hand trembled as I pulled out a Christmas tree made from the folded pages of a 1981 Readers Digest. It was a tad limp and a bit worse for the years spent banged around in the box, but it brought memories flooding back. Matthew's mother had made it and it was one of his most cherished belongings. We had a celebration every year as we unpacked it and placed it in an honored spot on our mantel. The first year, I remembered, I'd considered it tacky. But Matthew's emotional attachment and his obvious love for his parents made me consider it, even now, as spun from pure gold.

I thought I might break down, but the pain passed. As it did, I was left with warm sense of peace.

Oh, Matthew, I hope you and your mother are decorating heaven with a thousand magazine Christmas trees.

At that moment, I knew Matthew had sent this box to me. It was his way of saying, "Goodbye. Don't forget me, but live, love and be happy."

Finally, any doubt I had flew away like Santa in his sleigh. I believed in magic.

Jayne – Epilogue

"Mama! Mama!"

I heard Matt's excited cry just seconds before he shoved open my door early the next morning and scrambled onto my bed.

Glinda pounced up right beside him.

"Gracious." I barely had time to sit up and catch him. "What is it?"

"Look!" He held up a G.I. Joe. "Santa really is real."

Puzzled by his logic and the presence of the toy, I took the action figure and turned it over in my hands. Matt didn't have a G.I. Joe. "Where did you get this?"

"Santa brought it." He stared at the toy with wide-eyed solemnity.

Ah. One puzzle solved.

I kissed his cheek. "I'm happy that you believe in Santa now, Matt, but you know—"

"Kris brought it," he insisted stubbornly.

"Uh huh." Win must've snuck it under the tree last night, or Ingrid.

Matt took the toy when Glinda started sniffing it. "He tol' me to ask for somethin' and not tell you or Win. Or Ingie. I asked for this." He held the toy up triumphantly. "See? It was Santa night, and Joe's here."

Hearing the wonder of magic in my son's voice—so like his

father's—I recalled my epiphany the night before and realized I'd almost slid back into my mistrust of everything Christmas. Maybe Santa *had* brought the toy. Or maybe Matthew had found a way to give his son a Christmas present from heaven.

I was not going to question my son anymore. In fact, I vowed right there and then I would not ask Win or Ingrid if they were responsible.

I was a believer now. I would not backslide again.

𝔐𝔬𝔰𝔰𝔶 𝔆𝔯𝔢𝔢𝔨 𝔊𝔞𝔷𝔢𝔱𝔱𝔢

Volume IX, No. Three   Mossy Creek, Georgia

George Washington Highlight of Elementary School Program

by Sue Ora Bigelow

Apart from being a time when Mossy Creek celebrates its memories, Christmas is when all our traditions seem to gang up, draw a line in the dirt—or snow, depending on the weather that year—and dare us to change a one of them.

One of our brightest traditions is the Christmas Program held at Mossy Creek Elementary. It's invariably high entertainment, and this year's was no exception. Every dad-blamed kid in the school was in it, which brought out every parent, grandparent, aunt, uncle and cousin who lives within driving distance.

If you missed it, I'm sorry, but to wet your whistle for next year, here are a few highlights of this year's program:

- Forget the three wise men, the three kings and the three shepherds. The kids in Mrs. Anderson's third grade class decided if three was good, a dozen would be better. You've never seen so much gold,

frankincense and myrrh in all your life!

- If the fourth grade's herd of papier–mâché stage camels ever gets loose, they'll clean out every fruit stand from the mountains to Atlanta.

- Little Seth Bainbridge made an outstanding second-grade Santa, even though he forgot his lines a couple of times. Don't fret over his performance, however, because he was saved by the quick prompting of his friendly reindeer, Dasher.

- The fifth grade received the most applause and a rousing, impromptu singing of the *Star-Spangled Banner* by the audience when they presented the very patriotic story of Gen. George Washington crossing the Delaware on the evening of December 25, 1776. Kudos, Mrs. Dee Thrasher, fifth grade teacher, for thinking outside the traditional Christmas box.

Unless we make Christmas an occasion to share our blessings,
all the snow in Alaska won't make it 'white.'

—Bing Crosby

Joyeux Noelle

"Oh, shut up, Giselle!" I crawled out of bed and hurried into the twins' room. I hesitated at the door long enough to scratch behind the ears of the capering, barking alarm clock disguised as a dog. Giselle bounded into the nursery and cavorted between the cribs. "Coming, babies!"

When I reached the room, I stopped and gazed at my babies. I always did. God, what miracles they were.

Red-faced and squalling, Dooley clenched his fist, hiccoughed and howled again. I shifted my gaze to the more dainty of the twins. Dayna burbled and gurgled softly, but within moments, her cooing would resound through the rafters loud enough to rival Dooley's crescendo in volume.

"Mommy's here, precious."

With a silent prayer that Patty wouldn't be late this morning, I crooked an arm around each of my babies and hurried for the rocker. Feeding time came early at the Hart—no, make that Garner—household.

The off-beat warble coming from the shower made me smile. Tag hadn't left yet. Fixing a hungry-mouthed babe to each breast, I began steadily rocking back and forth, humming *Santa Claus is Coming to Town* softly.

"Santa Claus is coming to see you two, you know," I murmured, thinking of all the items piled in the storage closet in the shop downstairs.

Dooley gripped my finger, and I grinned. I couldn't help it. I was so crazy about these babies it was ridiculous. Nudging Dayna's little hand, I gazed at her, and the smaller baby responded by grasping my finger. How I loved such quiet moments with my babies.

"My daddy always said that as long as I believed in Santa Claus, he'd come to see me." I hugged the babies closer for a second. "I guess Santa brought you two to me for Christmas a little early. Always believe," I cooed and kissed the soft hair on each of their heads. "Always believe."

How I loved Christmas. My house rivaled any in Mossy Creek when it came to decorations, except I managed to keep mine within the realm of tasteful as opposed to "visible from outer space." I started humming again and soon shifted to *White Christmas.*

"Not very likely," I whispered to the babies whose bright blue eyes darted to my face immediately. From the time I'd been a little girl, I'd wished for a white Christmas. Living in Mossy Creek, Georgia, almost always assured I didn't get my wish.

The twins were another matter. I'd always wanted children, but because of my age, I didn't think it was possible to get pregnant. The resulting double surprise lay in my arms. Tag had been terrified when we'd found out I was pregnant. I'd been pretty worried myself. My delivery had gone without a hitch, albeit it six weeks early—unless you took into consideration that Tag's old coach and dear friend had had a heart attack on the same night. Luckily, he was fine as were the twins and me.

Dooley—named for the famous Vince Dooley, former coach and athletic director of the University of Georgia—reached out and grabbed a handful of Giselle's fur. Giselle gave me a doleful look as she waited to be extricated. I carefully pried Dooley's fingers out of Giselle's fur.

"That's what you get for staying so close," I scolded the dog who yelped gleefully and spun around before settling on the rug.

Barely two months old, the twins were already alert. I'm sure they are probably the smartest two babies ever born at Bigelow Hospital.

The susurration of water through the old pipes stopped, along with whatever country song Tag was belting out at the time. He suddenly appeared in the doorway and grinned at me. "I heard Giselle. Sorry. I hoped to get to the babies first."

"And do what?" I teased. "They're hungry. Not much you can do in that department."

He strode over, bottom half of his body wrapped in a damp towel and dropped a kiss on my forehead. "I can heat some of that expressed milk you put in the fridge."

I cuddled the babies closer and smiled up at him. "You know I'd rather do it myself."

He knelt down beside me and looked from one infant to the other and then at me. "I want to take whatever part of the burden I can off of you."

I chuckled. "All right. What you can do is get dressed and take that prancing horse you call a dog outside for a walk."

He rose and kissed me again, this time on the lips. "Your wish is my command."

"Good to know for future reference." I knew he adored me as I did him. We'd been married only moments before the arrival of the twins, but I'd been looking for him all my life. Maybe not precisely Tag, but someone just like him. He'd begged me to marry him when we'd found I was pregnant. I had foolishly refused. Only at the last moment did I realize I wanted more than anything for marriage to be a part of my life experience, especially now that I was having two babies.

"C'mon, Giselle." He rose, walked toward the door, jerked off the towel and wiggled his athletic butt suggestively. "We can always start on another pair of babies, Magster. You name the time and place."

I glared at him. He never called me by my name. It was always Magster or Mags or something else "endearing" he plucked out of thin air. After our initial introduction, thanks to Mom's kleptomania, he'd forgone Maggie and used some sort of substitution.

He waggled his eyebrows and made kissy faces.

I sighed in regret and blew a kiss at him. "Not yet. My six-week appointment is Tuesday, and you heard the doctor as well as I did—no sex until then."

I didn't know what I did with myself before Tag came along, but I couldn't imagine life without him.

He grinned, nodded and left. In under thirty seconds, he erupted from the bedroom, clad in sweats and bounded down the stairs with Giselle barking and dancing happily around his feet.

A moment later, I heard a crash and a yell. "Damned dog! You're gonna kill me."

Giselle had tripped him again.

"You okay, honey?" I called, unable to control my laughter.

"I heard that!" he grumbled. "Just for that, you get toast for breakfast. Women! Dogs!"

The front door slammed and the bell jangled. I smiled as I burped Dayna and waited on Dooley to finish. He always ate more. Before long, I burped him and tucked the two of them back into their cribs.

Marveling at the ease of the beginning of the day, I dashed into the shower and lathered up with my favorite honeysuckle soap. Sighing, I rinsed off and stepped out. Today wasn't a day of leisure. The soap reminded me that I needed to make a new batch for the shop. With Christmas just days away, everything was selling out. Too many things to do, too little time.

Tag's phone rang, but stopped before I could grab it. I heard the front door bell jangle and smiled. Patty English was a little early today.

"Come on up, Patty," I called, happy to have a few extra minutes for the shop.

"Maggie?" came the reply.

"Mother?" I leaned over the railing and looked down to see Mom standing at the foot of the stairs. "What are you doing out and about this early?"

"Oh, the bus is taking some of us shopping over in Bigelow. I'm planning on picking up a few things for the babies." Millicent Hart Lavender mounted the stairs with the vigor of a much younger woman. "Are they awake?"

I sighed. If they weren't, Mom would wake them up. "Just put them down after they ate. Maybe they're still awake." I turned to go back upstairs. "Wait. What do you mean by 'pick up a few things?'"

"You know, for the babies for Christmas." Millicent sauntered past and entered the nursery. "There you are, my precious darlings."

"Mother!"

"Don't bother me right now. I'm playing with Dayna. Or is it Dooley?"

"Mother!" I repeated, getting that funny feeling I used to get every time Mom walked out the door. Millicent Hart Lavender was a kleptomaniac and used to always be in trouble because of it. "What do you mean?"

The door downstairs opened and closed. "Maggie, where are you?"

I took one last questioning glance at Mom and sighed. I'd get no more from her. "Hi, Patty, we're still upstairs."

"Be right up."

The noise coming from the kitchen told me that Patty was putting on a pot of coffee. "Thank goodness," I murmured and finished getting dressed for the day.

Patty came hurrying up the stairs. "I know I'm early. I just—"

"Don't worry. It's a blessing today." I hugged Patty affectionately. "I've got a ton to do. Christmas is coming so fast, I'm way behind. People want gift baskets and I've got to finish up those batches of soap I started. They're ready to be cut into bars and packaged. Plus, I've got some I need to pour into molds. I'm trying some new scents."

Patty sniffed the air. "I love working here. This place always smells so nice."

"You don't know how glad am to have you." I eyed Mom again and motioned with my head. "Might as well get to it while Mom's here with the babies."

"Oh, no, don't count on me to babysit. I told you we were going shopping over in Bigelow to the Walmart."

"Mother, you should shop here in town. It's better for our economy and—"

"Going to Walmart. Got to pick up a few little things. Can't get everything in Mossy Creek, for goodness' sake."

Patty grinned and picked Dayna up. "I'll take her down with me. You can bring Dooley when Miss Millicent's through playing with him."

Mom rose and handed the baby to me. "Just stopped by to kiss the babies. Gotta run."

I hugged Dooley close and followed Mom down the stairs. "Mother, about your 'picking things up,' please behave yourself."

"I always behave myself."

Once again, I sighed, kissed her cheek and watched her practically sprint out the door. Past experience told me that Mom was up to something.

Tag's phone rang again. I simply let it ring. I wasn't about to race back upstairs to answer it.

Five seconds later, my phone rang. I handed Dooley to Patty and picked up the receiver. "Merry Christmas, this is Moonheart's."

"Oh, Maggie, glad you're in the shop. Is Tag around?" came Hayden Carlisle's voice.

"No, he's out walking Giselle."

"So that's why he didn't answer." Hayden chuckled. "Now, that dog is more like walking a pony."

"I totally agree. You should be here during a thunderstorm. You'd think she was a poodle instead of a Briard."

"How are you and the babies?"

"We're fine. You and Tiny?" I knew he called his wife Clementine Tiny, though few other people called her that.

"Fine and fit. You know us."

"I do. Is there a message for Tag? I'll be glad to have him return your call."

"I don't reckon so," he said slowly. "Well, might be. I need a substitute Santa Claus for Magnolia Manor's Christmas party the Saturday before Christmas."

Imagining Tag as a Santa made me laugh. It was really appropriate, now that we had two babies. "He'd probably love that."

"Just ask him to call me, and I'll fill him in on the details."

"Will do."

I replaced the receiver and glanced at the blinking light that meant we had messages. Probably more orders for baskets for the holidays. I was beginning to regret putting those up on the Internet. Especially the baby ones. I had to be so careful with those products that I hated to sell them in the baskets rather than as single items. My profit margin was much higher on the single items than on a group of them included in the baskets, even though I technically sold more items. Sell more, make less

. . . how does that make sense to anybody? But it was the way other companies operated, so if I wanted to compete, I needed to do the same.

After removing the freshly cured soap from the "resting closet" I began to slice it into rough-cut bars and then wrapped them. The labels were already printed, so I carefully placed the sticky label on the top, along with a tiny sprig of a silk flower.

Tag's phone rang again. I wondered if Hayden didn't trust me to pass along the message. I'd assumed all the calls were coming from the same person, but I could be wrong. I considered dashing up the stairs to see who it was, but the front door opened. Giselle bounded into the room and chaos ensued. She loved Patty and, as a result, the wide swoosh of her tail sent a neat pyramid of potpourri mini-bags skittering across the wooden floor.

"Giselle! Bad girl!"

Giselle turned to face me, loped over and licked my hand. "Cheater," I said with a chuckle. "Pick that stuff up."

She wagged her tail again.

Tag shrugged sheepishly. "Uh, I'll help her."

"Thanks. Oh, Hayden called."

"What did ol' HeyDay want?"

"He needs a replacement Santa for Magnolia Manor. I told him you'd probably do it, but you need to call and confirm." Carefully inserting myself between the wide sweep of Giselle's tail and the now-rising pyramid of potpourri, I looked at my adorable husband. "Your phone's been ringing off the hook."

"Better check it. Might be important." He started up the stairs and tripped over Giselle again. "Giselle, you're mighty troublesome this morning."

I returned to my task of label-making.

A few minutes later, Tag came bounding down the stairs. "Mags!"

I glanced up to see his eyes dancing in excitement. "What?"

"Guess."

"Santa called and asked if you'd guide his sleigh."

"Ha ha. No." His eyes sparkled with excitement. "You're going to be stunned!"

"Please just go ahead and tell me. You know I'm terrible at guessing when I haven't a clue what the subject is." I sealed the labels on the soaps and started arranging them in a basket.

"The phone calls—four of them actually—were from the general manager of the Raiders. They want me as head coach. Can you believe it?" He brought both fists down in the universal gesture for "Oh, yeah!"

Stunned? That didn't come near describing my feelings. More like devastation. It wasn't like it was the Falcons, just down the road a ways. This was all the way out in California. Football practice, pre-season and the season runs from August through the end of January. Five months.

He looked at me with a puzzled expression on his face. "Aren't you thrilled?"

As he lowered my feet to the floor, I tried to think of what I could say. "Thrilled? Not exactly. I mean, I'm really happy for you, but—"

"But? How can there be any but? This is the NFL. I've always wanted to coach."

He resembled a giddy little boy who'd gotten the greatest toy in the world. I felt like I'd been punched in the stomach. Nauseated. "Tag, California?"

"Right." He clearly didn't understand my feelings on the subject. "The Raiders.

California. "We have two babies. You'd have to live in Oakland."

"Right. We could—"

Fighting to hold back tears, I shook my head. "Tag, I can't move to California." I gulped the lump that had risen in my throat, but it refused to move. "No, I can't. I just can't."

He stared at me, apparently as stunned to hear I couldn't move as I was to hear he wanted to. Seconds crept past as my heart thundered in my chest. Dooley suddenly shrieked. I seized the moment and ran up the stairs. At this low point in my life, I needed to be with my babies.

Patty was reaching for him, but I got there first. "I'll get him. Please go watch the store."

She opened her mouth as if to say something, but just nodded and headed out the door.

I practically snatched Dooley out of his crib and clutched him to my chest as I sank into the rocker. Tears flowed freely, dampening the top of his head. I tried to smooth away the dampness with my sleeve. It wasn't fair to him that I was so miserable. How would this affect our lives? I was facing the most frightening two words in the English language: single mom. Rising, I wondered if I could do it. I wasn't as young as I once was. I lifted Dayna out of her crib and returned to the rocker.

A shadow cut across the sunlight gleaming across the floor. Tag stood there, hurt marring his handsome face. "Mags—"

"I can't move to Oakland, Tag." The trembling of my lower lip barely indicated the shock that I felt at that moment. The idea of leaving Mossy Creek, particularly so soon after giving birth to my precious twins, and moving to Oakland was almost more than I could fathom.

He stared at me, a blank look on his face before his slowly wrinkling forehead showed his uncertainty. Obviously, he hadn't expected that kind of answer.

"Tag, we have two babies. Do you really want to raise them in the smog, chaos and madness of California?" Maintaining a normal pitch to my voice wasn't easy at this point. I could feel the hysteria rising, along with the tone of my voice. If I kept talking, I'd soon be screeching.

"But Mags . . ."

Patty sailed into the room and stopped, apparently sensing the tension. "Oh, um, I've got to run out to my car a second."

I could barely look at her, but I managed a nod. Tag looked at her as if he didn't even know her.

She rushed down the stairs. Knowing she'd be right back, I inhaled deeply and shook my head.

"Magster, we can talk about this later." Tag continued to gaze at me as if I'd grown another head. "I need to go to the gallery."

Before I could answer, I heard Patty re-enter the shop. Tag took the stairs three at a time and disappeared into the lower story of the house.

After a short time, I put the babies back into their cribs. The day had to be faced, bad news or not.

I thudded slowly down the stairs, my mind swirling with the possibilities Tag's news had brought forth. None of them were pleasant. None of them boosted the optimistic attitude I'd started the day with. When I got to the bottom stair, I tried to smile at Patty.

"We've got a ton of orders to fill." I nodded at the filigree tray that served as our Internet order in-box. "Let's get them ready. They've got to be shipped today."

The morning dragged by like a slug oozing its way across a salt lick. Patty kept busy, occupying herself with filling those orders while I continued wrapping the soaps and displaying them in the shop. Customers came and went, leaving me little time to brood. Tag hurried out the door with barely a kiss on my cheek.

What could I possibly say to Tag? This was a chance in a lifetime for him. How well I knew that, but what about me and the twins? Could I really face a move to California? Even on the presumably excellent salary of a head pro-football coach, we'd still be in the city that claimed to be the biggest rat-race in the world. Gone would be the verdant mountain backdrop I loved so much. Gone would be the tranquility of a small north-Georgia town that had one foot in the twentieth century and one in—well, almost in—the twenty-first century. Gone would be the leisurely visits with friends and family.

Everything I treasured in life, with the exception of Tag and the babies, would disappear.

There was another possibility. Tag could live in California during football season. The idea of being separated from him that long flushed my eyes with tears again. This time, I couldn't stop them.

"Patty, I'm going to feed the twins," I called as I trudged up the stairs.

When I had a baby nestled to each breast, I held them close. I was practically doomed to be a single mom. There was nothing I could—or would—do to stop it. Tag deserved to follow his dream as much I deserved to follow my own. I never dreamed, not once in the past two months of wedding bliss, that my world would begin to crumble.

• • •

My cell phone rang. I ignored it. I couldn't talk. The number was not in my phone directory, so I burped the babies, changed them again and tucked them into their cribs. I gazed at them, picked them back up one at a time and hugged them close. They were the saving grace in all of this. No matter what happened, I still had my babies, my friends and, of course, Mom. The only question mark was Tag.

The phone rang again. And again, and again. I reluctantly answered.

"Maggie, thank God," came Mom's frantic words. She immediately started into a tirade I couldn't begin to understand.

"Hello to you, Mom. Slow down. I can't understand you." I dropped into the rocker, propped my elbows on my knees and listened as a sob caught in her throat.

"Maggie, you've got to help me. Immediately. I don't have much time on the phone. Come over to—"

The line went dead. I waited a full minute, thinking she'd call back. She didn't. "What a day," I murmured as I hurried downstairs. "The hits just keep on coming."

As I reached my office, I hit re-dial and got a recorded message. This was a one-way phone, dial-out only, from the Bigelow police office. "Oh, crap!"

I knew what that meant. Mom was up to her old tricks again. I dialed Tag to see if he could go and bail her out. No answer.

"Husbands," I grumbled. "Just when you need them, they're not around."

I dropped my phone into my purse, grabbed my parka and headed for the door. "Patty, I've got to run an errand. I don't know when I'll be back."

She popped out of the supply closet. "Okay. Anything I can help with?"

She didn't know how tempting an offer that was. "No, not really. Just hold things down here. I fed the babies. If it gets too hectic, just bring them down here. Oh, hell, if it gets that hectic, call one of the Drummond girls to come and help."

Without waiting for an answer, I sprinted out the door. It took thirty minutes to get to Bigelow due to a traffic jam caused, no doubt, by the Christmas shopping season.

Christmas! What would I do without Tag? Was he going to go for an interview? I wracked my brain, trying to remember if he'd said he had one already scheduled. Nothing but a quagmire of confusion about that. I hardly remembered anything at all after he'd announced he'd been offered a job in California.

I pulled into a parking place close to the police station and sighed. Where should I go? Nothing to do but ask. I walked around to the main entrance and walked up the marble steps. Inside, I found an information window. "Hi, I'm here to see if Millicent Hart . . . um, Lavender. Is—"

The young woman burst into laughter. "Oh, my God. The Chief will be soooo glad to see you." She blew a bubble with her gum and pointed to a large directory across the way. "Walk past that sign and go down the steps. The chief's office is on the lower floor. You could have gone in the back."

I fought with the idea of scolding her for bad manners or thanking her for the information. Before I got halfway across the floor, I heard her say, "Somebody's here to pick up that crazy old lady."

Crazy old lady. How dare she? I almost turned around and went back to give her a piece of my mind, but realized it wouldn't make any difference—especially since she was pretty close to being right.

Before I ever reached the door to the police chief's office, I heard a screech. "Oh, crap," I muttered and hurried down the stairs.

Loud voices assailed me as I wrenched open the door. Mother stood there, wielding a potted dieffenbachia like it was a sword. On the receiving end, a small woman, dressed as a deputy, cowered like a whipped dog in the corner. Several other deputies emerged from their offices with puzzled looks on their faces.

The police chief, whom I'd never had the occasion to meet, glared at the back of Mother's head, his hand hovering near his gun. He looked as if he couldn't decide whether attack by a large houseplant merited a drawn weapon or something less lethal.

"Mother," I yelled above the din. "Stop!"

She stilled, but kept the leafy end of the dieffenbachia

pointed at the cowering deputy. Without looking at me, she said, "It's about time you got here."

"Put the plant down, Mother," I commanded in my most decisive voice. Whether she heeded me or not remained to be seen. Finally, she leaned down and placed the plastic pot on the floor, fluffed the leaves and turned to me. "Hello, Maggie. Just let me get my purse. I'm ready to leave when you are."

"Hold on, there, little lady." The police chief moved in closer, removing his handcuffs as he slowly approached her. "You're not going anywhere."

Panic gripped me as I calculated the best way out of this situation. Maybe honesty would prove to be the best policy. "Chief, could I speak with you for a moment?"

"I'm listening," he said, stopping his advance, but never taking his eyes off Mother.

"Mother, sit right there!" I pointed to a row of gray metal chairs. "I'll be with you in a minute."

She eyed the police chief and then the deputy again, but obediently moved toward the chairs. The police chief and deputy both followed her with their eyes. Clearly, she'd been on her worst behavior since her arrival.

I stepped closer to the chief, hoping to keep our conversation private. "Sir, I realize my mother may have disturbed—"

"Disturbed doesn't half cover it, lady." He nodded toward Mother, who by this time sat contritely with her legs crossed at the ankles, her hands primly folded on her lap. "We've had less trouble bringing in vicious criminals. That woman is a menace to society and needs to be put away where she can't hurt anybody."

This wasn't going to be easy. I cast her one of my "what have you done now" looks and then offered a wan smile to the police chief. "Sir, my mother suffers from kleptomania. If you'll contact Chief Royden in Mossy Creek, he can confirm—"

"Amos? Your mama said he'd vouch for her." He eyed me closely. "That right?"

"Chief, Amos has been a good friend for a long time. He knows her well."

"Is that right?" Finally devoting his complete attention to me, he shifted his hand away from the cuffs and extended it. "Police Chief Hucklebee."

I shook his hand and tried a warmer smile. God, what a day! "Chief Hucklebee, Amos can definitely fill you in on details that might help you . . . dispose of this case without further inconvenience to your department or to the court."

He leveled his gaze at me. "I hear tell of strange things happenin' in Mossy Creek. Something to do with a fella actually named Kris Kringle, and there was a story about a 'possum spellin' out Noel with a string of Christmas lights."

I felt sure he was about to relent, that maybe he needed just a little push. "Sir, I realize that information is entertaining, but I would like to do whatever I need to do to remove my mother from your premises with the least amount of damage and embarrassment. She's an elderly woman who has a mental illness and—"

"Oh, no you don't!" Mother sprang to her feet. "I'm not crazy. That's what got me going at her in the first place." She motioned to the still cowering female deputy, who was now removing dieffenbachia leaves from her uniform and hair. "I'm as sane as anybody in this room."

I glanced at her and then back at the police chief. He must have seen the pleading in my eyes. "Sir, you must see that my mother needs help, not more legal difficulties." I sighed, a tear sliding down my cheek. "My husband, Tag Garner, would have—"

"You're married to the former Atlanta Falcon football player?" He strode forward and clasped my hand again, all mention of the spelling 'possum forgotten. "Always been a fan of his. I heard he's gonna be the new coach of the Raiders. Wish it was the Falcons."

Okay, he'd just crossed into territory I didn't want to discuss with anybody—least of all a man I didn't know. I smiled my most winning smile and raised my eyebrows conspiratorially. "I'm not at liberty to discuss this. I'm so sorry."

He nodded as if I'd just confirmed his assumption that Tag would accept the job. In fact, I couldn't imagine Tag turning down a choice position like that. I just didn't know what I was going to do about it, and I sure didn't want to talk to Chief Hucklebee about it. "Now, about Mother."

He glanced at Mother and shook his head. "Any way you can keep her out of Bigelow?"

Mother leapt to her feet with the energy of a teenager. "Just a minute. You have no right to bar me from coming to Bigelow. I'm an American citizen. I know my rights."

I couldn't keep from rolling my eyes. She'd never mastered the art of politely ignoring something she didn't agree with. "Chief, I can arrange for her to be barred from the bus when it comes here."

Mother glared at me, but I ignored her.

"Well, I guess we can overlook it this once." He motioned to the female deputy who was, by now, creeping across the floor as far as she could get from my mother. "Dismiss the charges."

Mother smiled and batted her eyes at Chief Hucklebee. "Thank you, sir. Now if you'd be so kind as to return the items I brought from Walmart."

Oh, God! How could she? "Mother!" I practically shouted, finding my temper flailing in the wind like a football thrown against a stiff gale. "You didn't pay for those things. Come on, before this nice man changes his mind."

Mother glared at the police chief, but began walking toward the door. The deputy handed Mother's purse to me. I noticed the bite marks on the woman's arm and tried to smile at her. She responded by raising her eyebrows as if I might attack her, too.

"Um, say, Miz Garner," the Police Chief said and cleared his throat. "Mind asking that husband of yours if he'll come by for our annual policeman's ball the week after New Year's?"

Reeling in my temper, I nodded. "I'll ask him. I'm sure you realize his plans are up in the air at the moment."

"Sure, sure," he agreed and turned back to his office.

I handed Mother her purse as we walked to the car. "I can't believe you did that. Of all things. Why? Tell me why."

It was anger talking. I knew there were no real answers. Mother's condition was something she really couldn't control.

When we arrived at Magnolia Manor, the crowd in the day room clustered around her as if she was a rock star. I merely shook my head, kissed her goodbye and hurried on my way. I could hardly wait to get home to see what other catastrophe fate had in store for me.

• • •

Several days later, I pulled into the driveway. I'd been to the post office to ship another batch of purchases from Moonheart's website and from errands in Bigelow. Several cars were parked on the street and in the small parking lot. Thank goodness for that. Sales would probably continue to be brisk, what with Christmas just a few days away.

Grabbing my parka, I got out of the car and noticed that Tag's car wasn't in the driveway.

"Must be at the gallery," I muttered, wishing he would have been here to discuss what I now termed "the problem" lurking between us.

I skipped up the steps, realizing—from the fullness of my breasts—that my babies must be hungry. Patty was waiting on customers, so I dashed past her with a wave and hurried up the stairs to the sound of a wailing infant. Dooley sounded like the world had come to an end. I swear, the rafters were shaking as I turned at the landing and took the next steps three at a time. "Mommy's coming," I yelled.

The sound of my voice quieted him for a moment. Without wasting any time, I hurried into the nursery, opened my shirt and bra and grabbed my babies before collapsing into the rocker. As difficult as it is having infant twins, they could be counted on. Their schedule never varied. Feeding time, diaper changing, bathing, sleeping. All in its own order and time.

The chime on the front door jangled, and I heard Patty mounting the stairs. "Sorry," she said as she hurried into the room. "Dooley just started crying. Dayna's been an angel, as usual."

I smiled, planting a kiss on each of their heads. Every day I marveled at what a blessing they were in our lives. Somehow we were a complete family, even though it had never occurred to Tag and me that anything was lacking.

Patty stood smiling and then jerked to attention. "Oh, wait. Tag left this for you." She fished into the pocket of her Moonheart's apron and pulled out an envelope.

The front door chimed again and she hurried for the stairs.

I stared at the envelope. Why would he need to write anything? We were scheduled to have dinner with Coach tonight. We both carried cell phones. Anxiety crept into my heart as I burped the babies and put them to bed.

Sinking back into the rocker, I slid my finger under the flap of the sealed envelope. Whatever this was, it couldn't be good.

Dearest Magster,

Sorry I had to run without talking to you. Called but got your voice mail. Patty said you were on errands and she didn't know when you'd be back.

The GM of the Raiders got me a private jet to come out and talk to him. The flight is early tomorrow morning. I'm on my way to Atlanta to spend the night at a hotel near the airport so I don't have to leave in the middle of the night.

I know HeyDay needs me tomorrow, but I can't make it. He'll understand.

I love you and the babies. As soon as I know something, I'll give you a call.

Love and kisses,

Tag

I stared at the letter. I read it two more times. Nothing about my feelings about the job. Nothing I could object to. Just the facts as he saw them.

Tears welled in my eyes. How could this possibly be happening?

The phone rang. I snatched it up and answered before it rang a second time. "Tag?" I said, praying it would be him.

"Uh, no ma'am. It's HeyDay."

Tears rolled down my cheeks. I sniffed. "Oh, hello."

"Sounds like you're taking a cold," he said. "I hope not. I always hated being sick at Christmas."

"Oh, um, it's just allergies, I guess." The lie rolled off my tongue much more easily than the truth would have.

"Aw, too bad. Well, I know Tag can't play Santa, but I was wonderin' if you know anybody else that might do it?"

Santa Claus? As much as I loved Christmas, I suddenly began to view the holiday with dread. How could I face Christmas knowing this might be my last with my husband? I heard a noise on the other end of the line. "Oh, HeyDay, sorry. No, I really don't know anyone."

He spoke on for a few moments and the said, "You bring the babies over Saturday to the Magnolia Manor. I'm sure Santa—whoever he is—will have something for them."

I swiped at my tears and sniffed again. "I'm not sure we can. We're awfully busy."

"Don't ever be too busy for Christmas, Maggie," HeyDay told me. "Christmas is a time for miracles. Talk to you later."

I hung up the phone. Miracles? It would take a miracle for me to enjoy the upcoming Christmas, even though I'd been looking forward to it ever since I found out I was pregnant.

My babies' first Christmas had to be special. I was going to make it special, with or without Tag.

• • •

Tag's flight was supposed to leave at six a.m. I glared at the clock, but it still kept ticking. I'd been awake all night, convinced my marriage was over.

Tag would definitely be offered the job. He would definitely take it. He would definitely leave for California immediately after packing his clothes. The only thing indefinite in the whole thing was that I still didn't know what would happen to us as a family.

After feeding the twins, I hurried downstairs. I rushed through my chores, printed out the seventeen Internet orders, placed them in the "in" basket, mopped, dusted and generally tried to wear myself out so I could keep from thinking about Tag who was now merrily on his way to Oakland.

I glanced at the clock again. It was almost time to go to Magnolia Manor. Mother had called and insisted I bring the twins. She wanted to show them off. Just everybody would be there.

They looked so adorable in their Christmas outfits, tiny as they were. Dooley wore a red stretch onesie with a Santa cap to match and a darling little candy-striped vest. Dayna wore her red velvet dress with the white lace trim and the tiny flower in her practically nonexistent hair. I pulled on a pair of black slacks, a black sweater and my parka, a true statement of my feelings.

The air was frigid as I hurried out to the car with the twins, buckled them into their car seats and climbed behind the wheel.

The sky was overcast and the chill air found its way through my parka and made me shiver.

When we arrived at Magnolia Manor, I took out the stroller and put both babies in their places. It had started to drizzle a bit, so I dashed for the front door. Once we got inside, we were practically attacked by Mother and her friends. Everybody wanted to hold them. While the babies were passed around, I poured myself a cup of punch, snagged a Christmas Star cookie with food-grade glitter on it and sat down.

Swarms of people rushed to and fro as the excitement built toward the time for the arrival of Santa. There was a photo booth, so I took my picture with the babies. I'd make ornaments and/or cards for next year. Dooley got hungry, so I fed them as discreetly as possible and put them back in their stroller.

Sudden, uproarious laughter drew my attention. There were not one, not two, but *three* Santas at the door. I could hardly believe my eyes, but not even that could lift my spirits.

The Santas took the situation in hand and began to greet all the folks who'd been awaiting their arrival. Then there were *four* Santas. The laughter increased.

I smiled, thinking HeyDay really should be here to see this.

The Santas all came by and tried to engage Dooley and Dayna, but both babies shrieked if one reached for them. Oh, well, so much for great Christmas pictures.

They moved on, a bit embarrassed to be the cause of such a ruckus. I smiled sheepishly. The newest Santa seemed a little beat up. His costume looked as if he'd grabbed it off the rack at some thrift store. But he did have a wide smile on his face. He meant well, I'm sure. I glanced at all the Santas, trying to figure out who they were.

My attention came back to the fourth Santa. He was headed straight toward me with a big grin.

Recognizing his athletic gait, I jumped up "Oh, my God! Tag!"

I flung myself into his arms, not caring what people thought. "I thought you were on your way to Oakland."

He kissed me, more vigorously than he had in a while and held me close. "Nope. I'll tell you about it later. "

I nodded as he picked up both babies and sat down to play

with them. Rather than screaming and screeching as they had with the other Santas, both of them began to coo and to wrap their hands in his not-so-pristine beard. People from everywhere began to snap pictures and take videos. Duh. I'd been so wrapped up in seeing Tag, I'd forgotten my camera. I made a mental note of who I could harvest the pictures and videos from later.

Another Santa brought over some gifts from under the tree. Mother leaned in close and whispered, "That damn cop didn't find everything."

I nearly choked on my laughter. I had no idea where the items were hidden when she was arrested—and didn't want to know.

We sang Christmas carols, drank eggnog and ate cookies. When we left Magnolia Manor, I was exhausted but I needed to hear Tag's story.

• • •

When the babies were asleep, I slid between the covers and snuggled into my husband's arms. Neither of us said anything for a moment, reveling in the joy of being wrapped in the warmth of the one we loved.

Finally, I couldn't take it any longer. "So?"

"So what?" he asked kissing my forehead.

"So what happened?"

A soft sigh escaped Tag's lips, and he hugged me tighter. "I couldn't sleep last night, Mags. I kept thinking about what you said about bringing Dooley and Dayna up in California. So this morning, I waited until I thought the GM of the Raiders would answer the phone, called him and turned them down."

"Tag! It's what you've always wanted."

"No, Mags. I realized I have what I've always wanted."

A tear slid down his cheek and melded with the tears on my cheek. "What's that?"

"I've always wanted a family. I've always wanted to live somewhere people actually liked other people, recognized them and appreciated them for who they are."

"And?"

"And that's what I've got. I've got the most precious babies in the world. I live in a home town that 'Ain't Going Nowhere and Don't Want To.'" He rearranged us so he could prop on his elbow and look into my eyes. "And I've got the best wife in the world."

"Oh, Tag, you don't know what that means to me." I choked out the words. "I love you. I was so desolate when I thought of living without you."

"Not nearly as much as I was." He kissed me, deeper and more intimately.

Happiness literally erupted from my body as I clung to him.

Suddenly a screech came from the nursery.

Startled, we jumped out of bed and raced across the hall.

Dooley and Dayna were shrieking at the top of their lungs. He grabbed Dooley, and I picked up Dayna. We carried them back across the hall and snuggled into bed.

"Merry Christmas, darling," he whispered. "Now, all we need is a little snow."

Tag's words made me realize how quiet it was outside. Settling Dayna in his other arm, I rose and drew the curtain aside. Looking out toward the streetlight, I saw that it was snowing. Big, fat flakes drifted down to ground already starting to disappear under a blanket of white.

"It's snowing." Another tear slid down my cheeks. "If it can hold out for a few days, the babies' first Christmas is going to be white."

"A good omen, don't you think?"

"I do. I really do." I let the drape fall back into place and looked at the love of my life with our babies cradled in his arms. "Welcome home, Tag. Welcome to the best hometown in the world. Welcome back to Mossy Creek."

Mossy Creek Gazette

Volume IX, No. Four

Mossy Creek, Georgia

The Bellringer

Christmas Blast from the Past

by Katie Bell

How would you like to get a message from beyond the grave? Octogenarian Mimsy Allen called to say she got a Christmas card in her mail on Tuesday.

Big deal, you say? Well, Mimsy's first clue this card was going to prove interesting was the return address: a place in Augusta where her sister, Sarah Fletcher, lived . . . fourteen years ago.

The second peculiarity was the postmark. The card was mailed from Augusta in December 1982. Sarah died in September of that year.

When contacted by yours truly, Hal Puckett down at the Mossy Creek Post Office said he found it behind an old sorting bin. "It obviously got stuck down there decades ago. We got a new one this year, you see, so when we pulled it out, we found the card. I thought the neighborly thing to do was to go ahead and deliver it. So that's what we done."

When asked to describe the card, Mimsy said, "Well, bless me. You might remember from way back that Sarah—God rest her soul—was a cat person. The card is Garfield the cat decorating Opie, his doggie friend, with Christmas lights and ornaments. Inside it says, 'May your holiday season be decorated with love and happiness.'"

Mimsy paused for a minute and, just when I thought she was going to cry, she said, "I hate cats."

At Christmas, all roads lead home.

—Marjorie Holmes

Secret Santa

Only two weeks 'til Christmas and I'd just now found the time to hang lights on the house. Which was unusual for Tiny and me. Christmas has always been Tiny's favorite holiday of the year. Without fail, the Thanksgiving dinner dishes were barely dry before Tiny was knee-deep in decorations. By the time the holiday weekend's over, the house would be nothin' less than a winter wonderland of homemade green and red decorations. Holly, laurel, berries, even sprigs of real mistletoe would hang in the doorways. Tiny was a master at decorating, bringing the outside in for the warm, homey feel, leaving no corner of our little clapboard farm house untouched.

But this year we'd gotten off to a slow start, leastwise on the outside decorating. What with last month's storm blowin' a hole in the barn roof and old man Chester's mule—who we let run in our back pasture for free, mind you—deciding he wanted to relocate my fence, it's been plenty busy around here. I don't know who was more ornery, Chester or his mule.

Anyway, sometimes women just confound me, the way they fret and fuss over the simplest things. 'Course, you'll never hear me say that around Tiny. The only thing "tiny" about my wife, Clementine Carlisle, is her stature and the nickname I gave her all those years ago in grade school. She can hold her own against anybody, even a big ol' ex-jock like me. And if that don't work, she's always got me to run interference. They don't call me HeyDay Hayden for nothing.

But I suspect my delay in helping with the Christmas decorating had less to do with the chores of running a farm and more to do with keeping a secret. Yep. And I had a big one.

169

You might recall me saying that Tiny and I don't keep secrets from each other. And that's what I was gettin' at. The more time I spent keeping busy on the farm, the less time I had to worry she's gonna find me out. Tiny has a way of just looking at me that made me want to spill my guts. But not this time. A promise was a promise. But dang, this secret was about to eat a hole in me to rival Wolfman's best moonshine. Keeping a secret from Tiny was like to tear me apart.

Lately, I've caught her staring at me kinda funny, like she's gonna say something, then changes her mind. Like she knew I was sitting on dynamite and couldn't decide if she should warn me or not.

It would all be worth it in the end, though, when Tiny got the best Christmas surprise ever. I just hoped I was still in one piece to see it.

"Earth to Hayden!"

I glanced over my shoulder to find Wolfman standing at the foot of my ladder, grinning up at me. Strings of Christmas lights were looped around his bull neck like a multicolored wreath. He pointed at the gutter where I was attaching the lights. "You missed a spot."

"Hush up and make yourself useful. Toss me the next section." I caught the free end midair and turned back to the gutter.

Wolfman Washington and I go way back. In fact, I can't remember a time we weren't friends and our daddies before us, which is why I put up with all his silly grins and winks at my expense. See, Wolfman never did settle down and it amuses him no end to poke at me every time he catches me doing something all husband-like. Hmmph. As if he doesn't hang Christmas lights on his own place.

Just then Tiny came around the corner of the house wrapped up like a Christmas present in her green plaid coat with the red scarf she knitted for me last winter wrapped around her neck. She carried two steaming mugs with smiling melting snowmen painted on them. Blue eyes twinkling, she smiled up at me as I stepped to the ground and handed a mug to each of us. Married all these years and that look she gave me still had the power to make me feel just like that snowman.

"Saw you drive in, Wolfman, and thought I'd bring y'all a cup of hot chocolate."

"Much obliged." He wrapped his large hands around the mug and blew into it.

"Thanks, hon." I pulled her against my side as I took a sip, eyeing Wolfman over the cup's rim. Now it was my turn to grin. He and I both knew who had the sweeter deal.

Tiny stepped back and pushed her hands deep into her pockets. "Hayden, I just got a call from Toby Holler, my student I told you about—he's not going to be able to play Santa at the Magnolia Manor Christmas party after all. His family decided to celebrate at his grandparents in Tennessee this year."

She shot a beseeching glance at Wolfman. His eyes got wide, and I could swear I saw a bead of sweat on his forehead, despite the forty-degree temperature. Wolfman didn't do well in large groups of people, even if most of them were in wheelchairs and wouldn't be able to hear what was going on, let alone see him very well.

"When did you say this was exactly?" Wolfman asked.

"The Saturday before Christmas. The kids in my home economics class have been working on a lap quilting project this year. Each one of them is making a nine-block quilt with the theme *What Mossy Creek Means to Me*. The plan is to give one to each of the residents at Magnolia Manor during their annual Christmas party. After dinner, we'll have cookies and eggnog, play the piano and sing carols, and then Santa will come and hand out homemade gifts from the kids." She paused for dramatic effect that would have made the drama teacher, Hermia Lavender, proud and pinned us both with a stare. "It won't be the same without a Santa."

"I'm sorry, Clementine," Wolfman said. "I promised my momma I'd carry her down to her sister's in Bigelow. They've got big plans to spend the day doing all their Christmas baking."

"That's all right, Wolfman." Tiny put her hand on his sleeve. "Tell your momma I wish her a Merry Christmas."

Wolfman's ears turned a shade of red I don't think had anything to do with the cold air. "I sure will." He nodded in my direction, "But what about Hayden?"

"I already asked him, before Toby agreed to do it." She raised hopeful eyes to mine. "I still think you'd make the perfect Santa."

Sacked again. Wolfman never did know when to stop talking.

That secret started burnin' a hole in my gut. "Tiny, it's like I told you before, I can't be Santa. I'm no good at that kinda thing and besides, I've got too much to do around here." I took hold of the ladder again, as if to prove my point. Or maybe I just needed to wrap my hands around something and hold on, what with the churning in my stomach and all. I hated lying. And more than that, I hated saying no to Tiny. "You know how I get around old people."

Which was, after all, not entirely a lie.

A knowing look passed between Tiny and Wolfman, but neither said anything. They didn't have to. I knew exactly what they were thinking. And if that settled the issue of Tiny expecting me to play Santa at Magnolia Manor, then so be it.

Tiny tucked her perfect slender hands deep into her coat pockets. "It's all right, Hayden. There's still time to find someone else." Right then and there, I wished I was one of those ridiculous snowmen so I could melt right into the ground.

The specter of my Great Uncle Percy rose up between us. Like old Jacob Marley, I could practically hear him rattling his chains at me and laughing his fool head off.

You see, it all goes back to when I was in grade school and my momma used to make me go with her to visit Uncle Percy at Magnolia Manor once a week.

He was a WWII veteran who lost his right foot in the war. He'd settled in South Georgia, but then outlived most all his family, and when he had a stroke and couldn't fend for himself, Momma brought him up to Mossy Creek where she could keep an eye on him. Around these parts, family looks out for family.

Percy was a tough old codger and the bane of my existence when I was all of eleven years old. He had a fake foot to help him get around, though he didn't do all that much walking after the stroke. The first time I ever laid eyes on him, he thought it was great fun to pretend to trip and turn his foot around backward.

I had nightmares for a week.

But Momma said I had to go back. That Uncle Percy was just

a lonely old man who liked to make people laugh. But I knew better. That old man had it out for me.

I suffered through runaway wheelchairs, fake heart attacks, whoopee cushion impersonations (if you know what I mean) and false teeth showing up in the most unnerving places. And when he wasn't playing practical jokes, he was holding fast to my arm, recanting one old war story after the next. His body may have been failing him, but his mind was sharp as a razor.

It didn't take long for the Mossy Creek rumor mill (even for eleven-year-olds) to pick up on the fact that I bore the brunt of old man Percy's jokes. A few kids tried to start something up at school, but Wolfman and I tackled that problem quickly enough. Even back then, we were obviously destined for the football team and thus, jock status.

But the worst day came just after school let out for the Christmas holiday. Momma sent me on to Magnolia Manor without her, saying she had to stop by a friend's house first, but she'd be along in no time. So I trudged into Uncle Percy's room, sneakers dragging, book bag heavy as a load of bricks on my back and braced myself for another full-on assault.

He was sitting by the window, staring out at the Christmas lights in the trees on the back lawn. Snow flurries bounced around in the wind, but melted as soon as they settled on the ground. Palms sweaty, I set a plate of homemade gingerbread cookies on the table and sat across from him, waiting.

He didn't start talking right away, preferring to just watch the snow float past the window. But eventually he started telling me about some of his old war buddies, the ones who hadn't made it home for Christmas—and never did. "Ya gotta learn to laugh at life, boy. It sure beats the alternative."

He leaned back with a heavy sigh and closed his eyes. Then his head kinda slumped to his shoulder. I thought to myself, here we go. He's playing 'possum again. Sure as I raised the alarm he'll jump at me and start cackling. So I sat. And waited. And waited some more. Felt like forever, but it was only about ten minutes before Momma walked in and discovered what I was seriously beginning to suspect. Uncle Percy had had the last laugh.

I think about that old coot every once in a while. Sometimes when I do something downright stupid, I can hear him laughing. Guess it reminds me not to take myself too seriously.

But I can't hardly walk past Magnolia Manor without breaking out in hives.

I'd risk it for Tiny, though. If it was any other day. Any day but that one.

Because her brother, Orin, called me last month—from Afghanistan—and asked me to keep a secret. Seems there'd been an accident and he injured his leg. Nothing a long rest and physical therapy wouldn't fix. But it was enough to bring him home eight months early. I promised to pick him up at the airport down in Atlanta the Saturday evening before Christmas. Yeah, the same night as that danged party.

No way could I ask anyone from Mossy Creek to go in my stead, not without Tiny finding out in two shakes of a lamb's tail and ruining Orin's surprise. Nope, it was my job to bring Orin home, and I aimed to get it done.

• • •

With just a few days left before the Christmas party at Magnolia Manor, Tiny still hadn't found a Santa replacement, so I figured I'd come into town and see if I could help scrounge up a volunteer. It was getting harder every day to ignore the glances and pointed sighs she sent my way. But she never put me on the spot or ridiculed my reason for not wanting to be Santa—which, of course, only drove my guilt deeper.

Women are wily creatures.

A handful of years back, Tiny's grandma went to live at Magnolia Manor. Tiny visited her regularly, taking her out for the day, shopping or to lunch. But when it came to holidays, well, Christmas was just about as special as it could get. I told you Christmas is Tiny's favorite time of the year. She'd take a little tree over to Magnolia Manor and she and her grandma would decorate it with homemade ornaments, some dating back to when her grandma herself was a little girl. They'd listen to carols, eat Tiny's most recent attempt at cookies (thankfully she's gotten better over the years) and exchange presents.

Over time, other residents joined in—some forgotten by

their own families, some who didn't have family at all. And being the warm-hearted home economics teacher that she is, Tiny even found a way to include her students. Said it was good for them to be around the older members of Mossy Creek and stay involved in the community. It sort of grew into a tradition after that. Even now, with Tiny's grandma several years gone, she still has a Christmas party at Magnolia Manor. I reckon she always will.

Up until now, Tiny never expected me to get involved, understanding my penchant for giving Magnolia Manor a wide berth. But I think her understanding nature was running out. There had to be someone in Mossy Creek with time to play Santa, or I was gonna have to find a way to be in two places at once. I opened the top button of my coat collar, feeling hot and itchy just thinking about it.

I wouldn't be in this predicament if poor old Ed Brady hadn't up and died—God rest his soul. He'd been the official Mossy Creek Santa for as long as I could remember. He even lived at Magnolia Manor for a bit while nursing his dear Ellie in her last days.

I hung my head and hunkered deeper into my coat. I'd sunk to a new low, blaming a poor dead fella for my woes.

I crossed the street, heading over to Hamilton's Department Store. Maybe that new guy playing Santa for them would be obliging. Word is his name's Kristopher Kringle, if you can believe that. I couldn't help noticing Hamilton's Christmas window display looked top-notch, made me feel like I was in the big city.

After Miz Inez and Lucy Belle's near-disastrous attempt at a contest to pick this year's decorating theme, another skirmish in the Christmas war with Bigelow, everyone finally settled on *The People of Mossy Creek*. Houses and businesses all over town were decorated to reflect their own personalities and love of Christmas. If you asked me, walking through Town Square was like walking back in time. The spirit of Christmas was everywhere, and I was beginnin' to feel more like the Grinch with every step I took.

I stepped into the winter wonderland of Hamilton's Department Store on the east side of the Square and headed straight for the Santa staging area.

It was empty.

Then my eyes lit on Spiva Quinlan tidying up a display of children's Christmas footy pajamas.

"Howdy, Spiva. Do you know where I can find Kris Kringle?" I felt like three kinds of fool just saying that out loud.

"Sorry, Hayden. I'm not sure where he is or when he's due back." She paused in her folding and pursed her lips. "It's funny, but he just shows up, does the Santa thing and then disappears. I'm not even sure where he lives."

I studied my feet a second. Dang it. This was gonna be harder than I thought. "Well, do you know where I can find Rob?"

Rob Walker was owner and operator of Hamilton's department store and Mayor Ida's only son. He'd make a right spiffy Santa.

Spiva stopped folding and gave me her full attention. "What's this about, Hayden?"

"I'm trying to help find a Santa for the Magnolia Manor Christmas party."

She pursed her lips again, raising a questioning eyebrow. I knew that look. I'd seen it half a dozen times already today. *Why not you, Hayden,* they all seemed to be asking. Then she shrugged and turned back to the P.J.'s. "I don't know where he is either, but I doubt he'll be able to help. Last I heard, he and Teresa had plans for a big night out. Sorry, Hayden."

The bell over the door jingled a merry goodbye as I stepped back out into the cold and shoved my hands deep into my pockets. This was getting downright serious. I scanned the street, mentally crossing off those I'd already asked and those I knew I could rule out.

Then I saw Tag Garner step into the Naked Bean coffee shop and hurried in after him. Tag was a good guy. Assistant football coach at Mossy Creek High, he'd make a great Santa. And his mother-in-law Millicent Hart Lavender lived at Magnolia Manor now. It was perfect. Besides, didn't he owe me one? He'd wrangled me into helping out during the homecoming game after Coach Mabry had a heart attack. Truth be told, I probably still owed him for pulling me back onto the ballfield after all these years. It had been one heck of a game.

Tag stood at the counter while Jayne Reynolds bagged up

his order. They both looked my way as a gust of cold wind followed me in. I opened up my coat, soaking in the warm air and scent of coffee mixed with Ingrid Beechum's baked goods. One of Betty Halfacre's famous pecan pies sat in the display.

"Howdy Tag. Jayne." I stepped up to the counter, and Tag slapped me on the back.

"Hayden, my man. What are you up to these days?"

"Me? I've heard the Raider rumors. Any of that true?"

Tag winced. "Sure can't keep a secret in Mossy Creek."

I grinned. "Nope. So you're moving out to California to be their head coach?"

"We'll see." He shrugged and changed the subject. "You ready for Christmas?"

"Funny you should mention that." I thought I caught a flash of sympathy in Jayne's eyes. So she'd already heard, no doubt. I cleared my throat. "Um, how are Maggie and the babies?"

"Amazing! Being a father is every kind of wonderful." His smile couldn't possibly get any bigger. Tag's wife, Maggie, had given birth to twins, a boy and a girl, that same homecoming game night just a couple of months ago.

Jayne caught my attention. "Hayden, can I get you anything?"

"Just a coffee to go. Black. Thanks." I cleared my throat again. "Listen, Tag. I don't know if you've heard or not, being busy with the babies and all, but I'm trying to help Tiny find someone to play Santa at this year's Magnolia Manor Christmas party." I tried not to squelch the tiny flare of hope in my gut.

Tag wrinkled his brow and took his bag from Jayne. "That's Saturday, right? I'm sorry, Hayden, but Maggie needs me to help fill some orders from the store. She's been slammed with Christmas sales. And honestly, she's not been feeling too well. The holidays and Dooley and Dayna are really wearing her out." He took a step toward the door. "I think she'd kill me if I tried to skip out, even for a few hours. You have *no idea* how demanding two babies can be. I'm just glad we're on winter break from school, so I have more time to be here for her."

He paused with his hand on the doorknob. "If you don't mind me asking, why don't you do it, Hayden? Seems like you'd make the perfect Santa."

I avoided eye contact with both of them as I took the cup of coffee Jayne held out. "I, um, have something else I gotta do." I glanced up and caught Jayne frowning at me, before she covered with a smile.

"Well, good luck, Hayden." Tag said, stepping out the door. "Maybe next year . . ."

A burst of cold hit me in the back as I took a sip of coffee. "Think Win might be interested . . . ?"

I let the question trail off in the face of Jayne's disapproving frown. She'd obviously given up all pretense of understanding my dilemma. No doubt Tiny had shared her tale of woe with her good friend.

"Sorry, Hayden. Win's entirely too busy with the town council and all the other Mossy Creek Christmas activities. Matt and I barely see him as it is." She wiped an imaginary crumb from the counter and took a deep breath.

I braced myself.

"Don't you think it's time to let go of the past?" she asked.

"Jayne."

She met my gaze squarely. "Yes?"

"I'd like a piece of pecan pie to go with my coffee, please."

She sighed and reached for the pie.

Two minutes later, I stood on the street corner debating my options. Keeping Orin's secret was getting downright painful. I'd give it one more day, two tops, before the whole town was going to think I really was some kind of Christmas Grinch.

As I stood there drinking hot coffee, a piece of pie wrapped up and growing cold in my pocket, a plan began to form. It just might work—if the old "Heyday" Hayden good luck would hold out a little longer.

Feeling better than I had in weeks, I tossed my empty cup into the curbside trash bin and started for home. I had a phone call to make.

• • •

Orin and I pulled into the Magnolia Manor parking lot at half past eight. A good hour late for the party. I could only hope my plan was working.

To say Orin and I made quite the picture at the airport

didn't do the scene justice. In order to save precious time, I had stopped by the costume shop in Bigelow on the way to the Atlanta airport and picked up the Santa suit (their last one) I had reserved that day coming out of the Naked Bean.

Taking full advantage of the dressing room and the clerk's offer to help with the hair and beard (bless her heart), I decided to change before I drove down to Atlanta. I confess, I did get a chuckle out of the funny looks and excited kids I drove past on the highway.

Airport security wasn't so amused.

A few wiseacres made cracks about me leaving my sleigh and reindeer on the runway. But everyone forgot about the guy in the Santa suit when Orin came through security in army fatigues, balancing on crutches. Knowing Orin, I'm sure he'd refused the airline's offer for a ride in a wheelchair or a cart. The steel cage around his right leg, holding pins in place, looked like something out of a science fiction movie, except that he'd wrapped a string of battery-operated twinkling Christmas bulbs all around it. Yeah. As if we wouldn't already look ridiculous walking together.

A quick hush fell over the busy, noisy crowd of people waiting to welcome their families and friends, then they erupted in cheers and applause. Even an old grump like me had to blink back tears as I grabbed Orin in a big Santa bear hug. Tiny's baby brother was safe at last. The crowd cheered louder. Santa hugging a wounded soldier. Don't see that every day.

It was a Christmas miracle in and of itself that we hadn't been pulled over for speeding, I thought as I pulled into the parking place at Magnolia Manor. I doubt the real Santa and his sleigh could have been any faster.

I shut off the engine and turned to Orin. "You ready?" I'd explained about Tiny's lack of Santa on the way home.

"Yes sir, Santa, sir." He grinned and gave me a mock solute.

"Will you stop that?" I growled at him and gave him an affectionate pop on the shoulder. I helped him out of the car and we sneaked in through the back door.

If all was going according to plan, Snow Halfacre, Magnolia Manor's administrator, had found a way to slow the party down. I knew I couldn't call her too far ahead of time without risking a ton of questions, so I'd called her on our way back from Atlanta and told her I needed a little time because I had a surprise for Tiny. She seemed only too eager to help. As eager as a stoic half-Cherokee can get, that is.

I'm still not sure how much of what we walked in on had to do with my plan or divine providence or was just a good ol' Christmas miracle, but the timing was, well, interesting.

I settled Orin across the hall in one of the rooms where he could hear when it was time for his entrance. Right outside the door to the recreation room, as if someone was expecting me, I found a giant red Santa sack full of the lap quilts. Go figure. I dropped my empty sack in its place and hefted the full one over my shoulder.

With the deepest, loudest "ho, ho, ho" I could muster, I stepped into pandemonium.

Everything happened at once. Tiny looked up and grinned at me as if I was the real deal. "Hayden!"

But before she could take even one step forward, the front door opened and Wolfman bounded in like some kinda Santa Superman, *ho, ho, ho*ing at the top of his lungs. An empty, flapping red bag hung over his shoulder.

It took a few seconds for the shock of seeing two Santas to sink into the befuddled minds of the elderly group gathered around the Christmas tree, cookies and eggnog held midair.

"Ho, ho, ho!" We turned as one in the next breath when Tag Garner sauntered into the room, as yet another Santa, only he'd had the foresight to stuff his sack full of . . . something.

Twinkling lights beat a reflection on stunned faces and Frank Sinatra crooned *I'll Be Home for Christmas* on the stereo.

I coulda sworn I heard Uncle Percy laughing his fool head off. My arms and legs began to itch.

Just then, Tater Townsend, one of Tiny's students, came rushing in through the same door I had just entered, sneakers squealing to a halt, a bushy white beard down around his neck, holding on to his oversized red Santa pants with one hand. "Ms. Carlisle! I can't get my pants to stay up and now someone stole the quilts!"

Well, that did it. Everyone started talking and laughing at the same time. Old man Forester laughed so hard he started choking on his false teeth. Millicent Hart Lavender pounded on his back and they fell into his lap.

Tiny rushed over and gave me a bear hug. "Hayden! I knew you wouldn't let me down."

I let the sack slid to the floor and held onto her real tight. "Merry Christmas, honey."

Tag and Wolfman made their way over, each trying to explain at once how they'd managed to free up some time for a good cause and an old friend. I was touched.

Leaning down, I whispered in Tiny's ear. "I've got a Christmas present for you that wouldn't fit in my sack." I gave the signal and stepped back to watch the look on Tiny's face as her brother, Orin, stepped into the room.

"Orin!" She leaped into his arms, practically knocking him off his crutches. The room grew quiet again as brother and sister hugged and cried together. Finally, Tiny let go and turned to me. "Thank you, Hayden," she whispered through tears. Then in a stronger voice, "Everyone, you remember my baby brother, Orin. He's come home for Christmas."

Orin squeezed her to his side. "Home for good, sis."

Some of the men, those who had been in the military, rose slowly, painfully, to their feet and saluted. There wasn't a dry eye in the house.

A little while later, the party in full swing, lap quilts strewn here and there, some tucked over frail, elderly legs, Tiny pulled me into a quiet corner.

"Hayden, I know it's a few days early, but I wanted you to have this now." She reached under the Christmas tree, then handed me a tightly folded quilt, wrapped with a big red bow.

"How did you know I'd be here?"

"You've never let me down, Hayden. Not once." She kissed my cheek. "I love you."

Struck silent by her faith in me, I tugged open the bow and spread open the quilt. Nine blocks, in every color of the rainbow, reflected what Mossy Creek meant to Tiny. The Mossy Creek Silo, where we'd shared our first kiss; the creek bed we used to picnic beside when we were dating; a magnolia for Magnolia Manor; Colchik Mountain in Bailey Mill where we lived; our little white clapboard house; our barn; an apple, for Tiny's family apple orchard; a shepherd's staff like the one I gave her all those Christmases ago when I first fell in love with her during our elementary school Christmas play. And finally, wedding rings woven together.

"Merry Christmas, Hayden," she whispered.

Lost in her lovin' blue eyes, I pulled her down onto the quilt draped over my lap and kissed her.

"The Voice Of The Creek"

Hey, folks! It's your friendly Man-On-The-Air, Bert Lyman.

Did you hear all the commotion over on Spruce Street yesterday morning? Such excitement! Five-year-old Ernie Finch, son of William and Nancy Finch from over in Yonder, got stuck in his grandparents' chimney—Eleanor and Zeke Abercrombie.

Poor little Ernie was stuck there for three and a half hours.

"Can you imagine?" Zeke said. "Eleanor and me were beside ourselves."

First they called in the Mossy Creek Volunteer Fire Department. Bill Bainbridge and crew rushed over. They yanked and pulled the squirming youngster to no avail. Little Ernie wouldn't budge!

In the meantime, Police Chief Amos Royden showed up. Studying the situation, he called in the able help of our local handyman and construction guru, Dan McNeil.

Now Dan's suggestion was to take the brick chimney apart but, "I put my foot down," Eleanor said. "No way was I having my house destroyed a few weeks before Christmas. I've already decorated."

Amos sized up the predicament for a spell, then asked Eleanor to get her jar of mayonnaise from the fridge. When she did, our esteemed Police Chief worked it all around that little boy and he slid out like a greased pig at the county fair. Well done, Chief!

When asked why he climbed up the chimney, Ernie said, "We're spending Christmas Eve at Nonnie and Poppy's and I just wanted to make sure Santa could get down their chimney."

Don't that beat all!

Christmas waves a magic wand over the world and behold,
everything is softer and more beautiful.

—Norman Vincent Peale

Harry's Christmas Surprise

On top of Colchik Mountain, a rocky knoll opens into a 360° view of the Blue Ridge Mountains. From that vantage point, you could see as far away as North Carolina, and as close as the valley below that enfolded Mossy Creek.

If you happened to be there on a clear morning right at sunrise, there was a moment—just a small, brief span of time—when you couldn't tell which way was east. It appeared as if the sun was coming up all around. Earth's entire circumference glowed a pale pink rising into the blue morning sky.

Every time I saw it, I set aside the scientist within and basked in a moment so magical, it defied description. But wasn't that the essence of magic?

I smiled to myself as I drank in the mystic morning.

Josie would be proud. Sometimes she despairs of my logical mind needing proof before I believe.

I've tried to describe this sunrise to Josie. I've even tried to show it to her several times. But each time we've come, the weather refused to cooperate. It rained one time, snowed once, but all the other times brought the smoky tendrils of low-hanging clouds for which the Blue Ridge Mountains were so famous.

But even though Josie didn't fully understand the beauty of the moment, she understood the magic of it.

Sometimes I think my sweet, loving wife is half witch. She's so observant, so keenly intuitive, she can see into the heart of a moment, or a person. She knows me inside and out. When we first met, that made me uncomfortable. I had as much darkness inside of me as she had light.

But that time was long past. After being alone for so long, I found someone who cared enough to look inside me and who didn't cringe at what she saw there. It would be a colder day than anything Colchik Mountain could throw at me before I'd let her go.

I frowned at the thought. Josie was due to deliver our child in early January—a little over a month from now—and I was worried. Sometimes babies came early. I did not have a single reason to worry. She was in perfect health, still running around decorating Mossy Creek homes and businesses for Christmas. Still I worried, but I considered that a good thing. Worry created vigilance, and vigilance could be the difference between making it to Bigelow Hospital or not.

So what was I doing here, marveling at pink light? I needed to get my readings and go home.

As I turned, I stopped short. There, not thirty yards away, stood a small, rather portly man enjoying the same view.

"Not much comes close, does it?" he said with a smile.

"You certainly came out of nowhere," I said, a bit irascibly for being startled.

He shrugged easily. "I travel quietly. And you were . . . in the moment. I didn't want to disturb that."

Mollified that he understood, I extended my hand. "Harry Rutherford."

He shook it heartily. "Yes, I've heard about you. The mountain man with a PhD."

"Not born a mountain man, to be sure, but I'm getting there." I smiled ruefully. "I hope."

"Yes," he said. "PhDs don't fit Mossy Creek all that well, do they? But mountain men do."

He surprised me again with his acumen, and I felt like I needed to explain what he saw inside me. "No one has ever been ugly to me or anything about my education. It's just that some Creekites seem uncomfortable around me."

He nodded. "Education is as intimidating to the uneducated as wealth is to the poor."

Again, I was impressed. This man seemed every bit as astute as Josie. "You're new to the area, aren't you?"

He nodded. "Just arrived a few days ago. I've been hired as the new Santa at Hamilton's Department Store."

"Ahh. That's why you look so familiar." I took in the white hair and beard, the rosy cheeks and rotund form. He was a perfect Santa. "I should've known. We have enough likenesses around the house now."

He chuckled. "Josie does love Christmas, doesn't she?"

"You know Josie?"

"I met her at The Naked Bean yesterday. She decorated that, too, I believe."

"Among about two dozen other homes and businesses. This time of year is her decorating bread and butter. She starts in early November and goes . . . well, she should be busy another week or so."

He nodded, and I said, "Well, I'd better get going. Have a bit of work to do before I head back down the mountain."

"May I walk with you?"

Again he surprised me. People who enjoyed the solitude of a mountain hike usually wanted just that—solitude. "Of course."

"Thank you. What kind of work do you do, exactly?"

As we walked, I described my research on the effects of acid rain on the southern Appalachian Mountains. It was no longer a sexy topic, being very little in the news these days. Even though the Clean Air Act helped reduce acid rain in the US, it was a very real concern all over the planet and my grant had been renewed just last year for another ten years of study.

The small man beside me surprised me again not only by how easily he understood my methodology, but how easily he kept up with my long strides. He was at least a foot shorter than me and didn't appear to be in the best of shape, but he wasn't even breathing heavily by the time we'd reached the cabin.

"Is this your house?" he asked.

"Yes, one of them." Realizing that made me sound rich, I added, "I built this cabin when I first started my research, and I lived here for several years before I married Josie. Since her work is in and around Mossy Creek and since my need to be up here is sporadic, we mainly live in a house at the base of the mountain."

"Ahh."

"As a matter of fact, one reason I'm here is to close it up for the winter. Normally, we'd come up here Christmas Day after Christmas dinner with her folks, but she's pretty darn pregnant. In fact, the baby should be here just after Christmas."

"Yes, I noticed her condition," he murmured. "Do you know if you're having a boy or a girl?"

I shook my head. "Josie insists on being surprised."

"Insist" was putting it mildly. Josie was so set on not discovering the sex until birth that she wouldn't let the doctor, nurses or technicians tell her any results from the sonograms except the health of the baby.

The small man's blue eyes actually twinkled. Must be a trick of the dawn light. "Ah, yes. Christmas surprises are the best."

I shrugged. "I don't know what the difference is. You're surprised whenever you hear. Now or later, what's the difference?"

"So you're indulging your wife. You love her very much."

It was statement more than question. "I have to plead guilty."

The little man nodded as if satisfied. "So your cabin is going to be empty for a few months? Would you consider renting it to me?"

He surprised me again. "Seriously?"

"Absolutely. I love it up here."

"But . . . it's rather primitive. No running water. The only electricity is from a cantankerous old generator fed by an old solar panel. It's heated solely by the wood stove."

"That's no problem. Really. I'm from . . . up north. I'm used to the cold and used to living simply. In fact, I prefer it."

"To tell you the truth, I've never thought about renting it, but I guess I'd prefer someone be living here to its sitting open to critters of the two- and four-legged varieties."

"I only need it for December."

I dragged a hand through my thick hair. "You work in town. It's an hour's hike downhill and at least twice that coming up. Do you have an ATV?"

He cocked his head to the side. "In a manner of speaking. Don't worry about that. I'm accustomed to long commutes."

"Okay, then. It'll be nice to have a little cash for Christmas."

We agreed on the rent. To my surprise, he pulled out a wad of cash and paid me for two months.

"But you said you only needed it for December."

He shrugged. "I might need a little time after Christmas, to clear out my things."

"Okay, then. Do you want to move in today or are you working?"

He nodded. "My shift starts at noon, but I'll move in after that."

"All right. Since you're staying here tonight, I'll leave the stove going, but just barely. You'll need to turn up the airflow when you come in, possibly add some wood."

"That would be nice. Thank you. I've used one before."

"There's plenty of wood out by the shed."

"Wonderful." He looked around, pleased. "Good. Well, then. Guess I'll head back to town. I need to check out of the Hamilton Inn and pack my things."

"Okay. I still have a few things I need to do here before I leave. I'll see you around town. "

"No doubt you will."

He started to leave, then I realized, "Hey, I never asked your name."

"No, you didn't." He turned and I swear his smile twinkled. "It's Kris Kringle."

He was gone before the full meaning of that sunk in.

• • •

"Whooooeeee! Ain't that somethin'!"

I stood back and shoved my goggles on top of my head.

It boded well that Randy McPherson—better known as Punch, especially to the crowd at O'Day's Pub—was impressed with what I'd done so far. He worked at the Mossy Creek Furniture Factory which was still in business because it made custom rustic furniture that was handmade from the tree down.

Punch caressed the eight-foot-long, three-foot-wide, two-inch-thick slab cut from a black walnut that I'd wrestled down the mountainside with my four-wheeler. "This here's gonna make one bee-yoo-ti-ful tabletop. Yessirree."

I stood in Punch's workshop, which was in an old barn behind his mother's house on the outskirts of Mossy Creek. "So you think it's dry enough?"

"You cut the slab from a tree that'd been down so long it had mushrooms growing on it like I told ya, didn't ya?"

"Yes, I did. I cut it back in March."

"An old trick my daddy taught me. Don't nobody know why, but mushrooms let ya know that log has cured naturally so you don't have to worry much about it cracking or splitting like you would a green log. I think they're kinda like one of those button things that pop out of a turkey when it's done." He bent down and peered down the surface. "Good slab. Pretty darn straight. When did you cut it?"

"Back in May."

"So the slab's been drying six months. That's good. That'll pretty much guarantee that it won't warp." He paused, his eyes falling on an old lathe across the room. "Did I ever tell you about my daddy?"

"I believe you did, yes." Somehow I stopped myself from rolling my eyes, because I knew the story was coming again anyway. This would be the fourth time I'd heard it, but it was a cheap price to pay for Punch's help. I'd enlisted his expertise soon after Josie told me she was pregnant.

I'd been planning a while to get her a rustic dining table like the ones she so admired in some of the decorating magazines she read. But she kept putting me off, saying they were too expensive.

As we talked about the baby over the first weeks of pregnancy, I suddenly got the urge to *make* a table with my own two hands. Josie was creating something and I wanted to, as well. It was such a *mountain man* thing to do. The only trouble was, my education was in botany and chemistry, not more practical technologies. I had no idea how to go about it.

But I knew that Punch did.

The Mossy Creek Furniture Factory specialized in rustic, high-end tables made from ancient slabs of wood that were seen on those home television network shows about multi-million-dollar mountain retreats owned by rich CEOs and movie stars. The tables had price tags that said they belonged in those homes. While I could afford one, Josie would not be pleased at my extravagance. Quite the opposite. However, she *would* be pleased if I made it myself, even with help. So I'd enlisted Punch's aid.

Punch came by his expertise honestly. Three generations of McPherson men had worked in the Mossy Creek Furniture Factory. That was, no doubt, going to end with ol' Punch here. He was fifty-three and had never been married. He still lived with his mother, Alameda. They were drinking buddies down at O'Day's. Both loved games of darts.

And stories.

"My daddy was eighty-seven when he died, sittin' right there at that table over there," Punch said. "Mama found him with a fancy finial nearly done and still spinnin' on that there 1923 Oliver lathe. He was still sittin' up and still had his finger on the lathe. Mama said he had a sorta thoughtful look on his face, like he was tryin' to decide if he needed to strop his gouge."

"That's amazing," I murmured. Actually I *was* amazed I now knew that "strop his gouge" meant he was sharpening his chisel on a specially-treated strip of thick leather.

"Daddy always was fussy about his edges. That's just right for a man who made some of Mossy Creek's finest furniture."

"A good man, your dad." Though I never knew him.

"It didn't surprise Mama nor me neither that Daddy died without dropping his gouge and without falling off his stool."

I beat Punch to the next line. "I'll bet the first thing he said to Saint Peter was he wished he'd had some warning so he could've turned off the lathe."

"Ain't it just so." Punch nodded as if he'd never heard the phrase before. Then he shook himself out of the past. "Now, let's get this puppy into that planer. We've got some work to do."

• • •

"Have you been on the mountain all this time?"

I turned from hanging my coat on the hook next to the back door to see Josie standing in the door to the kitchen. With one hand on the doorjamb and the other on the bulge of her stomach, she looked like Gaea, the Greek goddess considered by many to be Mother Earth.

I had my excuse ready. "No, I had to do some research down in the library in Bigelow."

Her lips pursed as always at the mention of Bigelow, but relaxed as I kissed them.

"Do you have to go down there?" she asked with a sigh.

"Yes, I do, occasionally. Not everything's on the Internet. And though I love the quaint Mossy Creek library, Bigelow's is state-of-the-art, thanks to our infamous governor." I looked away, so she wouldn't see the lie in my eyes. "As a matter of fact, I'll be spending several days a week down there between now and Christmas."

"Yeah, yeah," she muttered, then brightened. "I invited Jayne and Win over for supper next Tuesday night. Win cooks so much for us, I thought it'd be nice for us to reciprocate."

I nodded. "Sounds good."

"Have you had supper?"

"No. Have you?"

"No. Leftover pot roast okay?"

"*Okay?* I *love* your leftover pot roast."

I followed her into the kitchen and sat at the ancient linoleum kitchen table we'd moved from her grandmother's house, where we'd lived the first few years we were married. The table was rickety and literally on its last stable leg. Though it had sentimental value, it badly needed to be replaced. The rustic slab table I was making would fit nicely in the kitchen. Even though the kitchen was brand-spanking-new—as was the whole house—it looked like a larger, more functional copy of her grandmother's kitchen.

Several years ago, we'd purchased seventy-five acres of land at the bottom of Colchik Mountain and built a new house within earshot of a year-round stream and small waterfall. Though I'd given my decorator wife carte blanche in building the house, she'd chosen to rebuild a larger, better-built version of her grandparents' country cottage instead of the Martha Stewart mini-mansion LuLynn had practically insisted on. I was pleased at Josie's choice. More than pleased . . . I was proud of her. She'd finally gained the confidence to break the chains of LuLynn's smothering influence.

"How was your day?" I asked, so she wouldn't ask about mine.

"Hmmm? Oh. Interesting. I got a new commission."

"Really? With who?"

She looked up suddenly. "Oh, I just remembered. Did Mr. Kringle talk with you about renting the cabin?"

Once again, I was taken aback. "Well, yes. Did he talk to you about it?"

She nodded as she slipped a glass pot into the microwave. "Yesterday. I forgot to tell you last night. He mentioned he was looking for a more remote place to rent and I knew we couldn't use the cabin for a few more months, so I suggested he talk to you about it."

"Hmmm. Yes. He found me on the rocky knoll on Colchik Mountain."

She looked up. "At dawn?"

I nodded.

She seemed peeved. "You mean he got to see your sunrise?"

"Well, it's not *my* sunrise—"

"That's not fair!"

I shrugged. "He made the climb on a clear day. What can I say?"

She pulled out yesterday's broccoli salad from the fridge. "I'll make it up there one of these days."

"I wasn't trying to be snide," I said softly. "There's plenty of time. It happens every day, as far as I know. It's just that a lot of days you can't see it."

She met my eyes across the room. "I know. I just want to share the things you think are special. It's not every day that you describe something as 'magical.'"

I grinned. "Who gave you this new commission?"

She stared down at the broccoli salad she'd just uncovered. "Pearl Quinlan. It's not exactly new. She'd been planning on a remodel after Christmas, but has decided to go ahead now to fancy up her shop for the Christmas trade. Dan McNeil assures us it can be done in a few days."

Part of me was glad she'd be distracted so I could work on the table without suspicion. Still, I looked from her tired face to her swollen belly. "Are you sure *you're* up for that?"

"Harry, please don't worry." Her hand went to her belly as it so often did these days. "I'm okay. The baby's okay. Everything is going to be okay."

See there? She was reading his mind again.

"How can you be so sure?" I asked softly.

She stepped across the kitchen and, placing a hand on either side of my burn-scarred face, kissed me. "Because I'd know if something was wrong. Women know these things."

I pulled her between my legs and wrapped my arms around her. Even though our baby lay between us, Josie felt small, frail. "*How* do you know? And don't say intuition."

Giggling, her arms went around my neck, which she kissed. "Okay, Mr. Scientist. Even though intuition is how I know, I also have the scientific medical world telling me our child is okay. We go every week, and every week they tell us we have a healthy child."

"I know. I just . . ." I breathed deep of her delicate fragrance. During the last few weeks, she smelled like Christmas trees. "You're all I have."

I felt her shake her head as she pulled away just far enough to meet my eyes. "I'm not going anywhere, Harry Rutherford. But even if the worst were to happen—"

I started violently but she held on, calming me with fingers digging through my hair.

"The worst is *not* going to happen," she insisted. "But if it did, you're not alone. You're a bona fide citizen of Mossy Creek now. You never have to be alone again."

I nodded. Part of me knew that, but part of me still felt like the Bigfoot on Colchik Mountain. "Say it again."

Somehow, she knew exactly what I meant. "The worst is *not* going to happen. How could it? It's Christmas, and you know I love Christmas in Mossy Creek way too much to go anywhere. Even heaven. See? You don't have anything to worry about."

I pulled her close so she couldn't see that I would worry until both she and Baby Rutherford were safe.

• • •

On Saturday that same week, I was hovering so close Josie chased me up on Colchik again to check my instruments.

Average rainfall in North Georgia was slightly higher than other parts of the state, and winter was usually wetter than summer. Especially in the higher elevations where it snowed more than below. In fact, the snow that had come through three days ago left two inches on the mountain, but hadn't stuck at all in Mossy Creek.

It was threatening snow again, but wasn't supposed to start until late. If it started sooner, I didn't much care. A little snow didn't daunt me at all. I was a big man with big feet, and sure-footed on most terrain. So I assured Josie that I would be home well before dark and left.

Little did I know that one of my instruments had run out of battery life and another had been torn apart by what had to be a bear, judging from the tracks surrounding it. Bears in these parts might find a cozy cave in the worst weather, but they didn't hibernate like their northern cousins.

It happened occasionally. Who knew why? There was certainly nothing edible in the instruments. Maybe the slight hum they made drove certain bears crazy.

Whatever it was, it had to be fixed. If I didn't go ahead and do it, I'd have to come back in the next day or so. Might as well save myself a hike.

After calling Josie on my satellite phone and leaving a message that I'd be later than I thought, I hiked back to the cabin to get replacement parts for both sites. It was almost one-thirty when I arrived at the cabin, and there was no sign of Mr. Kringle. I hadn't expected to see him. He was no doubt still at work.

How he got up and down the mountain every day was a mystery, because I saw no sign of an ATV. But he obviously made it, because the wood stove was still on. It was turned as low as it could possibly go and still keep warm. Keeping wood stoves on while you're gone was tricky, so I was glad to see that he was keeping to the same safety rules as I did when I lived there.

Even though the cabin was mine, I felt like an intruder, so all I did was stick my head into the dark interior to make sure nothing was on fire, then I went to the shed to retrieve the parts I needed and headed back to the two damaged sites.

Clouds from the oncoming storm made dark fall even sooner, so it was the first stages of twilight when I headed back down the mountain. Smelling smoke on the air, I decided to run back by the cabin. Could Mr. Kringle already be home?

That was a little hard to believe. I checked the time on the watch Josie had given me last Christmas. Five-forty-seven.

Hamilton's closed at five on Wednesdays—even during the holidays—to allow its God-fearing employees time to get to Wednesday night church services. But still . . . even if Mr. Kringle took off the second the clock struck five, it would take more than an hour to climb up the mountain. Heck, it took *me* that long, and my stride was significantly longer than his.

Maybe they let him off early since it was about to snow.

As I came into the clearing, I spied smoke rising from the chimney.

Yes, that must've been it.

My next step fell on a small branch which crunched softly into the icy snow from last weekend. The noise startled me and stopped me short.

I wasn't the only thing it startled, because there were sudden scurryings all around the cabin. I watched in the dim light as what seemed like a rather large number of creatures scampered into hiding.

Now, I knew from personal experience that the mountains were home to all kinds of small creatures, but I'd never known them to hang around the cabin in such numbers. What were they? Squirrels? Rats?

Hmmm. Curious.

"Hello the cabin!" I yelled, not wanting to startle Mr. Kringle.

"Come on in," came the faint return.

As I approached, I saw hundreds of tiny footprints. I recognized birds and squirrels and rabbits and even a fox. But there were others . . .

I peered closer, shining my flashlight along what should've been relatively undisturbed snow. There were footprints leading up to and away from the steps that looked . . . almost human. Like tiny humans with incredibly small, narrow feet.

A crash from inside the cabin sent me dashing up the stairs. I threw open the door and stopped short.

Mr. Kringle stood on the opposite side of the cabin, bent over next to the bed as if he'd just shoved something underneath.

He straightened—guiltily?—and said with an over-bright voice, "Harry! What brings you up here on such a cold, blustery night?"

"I . . ." Glancing around the cabin, my gaze fell on the table. A kerosene lantern blazed in the center. Surrounding it were all kinds of toys, in various stages of construction. They were lined up in rows—all the dolls in one, all the toy trucks in another, and so on—as if there had been people sitting there working on each line.

What the—?

My mind swept back over all the strange things I'd heard about Kris Kringle during the past week. Half the town believed he was *really* Santa Claus—and I wasn't talking about the children. Josie was solidly in the believing half.

"I . . ." I swallowed hard, almost afraid. Toys were everywhere I looked, not just the table. Tiny teacups lined the hearth, some painted with tiny flowers, some plain. Toy airplanes in various stages of construction were lined up on the kitchen cabinets. Alphabet blocks were stacked along the wall along with uncarved blocks and wood shavings. For all intents and purposes, it looked like a scene out of a Christmas storybook depicting Santa's workshop.

"Where are the elves?"

Mr. Kringle frowned. "Beg pardon?"

His confusion seemed sincere and broke the spell. I laughed, shaking my head at my own foolishness. "I'm sorry. It just came out." I swept an arm around the cabin. "What is all this?"

He chuckled. "Ah, yes, I can see what you must've been thinking. I have a second job as a toy repairman."

"For Hamilton's?"

He waggled his head as he moved toward the wood stove. "Among others. Would you like to stay for supper? I've got a nice pot of stew here. Thought a hearty meal was just the thing with the weather coming in."

"No, thank you," I said quickly. "I've got to get back down the mountain or Josie'll have my hide."

"In this weather?"

I shrugged. "It hasn't started snowing yet, but it will. I need to beat it down."

He moved to the window. "Awfully dark out there. I was so busy, I hadn't noticed."

"Oh, don't worry about me. I've been up and down and

around this mountain for years now. I know every foot of her."

"Suit yourself." He turned back to me. "Let me at least warm you up with a cup of cocoa."

I hid a smile. Santa Claus *would* have cocoa and not coffee, wouldn't he? "Okay, sure."

During the next fifteen minutes or so as I drank the cocoa, I asked him about the toys. He was evasive about where they came from, and when I asked how he got them up and down the mountain, he just shrugged. "Oh, a few at a time."

But he loved talking about the toys themselves and—this was the strange thing—he knew the "owner" of every single toy. Mentioned the children by name. Just first name, of course. Still . . .

As he talked, I noticed they didn't look as if they were toys in need of repair, but rather toys in need of finishing. They looked like toys under construction, not broken toys.

Even more curious.

One thing was for certain—Kris Kringle loved to laugh. He did so at every opportunity and as he did, his stomach really did shake like the well-known poem described.

After a few minutes, I was enchanted. That's the only word I have to describe it. I liked Kris, as he insisted on me calling him. He was a kind, warm, funny man.

I'd just finished my cocoa and set it down when Kris perked up, like he'd heard something. My thoughts went immediately to the tracks I'd seen outside the cabin.

"What is it?" I asked quietly.

"My, my, look at the time," he said, standing and taking my cup. "I didn't mean to keep you so long. You'd better go."

I looked around for a clock, but didn't see one. So I checked my watch. A little after five. "You're right. It'll be dark by now. Josie might be concerned."

Kris seemed anxious. "Yes, Yes. I have. . . . She might need you."

I stood and pulled on my jacket, knowing if I were needed, I'd have been called on my sat phone. All pertinent emergency people had the number. Josie had seen to that.

He ushered me quickly to the door. "Goodnight."

"Goodn—" I blinked as he closed the door practically on my butt.

Darkness had indeed fallen, but instead of snowing, the clouds had cleared away and a bright full moon mitigated the murk.

Good. It would make traveling down the mountain that much easier, and a little quicker.

As I stepped onto the snow, I remembered the footprints I'd seen earlier but instead of pitted snow, I noticed an evenness to the landscape.

I turned on my powerful flashlight and beamed it across the yard. All the footprints I'd seen had vanished. The area looked like fresh snowdrifts, though the moonlight was proof it had not been snowing.

I had no idea what it all meant. Was Kris really Santa, or just a weird little man?

As I trudged down the mountainside, I finally decided that whether Kris was really Santa or not was irrelevant. He embodied the spirit of Christmas.

And I found that in the cold of the still, silent night, I wanted to believe.

• • •

Twenty minutes later, any thought I'd ever had about Christmas—magic or not—flew right out of my head as I rounded the last turn down the mountain.

What one would be kind calling a gravel road was the only access to Colchik Mountain. Approached from the Bailey Mill Highway barely a mile from our house, it snaked around the base and dead-ended on the north side at boulder-strewn Colchik Creek. The trail I used mostly hits the road half a mile from the creek.

What I saw were red and blue emergency lights of a police car flashing through the branches of winter-bare trees.

Startled at seeing anything near the trailhead, I stopped short. "What the blazes?"

Had there been an accident of some kind? So far from the highway?

If the worst were to happen, you never have to be alone again. You're a bona fide citizen of Mossy Creek now.

I started violently now as I had when Josie said those words just a few nights ago. *Had* the worst happened?

She'd been grumpy since they woke that morning and I'd caught her massaging the small of her back several times. Knowing labor sometimes began with back cramps, I'd questioned her, only to be growled at and chased out of the house and up the mountain. I'd gone only because she'd been so emphatic that she was okay and because it might be the last time I could check my instruments for weeks.

Shifting my backpack to get a better grip, I raced down the dark trail. As I cleared the thickest trees, I saw a small group of bundled-up people in the headlights of a Mossy Creek police car, giving every evidence of gathering supplies to head up the mountain.

They were looking for me. I knew it as surely as I knew I had to fly the remaining quarter mile down the trail.

"Hey!" I cried when I was close enough for them to have a shot at hearing me.

The group of four men turned as one. A second later, one of them pointed up the mountain, evidently spying the wild trace of my flashlight. Relief swept through the small cluster of men. I could see it in their stances.

One of them sprinted up to meet me. As I closed in, I saw it was Mutt Bottoms.

They'd sent a Mossy Creek Police Officer outside of his jurisdiction? I knew something was wrong. Seriously wrong.

I ran faster and nearly mowed him down as I skidded to a halt.

"What's wrong with Josie?" I bellowed.

"Noth . . . ing," Mutt said around gulps of air. After all, he'd had to run *up*hill.

I didn't care. "What do you mean, nothing? Then why are you here?"

Win Allen, Mac Campbell and Tag Garner came up behind. The only one not breathless from the quick climb, Tag said, "Nothing's wrong, but Josie *is* in labor."

"What? When? She's only at eight months."

"Jayne took her to the hospital around two," Win said. "Josie tried calling but said your sat phone rang and rang. They finally went on and sent me to get you. I rounded up a posse and here we are."

I dragged my sat phone out of my pocket, but it came out in several pieces. "What the heck?" But then I remembered. I'd taken off my jacket while I was repairing the worst of my instruments. At one point, I'd stumbled back and stepped on my jacket. The wind had been howling so loudly at that point, I hadn't heard the crunch.

Horrified that I'd made such a stupid mistake on one of the most important days of my life, I stared at the useless thing.

Tag slapped me on the back. "It's your first baby, so Josie will probably be in labor several hours yet. But let's get going. You want to be there. Trust me."

I led the way and all five of us reached the road in record time. Thank God, they'd thought ahead and brought two vehicles. We were all big men so the backseat of Mutt's patrol vehicle would've been cramped, to put it mildly.

As I reached for the door of the patrol car, newly-minted politician Win hesitated. "Mutt, maybe we'd better ride with Tag so you can head back into Mossy Creek. Mossy Creek is not high on Bigelow's list during the best of times. After the tree-lighting fiasco, I'm afraid we might start Bigelow County's own version of World War III."

"Just let 'em try to stop me." Mutt's eyes shone with repressed glee. "My lights and siren can cut fifteen minutes off the trip. Harry, it's up to you."

As an answer, I dragged open the door to his patrol car. "Let's go!"

With a sigh, Win climbed into the back.

"Y'all don't need us, so we're gonna head home," Mac called as he and Tag climbed into Tag's SUV. "Good luck, Harry. Let us know!"

I waved in response. I was grateful for their help, but just wanted to get the heck to Bigelow. "For God's sake, step on it, Mutt."

With a grin, he turned on the full-tilt emergency lights and sirens and took off down the road, sending gravel flying. Luckily, they'd already turned the vehicles toward town.

Now normally, I would've relished the high-speed race through town and down the dark road to Bigelow. But even though the usual thirty-minute ride from the city limits of Mossy Creek to the Bigelow Hospital took only eighteen, it seemed like an eternity.

Win called Jayne as soon as we got in the car, of course, but Josie had been taken out of the room for a test, so I couldn't talk to her and assure myself she was okay, assure myself I would be there in time.

Mutt picked up a Bigelow PD tail as soon as we hit the city limits, but it didn't slow him down. He ran all four red lights on Bigelow's Main Street.

As soon as he screeched to a halt at the emergency room entrance, I threw open the door, leaving him to deal with the fallout of our wild ride through Bigelow. I raced through the automatic doors which, mercifully, had been triggered by a wheelchair being pushed out by a tall, portly orderly.

The waiting room was nearly empty as I stopped and zeroed in on the front desk.

"Harry Rutherford," I all but shouted at the nurse. "My wife is having a baby. Where is she?"

Instead of buzzing me immediately through the doors, she turned to her keyboard. "Your wife's name?"

"Rutherford, for God's sake! Josie Rutherford! How many Rutherfords do you have in here tonight?"

She threw a baleful look at me and took her sweet time consulting her computer. Finally, she faced me, "Do you have ID?"

Realizing I didn't because I'd hoofed it all the way from home, I roared in anger. "No, I don't have an ID. For God's sake, woman, let me in!"

Win came up beside me. "I can vouch for him, Nurse . . . Tanner. I'm the mayor of Mossy Creek."

Her nose twitched. "I don't care if you're the sultan of Mossy Creek, I need to see an I—"

Just then, a gurney was pushed through the locked doors. Without permission, I sprinted through.

"Josie!" I bellowed.

"Harry?" I heard faintly.

Jayne poked her head of out a curtained partition halfway down the left side of the room. Her face cleared. "You're here. Good."

She held the curtains aside as I ran down the aisle.

I skidded to a stop. Josie lay propped up on the bed, her arms crossed over her stomach, looking every bit as cantankerous as she had that morning.

Confused, I asked, "Has it come?"

She glowered at me. "No, it hasn't come. It was false labor."

"But we've got another month to go."

She threw her hands up. "I know. Apparently this can happen."

"But you're fine? Everything's okay?"

"Yes," she admitted grumpily. "No thanks to you. Why didn't you answer your phone?"

Finally, I walked in and kissed her. "I'm sorry. I broke it without knowing. Two of my instruments needed repair, and I knew I'd better do it while I was up there."

"Next time . . ."

"There won't be a next time," I promised. "I'm not leaving Mossy Creek until after our son or daughter is born."

"Okay." She fidgeted with the IV. "Can we go home now?"

"I'll ask the nurse to release you," Jayne said. She hesitated. "I do have some news about the baby."

"No!" Josie shouted. "I do *not* want to know the sex."

I looked at Jayne's smug expression. I wanted to know what she knew, but Josie would have a fit. So I just asked, "Is it healthy?"

Jayne's eyes sparkled. "Oh yes. Very healthy. One might say twice as healthy as any other baby."

• • •

Over the next several weeks, I found it difficult to get away to work on the table. One thing after another crept up to keep me busy.

With Josie having been told not to lift anything heavier than a sack of sugar, I knew it was more important to be nearby in case she needed me.

I also had to take a trip down to Athens for a meeting with

my department. I insisted Josie go with me so I could keep an eye on her. She bought unisex Bulldog baby clothes at the university store while I had my meeting.

As Christmas Eve dawned, I knew time and Christmas had defeated my best intentions. I'd finish the table after the holidays, but I could still "give" it to her.

While she made breakfast, I called Punch to make sure it was okay if I took her over to his barn on Christmas Day to see what I'd done.

We spent Christmas Eve day with LuLynn and John. John and I watched football while LuLynn and Josie prepared for Christmas dinner the next day.

I had to admit that since Georgia had been passed over by the bowl games, I had no interest in the games John watched. Restless, I made regular trips to the kitchen, checking on Josie.

The fourth time I caught her with her hands kneading the small of her back, I had to ask, "Josie, are you in labor again?"

Both Josie and LuLynn looked surprised.

Then LuLynn turned to her daughter. "Are you? You've been stretching your back for several hours now, like it's bothering you."

Josie waved them away. "I'm a little crampy back there, but it isn't labor."

"How do you know?" I insisted.

"Do you see me writhing in pain?"

"No," I had to admit.

"I probably just strained it somehow."

"How? The heaviest thing you've lifted is your toothbrush."

She patted her baby bump. "I'm a little front-heavy, if you haven't noticed. My balance is all off. It happens. Don't worry, my love. When I think I'm in labor, I'll let you know. Now go enjoy your football."

Reluctantly, I rejoined John.

Just before we were going to sit down for supper, I heard a faint splash and then, "Oh dear."

Josie's water had broken.

We were at the hospital twenty minutes later.

Her labor went much smoother than I could've hoped. At eleven-fifty-eight, our beautiful, healthy, five-pound-seven-ounce son was born. I thought my heart would burst with love and pride as I heard his first furious cry at being separated from his mother's warmth.

As I watched the umbilical cord being cut, I squeezed Josie's hand and kissed her. "Jonathan is here. Thank you, my dear sweet darling girl. You've given me the best Christmas present I've ever received."

"I love you, Harry Rutherford." Her face was as emotional as mine until she winced.

Concerned, I jumped to my feet. "What is it?"

"I don't know," she said, "Probably the after—"

"Well, you've had the last baby on Christmas Eve," the doctor said, glancing at the clock. It was just past midnight. "Now let's see if you'll have the first Christmas baby."

Both Josie and I went still. "What?"

The doctor looked smug. "I tried to tell you two, but you wouldn't let me. You've got another baby . . . and here she comes."

Our daughter, Sarah Lynn Rutherford, was born at twelve-oh-five and the first Christmas baby in Georgia that year, it turned out. Though born just seven minutes apart, our twins would have two different birthdays.

As I carried them to the waiting room half an hour later to introduce them to their grandparents, I saw that snow was falling heavily. We were going to have a white Christmas. Smiling, I continued on, but came to a dead halt at the doorway.

Not only were LuLynn and John in the waiting room, they were kept company by what had to be thirty people from Mossy Creek. When they saw me, they all stood and started clapping.

Stunned at this display of love and support, I stammered, "Please meet our babies, Jonathan Harold and Sarah Lynn."

They gathered around to see. All our friends and family. So many, later I couldn't remember them all to tell Josie.

Her eyes filled with tears as she took Jonathan from me. "Why didn't they come to see me? I would've remembered who."

"Since it's snowing, I asked them to go on home and come back tomorrow if they could, after they've had their Christmas. You need sleep."

"Never mind. Mother will know who was there." She kissed her sleeping son's head. "What did they say when they saw the twins?"

I shook my head. "They all knew."

Her head came up. "What?"

"LuLynn found out when we were here with the false labor a few weeks ago, and you know your mother."

She nodded ruefully. "And I know Mossy Creek, bless their hearts. I'm surprised no one let it slip to us the past few weeks."

"They all love us and wanted to give us what we wanted," I said with pride. "See? They *can* behave when there's a darn good reason."

Josie's beautifully exhausted face beamed.

"What?" I asked.

"You finally believe—way down deep where it counts—that you belong in Mossy Creek."

I realized she was right. Somehow this scarred hermit of a mountain man had been enveloped by the love and gracious Southern hospitality of a close-knit community. They'd loosened enough threads to bind me up in their warmth and generous hearts.

I smiled at the beautiful mother of my children, who'd accepted me first. "Yes, my love. I finally believe."

• • •

Snow was still on the ground when I took Josie and the twins home the day after Christmas. After we settled them in the bassinet in our room, we walked into the kitchen and stopped short.

There, where the old Formica had been, sat my beautifully finished, black walnut table.

Josie went wild with joy. When I explained to her how I'd started it but hadn't seen it through, she asked, "Who finished it, then? Punch?"

"I guess."

That's when I saw a wood-burning pen lying on the kitchen counter with a note saying, "Artists always sign their work."

On a whim, I crawled under the table and looked up. On the end toward the hallway was a list of names seared into the walnut.

I read them to Josie. "Punch McPherson. Amos Royden. Win Allen. Tag Garner. Mac Campbell. John McClure. Hank Blackshear."

I climbed out to see tears streaming down her face. "They finished it for you?"

I nodded, emotion closing around my throat. "Each of them must've given up hours of their Christmas to help me."

She smiled. "As you would've for them."

I blinked, then admitted, "As I would've for them."

"No doubt about it," she said as her hand cupped my face. "You belong in Mossy Creek."

I shook my head then kissed her. "I belong *to* Mossy Creek. And there's no place on Earth I'd rather be."

Mossy Creek Gazette

106 Main Street • Mossy Creek, GA 30000

From the desk of Katie Bell

Lady Victoria Salter Stanhope
The Clifts
Seaward Road
St. Ives, Cornwall, TR3 7PJ
United Kingdom

Hey, Vick!

Well, Christmas is over for this year. It was a humdinger, too. A skydiving Santa crashed the Tree-Lighting Ceremony. A soldier surprised his sister for the holidays. We had runaway horses at the Christmas parade. And somehow, we ended up with a most amazingly authentic Santa.

About the decorations that were so up in the air, they turned out just fine. The committee—by that I mean Inez Hilley and her granddaughter Lucy Belle—hit the right theme with *People in Mossy Creek*. So essentially a theme without a theme, but it was perfect. Other people seemed to think so too. Tour buses were seen driving straight through Bigelow up here to see Mossy Creek's decorations.

Some were elegant, like LuLynn McClure's all-white lights covering her front porch. Some were religious, like Foxer Atlas's life-size manger scene with stuffed people and live animals. Some were downright redneck, like Orville Gene Simple's ten-foot "tree" made from beer cans. Quite impressive, actually. Can you imagine how many that took?

The decorations all over town were homemade and all reflected some aspect of the people in Mossy Creek. I loved each and every one!

Until next time . . .

Katie

Recipes from

Mossy Creek

Pearl's Festive and Healthy Spinach Salad

1 bag leaf spinach
1/4 cup chopped red onion
1/3 cup pecan halves
1/4 cup craisins (dried cranberries)
1/3 cup feta cheese crumbles

Mix salad ingredients in large bowl, then make dressing right before tossing.

Dressing:

1/2 cup extra virgin olive oil
1/4 cup light brown Splenda sugar substitute
2 tbsp. apple cider vinegar
1 tsp. dried onion flakes
1/4 tsp. dry mustard
1/4 tsp. salt

Mix dressing in blender right before serving. Pour over salad and toss.

(Courtesy of Angelle Buckley)

Clementine's Zucchini Casserole

3 cups zucchini, sliced thin
1 cup Bisquick
1/2 cup chopped onion
1/2 cup grated cheese
2 tbsp. snipped parsley
1/2 tsp. salt (or seasoned salt)
1/2 tsp. oregano
Dash pepper and garlic salt
1/2 cup oil
4 eggs, slightly beaten

Mix all ingredients and spread into greased 13x9 baking pan. Bake until brown (approx. 25 minutes) at 350°. Cut into squares and serve.

Lucy Belle's
Holiday Pimento Cheese Muffins

1-1/2 cups baking mix (like Bisquick)
3/4 cup buttermilk
1-1/2 tbsp. sugar
1 cup pimento cheese (Palmetto brand)

Preheat oven to 425°. Grease a mini muffin pan. Combine ingredients. Add a little more buttermilk if dough is too thick. Spoon into muffin pan. Bake for 10-12 minutes.

Inez Hamilton Hilley's No-Bake Reindeer Poop

1-3/4 cups sugar
1/2 cup milk
8 tbsp. butter, cut into pieces
3 tbsp. unsweetened cocoa powder
1/2 cup creamy peanut butter
1 tsp. vanilla extract
1/4 teaspoon salt
3 cups quick-cooking oats

Add sugar, milk, butter and cocoa powder to a saucepan over medium-high heat. Bring to a boil for three minutes. Remove from heat and stir in rest of ingredients. Drop large spoonfuls of mixture onto parchment paper and allow to dry for 15 minutes or until cookies are firm.

Spiva's Whiskey Balls*

1 large box vanilla wafers
1 cup powdered sugar
1 cup chopped pecans
1-1/2 tsp. cocoa
2 tbsp. white Karo syrup
1/4 cup bourbon

Grind vanilla wafers in food processor. Dump into large mixing bowl. Mix in finely chopped pecans and cocoa. Add wet ingredients—white Karo syrup and bourbon—and mix thoroughly. Form into small bite-sized balls. Pour powdered sugar onto small plate and roll whiskey balls around in the sugar until coated. Keep the whiskey balls in a very tight container, like one of those old holiday tins your sister hordes and line it with waxed paper. If you're not partial to bourbon, substitute with a good dark rum.

*A grown-up treat, not intended for young'uns.

Spiva's 151 Rum Cake*

1 cup chopped pecans (or walnuts since they're supposed
to be so good for you according to my sister)

1 package yellow cake mix (I prefer Duncan Hines)

4 oz. package vanilla pudding mix

3 eggs

1/2 cup cold water

1/3 cup vegetable oil

1/2 cup Bacardí dark 151-proof rum

Glaze

1/4 lb. butter (1 stick)

1/4 cup water

1 cup granulated sugar

1/2 cup Bacardí dark 151-proof rum

Preheat oven to 325° if using coating or dark pan, 350° for regular pan. Grease and flour 12-cup Bundt pan. Sprinkle nuts in bottom of pan. Mix all cake ingredients on medium speed with electric mixer until smooth, according to box directions for length of time. Pour batter over nuts and bake for 55-60 minutes, until toothpick comes out clean. Cool. Invert on serving plate and make glaze.

Glaze: Melt butter in sauce pan over medium heat. Once butter is melted, stir in water and sugar. Bring to a boil. Stirring constantly, let glaze boil for 5 minutes. Remove from heat. Stir in rum.

Prick top and sides of cake with toothpick. Spoon and brush glaze evenly over top and sides. Allow the cake to absorb glaze. Repeat until all glaze is used up. Cover your cake until ready to serve.

Serving suggestion: Serve with a scoop of vanilla bean or butter pecan ice cream for an extra special treat.

*A grown-up treat, not intended for young'uns, especially if you use the 151-proof rum in the glaze.

Clementine's Lemon Crumb Squares

15-oz. can condensed milk
1/2 cup lemon juice
1 tsp. grated lemon peel
1 1/2 cups sifted flour
1 cup brown sugar, packed
1 cup uncooked oatmeal
1 tsp. baking powder
1/2 tsp. salt
2/3 cup butter

Blend together milk, juice, rind and set aside.

Sift together flour, baking powder and salt.

Cream butter and blend in sugar. Add oatmeal and flour mixture, mix until crumbly.

Spread half of mixture into 8x12x12 buttered baking pan and pat down.

Spread milk mixture over top and cover with remaining crumb mixture.

Bake at 350° until brown around edges (approx. 25-30 minutes).

Cool in pan at room temp 15 minutes.

Cut into squares and chill until firm.

Clementine's Holiday Pumpkin Spice Cake

4 eggs, beaten
15-oz. can pumpkin
1-1/3 cups sugar
1 cup vegetable oil (or applesauce)
2 cups all-purpose flour (or gluten-free flour)
2 tsp. baking powder
1 tsp. baking soda
1 tsp. salt
2 tsp. cinnamon
1/2 tsp. ginger or nutmeg

Mix eggs, pumpkin, sugar and oil until creamy. Blend in dry ingredients. May add chocolate chips or nuts. Pour into 9x13 ungreased cake pan. Bake at 350° for 25-35 minutes (until center is springy to touch or dry-toothpick test). Cool, then top with cream cheese icing of choice.

Ingrid's Reindeer Food

6 cups Crispix
2 cups peanuts
3 cups Cheerios
2 cups stick pretzels, broken into pieces
12 oz. pkg. M&M's
1-1/2 lb. almond bark

Mix first five ingredients. Melt bark in double boiler or microwave and pour over dry ingredients. Spread onto wax paper and let cool.

The Mossy Creek
Storytelling Club
(in order of appearance)

Merry & Louise...................... Carolyn McSparren
The 96th Annual Mossy Creek Christmas Parade

Inez & Lucy Belle........................... Susan Goggins
The Christmas Competition

Pearl & Spiva .... Maureen Hardegree
You Get What You Give

Jayne & Win .... Martha Crockett
Miracle on Main Street

Maggie & Tag.....................................Nancy Knight
Joyeux Noelle

Clementine & Heyday ....Darcy Crowder
Secret Santa

Harry & Josie.............................. Martha Crockett
Harry's Christmas Surprise

The Mossy Creek Hometown Series

Mossy Creek
Reunion at Mossy Creek
Summer in Mossy Creek
Blessings of Mossy Creek
A Day in Mossy Creek
At Home in Mossy Creek
Critters of Mossy Creek
Homecoming in Mossy Creek
Christmas in Mossy Creek

Other BelleBooks Titles

KaseyBelle: *The Tiniest Fairy in the Kingdom*
by Sandra Chastain

Astronaut Noodle   by Kenlyn Spence

Sweet Tea and Jesus Shoes
More Sweet Tea
On Grandma's Porch
Sweeter Than Tea

Milam McGraw Propst, author of acclaimed feature film The Adventures of Oicee Nash
Creola's Moonbeam

All God's Creatures   by Carolyn McSparren

From *NYT* bestselling author Deborah Smith

Alice at Heart — Waterlilies series
Diary of a Radical Mermaid — Waterlilies Series
The Crossroads Café
A Gentle Rain

81321833R00136

Made in the USA
Columbia, SC
20 November 2017